Taking Wing

First Published in 2019
Crowvus, 53 Argyle Square, Wick, KW1 5AJ

Copyright © Text Clemency Crow 2019
Copyright © Cover Image Crowvus 2019

ISBN 978-1-913182-03-8

For comments and questions about
"Taking Wing"
contact the publisher directly at the_team@crowvus.com

www.crowvus.com

CHAPTER ONE
An Eye for an Eye

617 AD

Six women carried the body, laden with jewels from around her empire. Behind them, other women carried trays of gold and silver, emeralds and rubies. Somewhere in the crowd of people behind, a man was singing a tune without words, and a woman was wailing, but these were the only sounds. The footsteps made no noise and there were no birds to sing - everything else was silent.

Farmers, soldiers and nobles followed the funeral, looking ahead at the woman's body.

One man watched from a distance, his black eyes taking in everything around him, but they were focused on the woman. He had the same white hair, flecked with brown, as the lady on the bier, coming to the same sharp point in the middle of his forehead.

As the funeral passed, he joined them, standing directly behind her, never taking his eyes off the body. There were no tears, no sadness, but anger seeped out of him, causing the other people to keep a safe distance. His normally smooth face was twisted in anger and grief.

The procession soon came to a boat, looking out-of-place as the river was one mile away. Without a word, the women stepped into the boat and placed the body on a platform strewn with fur and bird feathers. Silently, they stood back and left the boat.

It was then that the man stepped up beside the body and bent down so that his face was almost touching hers. When he was close enough, he looked down to see the cut that had caused her death and whispered in her ear.

"You go before me." His whisper was almost like a hiss. "You will not rest until I avenge you, and I will not rest until that day."

On saying this, he spun around and did not look at her again. Knowing that he would not be able to stop his tears if he stayed, he did not watch the rest of the funeral but strode from the burial site, his face growing more twisted in rage.

A loud guttural croak caught the man's attention and he looked up to see an unusually large raven sitting watching him. The raven's black eyes were staring straight into his and it opened its rough beak again, making the same noise. It made the man shudder.

"No wonder you are called the bringer of death," he snapped and moved towards the bird, snatching at it wildly. His grief made him misjudge the distance and all the raven had to do was simply hop a few steps and watch as the grieving man fell onto the scrub. When he got to his feet, the raven had gone and was replaced by a large man. He wore body armour as black as his hair and neat beard but, more unusually, he wore a long cloak made from small twigs woven together. The white-haired man could not bring himself to look at him. Every time he met the raven-black eyes, anger and hatred overtook any other feeling he had.

"Raedwald." The raven man croaked. "Raedwald, please. Please look at me."

"How can you speak to me?" Raedwald, the white-haired man, hissed. He brought his eyes up to meet his and the same feeling of bitter hatred swept through him. "How can you speak to me when my wife is being buried? My wife that you murdered."

The other man looked at him without speaking. His black eyes glistened, and his mouth parted slightly as though he was about to talk, but he shook his head sadly.

"I demand that justice is done!" Raedwald shouted and drew his sword, staggering under the weight of his grief.

"We did not kill your wife, Raedwald." The other man pleaded with him. "Enemies as we are, I mourn Edweth's death. Let me help you find her murderer."

"You would blame an innocent to cover your guilt, Ethelfrith." He shook his head. "You may pretend to be a friend, but I know it was your tribe who killed her, and we shall be at war until I know that the murderer is dead. We shall be at war until I have avenged my wife!"

"No," Ethelfrith moved towards him, "I want to find Edweth's killer. I promise you that it was not the Crows who killed her. Please believe me. I don't know how to persuade you that I'm telling the truth."

Ethelfrith's face was serious as he begged to be believed. His voice never faltered and Raedwald looked at him for a moment, considering what may or may not have been the truth. Surely this raven could not pretend so well, but Raedwald was so certain that it had been a member of the Crow tribe who had killed his wife. Perhaps Ethelfrith was unaware of who it was, but it must have been a Crow, so he was clearly losing his grip on the tribe he once commanded.

Raedwald never doubted that he was guilty. Whether or not he was directly responsible for his wife's death, Raedwald was still unsure, but he should have stopped it from happening. Because of that, he *was* guilty.

An idea glinted in his pale face and a small smile, so slight Ethelfrith could not see it, touched his thin lips.

"You would put our past behind us?" Raedwald's voice faltered and he gave a false smile.

"For as long as it takes to find the guilty one. Until then, we are brothers again."

The white-haired man looked at him, feeling a fever of anger sweep through his blood, and nodded slowly. Despite the bitterness and hatred, he walked over to him and laid a hand on Ethelfrith's back in a sign of false friendship.

"Brothers again," Raedwald repeated his companion's words but, unseen by the other man, his face contorted into a twisted, ugly expression of hatred.

Determined to begin his revenge, Raedwald hissed a laugh and was too quick for Ethelfrith to defend himself. He pulled the raven's dagger from his waist and let his hatred control his actions.

CHAPTER TWO
Poltergeist

Present day

Freya walked along the quiet road, slouching as her back ached from standing for too long. Her feet were sore too, so each step sent jolts up her leg and made her back even worse. She had been on her feet for 5 hours, working in the shop after school. Now she had finally finished, she had to walk back up the hill to the flat. The sun had set some time ago, and the shadowed houses loomed over Freya as she walked past them, beyond the deserted warehouses that lined the harbour.

She hated the dark and it frightened her to walk home this way. She could go along the main road of course, with its busy traffic and beaming streetlights, but then she would be surrounded by people, which also made her nervous. Right now, though, as the darkness closed around her, she was beginning to wish she had chosen the crowded option.

Glancing back over her shoulder, she realised there was someone walking a little way behind her. This made her more uneasy and she stared ahead, taking deep breaths. She wasn't sure if she was imagining the quickening of feet behind her but, when she looked again, the person was still the same distance away. As she looked, the stranger looked straight back at her and, for a moment, Freya thought she saw a yellow glint in his eye.

It's just my imagination, she told herself, *don't be an idiot, Freya.*

Freya was a very sensible person, always getting the top marks in her class of Primary Sevens, the only one in her class who had a part-time job, and often trusted to stay at home on her own when her parents had long meetings with the lawyers. Tonight, though, she was heading to her Auntie Jessie's house as her parents were taking a couple of weeks away together to try and sort things out.

But being sensible was not stopping the fear that almost choked her, and she could not stop her heart from thundering so hard it made her sick. Her panic making her not think straight, she decided to turn down one of the small side-streets to see if the yellow-eyed stranger would follow.

Taking a deep breath, she turned right and crept close to the buildings, fingering her phone in her pocket. Looking nervously over her shoulder again, she let out a sigh of relief as she realised there was no one there.

Of course there's no-one there, she laughed to make herself feel better, *it was probably just someone else walking home. And the yellow light was probably just the reflection of the streetlight.*

She couldn't keep walking until her nerves had calmed down, so she leaned against one of the stone walls and tried to stop her heart from racing. Closing her eyes, she could hear her heart beat even louder.

Why do I do this silly job? she snapped at herself. As she was twelve, the money she earned for working in the shop was a pittance and not even enough to fund tickets to the Ed Sheeran concert her friends were going to.

Thinking about her friends brought her back to reality and she opened her eyes again, immediately wishing that she hadn't. In front of her was a building, hugged by scaffolding. This was not unusual, but the three pairs of eyes that shone out from the scaffolding caused her to let out a high-pitched yelp.

They weren't people's eyes. They were too close together for that.

The eyes seemed to come closer and closer and she realised that they were flying towards her.

Fear or darkness made it so she could not make out what animal they were. They were white, that's all she could tell. They weren't gulls. No, these eyes were bigger and further apart...and they were coming straight at her.

Just as the three birds were about to reach her head, Freya held up her arms to stop them. Unsure whether time was slowing down because of her fear - she'd heard it could happen like that - she realised the birds had not touched her and she peered up.

Next to her, the three monstrous birds were crowded around another person. It was difficult to make out who it was because the birds were covering him, clawing, snapping...

Although she wanted to, she could not run, feeling that she couldn't leave someone to be hurt because they had helped her. The birds were attacking so relentlessly that the boy was having to simply shield his face with his hands. He would manage to knock one bird away but the other two would attack even more ferociously until the third joined them.

Freya knew she needed to do something to help and she looked around for something to beat them off with. There was nothing useful that she could see so she was about to use her bare hands to pull at the fearsome birds, but she heard a sliding crash above her.

Freya watched in horror as several tiles from

the warehouse next to them fell onto the birds, who slumped to the floor. Her horror was not only caused by this, but as she watched the birds fall, they seemed to grow...and grow...until they were taller than her. It was only then she realised they were no longer bird-shaped, and they had arms and legs just as she did. There were two women and one man at her feet – breathing but unconscious. And standing in front of her was the boy who had tried to help when the birds or humans, or whatever they were, had attacked.

Trembling, Freya turned to him and realised this was the one who had been walking behind her. She could now get a clear view of his straight hair, which looked like it had not been brushed for days. Below his eyes, which still held a glint of yellow, was a long, hooked nose.

He couldn't have been much older than Freya herself and she realised he was looking straight at her as she was staring at him, but he was clutching his side, in pain.

Freya edged towards him, and he watched her with interest, apparently not concerned by the wound in his side. She looked away slightly, taking deep breaths to try and calm herself.

"They were going to hurt you," the boy said, his voice high pitched and clipped.

"I know, but I don't know why." Freya's voice shook. "Thank you for helping me, but I think they hurt you."

Freya pointed to the boy's side, but he hardly seemed to notice.

"It is an honour. And an honour to meet you. I'm Enna, by the way."

"Okay." Freya would have laughed at Enna's strange use of language, but the boy was hurt and clearly needed help. "I'll ring for an ambulance. This is my fault."

"No," Enna was insistent and became so upset that Freya paused in the act of reaching for her phone. "No, you can't get an ambulance. I'll be fine."

As he was getting so worried, Freya moved her hand away from her pocket, but the boy stumbled forward, growing paler.

"Okay, okay," she said, desperate, "come with me. We need to get you help."

She knew what she was doing was wrong as she led the boy up the stairs towards her flat. She was certain that Auntie Jessie would know what to do. Her auntie always remained calm under pressure.

As she rang the doorbell, she wondered what her aunt would think of her bringing a boy home. This was a first for Freya.

"What's going on, Freya?" Her aunt opened the door and peered out. "Who's this, and why is he bleeding?"

"My name is Enna," Enna said before stumbling onto Freya who tried to support him as best she could.

"Freya," her aunt began, "I know I'm always telling you to loosen up, but this is not what I had in mind."

"He's injured because he helped me. Please, we've got to help him."

Her auntie took another look at Enna's face, that was becoming whiter than the magnolia paint in the flat, and nodded. Freya wasted no time getting Enna inside and guided him over to the sofa. He didn't speak and he seemed to be concentrating very hard on staying conscious. Freya rushed over to her auntie.

"We need to get him help, but he's refusing an ambulance," she whispered urgently. Auntie Jessie looked across at him with interest.

"Perhaps he prefers different healing," she walked up to him and knelt in front of the boy. "Enna. I know what might help with the bleeding. Have you heard of the plant yarrow?"

At this, Enna looked up and nodded enthusiastically, but the action was too much, and he fell back on the sofa.

"I can't take you to my surgery, Enna," Auntie Jessie spoke calmly and quietly, "but I can fetch some yarrow and bandages and bring them back here. Would that be okay?"

"Yes," Enna mumbled, closing his eyes. Freya's aunt stood up and grabbed the car keys from the hook by the door.

"Freya," she whispered, "I'll fetch the supplies and you try and make sure he stays awake."

Freya nodded and felt another twinge of fear as she watched her aunt leave the house, shutting the door silently behind her. She glanced across at Enna whose eyes were half closed and, remembering the instructions her aunt had left, walked cautiously over to him.

"Enna," she whispered, and he opened his eyes even more. "My aunt's gone to fetch some herbs from her shop. She's a trained herbalist, and she'll make you feel better. But she might recommend you go to hospital once she's seen you."

"No," Enna shook his head. "No hospitals. No ambulance."

"Enna. You have a very bad wound," Freya insisted.

Enna didn't reply but closed his eyes. At first, Freya was worried he might fall asleep, but the worry was soon replaced by confusion as she saw a liquid-blue light appear in his hand. The light throbbed silently and grew until it covered Enna's wound.

"It's not working," the boy gasped, "I don't understand why it's not working."

"Calm down," Freya whispered, her voice had died away as she watched the blue light grow and grow.

The light was soon covering Enna's entire body. Freya took a step back, too puzzled to be scared, but her fear returned when she heard something smash behind her. Turning, she realised the windowpane had just shattered. Thinking it was some yobs throwing stones outside, she was about to go and get angry with them, when a vase which had been standing on the sideboard, narrowly missed her head as it flew across the room and smashed against the wall.

Looking back at Enna, she only had time to see that the blue light had not disappeared before she felt something hit her leg. She looked to see that the footstool, that had been next the sofa, had skidded across the floor with such force that she could feel the bruise appearing on her shin.

It was like a poltergeist, but Freya didn't believe in such things. In fact, she didn't believe in much at all, except things that were easily explained. The pain from the bruise showed her that she was not imagining any of it, but that made it no easier. If anything, it made it scarier. More inexplicable.

Her thoughts were scattered all over the place, like the now-littered Living Room, so she was only partly aware of something hitting the back of her head before her vision blurred and she fell forwards onto the carpet.

CHAPTER THREE
New Surroundings

Sounds were distorted as Freya took a few moments to realise that she must be waking up. Without opening her eyes in case it made her head hurt even more, she could still tell she was lying with her back on a soft carpet and with something raising her head off the floor. Someone placed their hand on her forehead.

Slowly, the noises came into focus and she could make out a girl's voice very close by.

"She's fine," the girl said. "She might just have a sore head for a while, but I've healed the wound."

"Good." Freya jumped as she heard a man's voice not quite as close.

"I think she's awake." Freya could tell that the

girl was smiling when she said it. Her voice sounded gentler and more soothing than the man's harsh tone. "It's alright. Open your eyes."

Freya did open her eyes and looked into the dark eyes of the girl who was speaking. It was her knee that her head was resting on and, as Freya tried to sit up, she pushed her gently back down again. Freya didn't complain, as her head ached so much she would have struggled to stay upright. She could make out the state of the room, though, and remembered the events which had left her unconscious on the floor.

Things were scattered all over the room, and three of the windowpanes had been smashed. Her initial thought was one of horror that Auntie Jessie or her parents would never trust her again, until she remembered the wounded boy who had helped her.

Determined for an explanation, she tried to sit up again and pushed off the girl's hand. Her head was slightly better for sitting up, but she felt wobbly.

The girl, who was now looking concerned, could only have been about sixteen. She looked striking with black hair that fell down her slender body to her waist.

Freya looked across at the man, who was now watching her with a disapproving glare. Although he had some similar features to the girl, he could not look more different. He had a large nose and the same dark eyes which gleamed in the light, but he was much taller than the girl, and he looked older. He looked foreboding, especially as his thin mouth was curved down slightly into a frown. His small beard and hair were so black they almost shone.

"Who are you?" Freya asked, uncertain, and unsure whether she wanted an answer. At this, the man grunted and turned back to Enna who was lying on the sofa, still unconscious.

"Will he be alright?" she asked, turning to the girl, and hoping for a response. She smiled but did not nod.

"I hope so." She laid a gentle hand on Freya's arm. "We've stopped the bleeding but that isn't what has caused this coma."

"Coma?" Freya gasped. "He's in a coma?"

The girl nodded and turned to look at Enna, whose face was peaceful and expressionless.

"That's because of me," Freya said quietly.

"No." The girl turned back to her and shook her head. "You mustn't think that. It was Enna's decision to help you, and a very noble and honourable decision it was too. He will get better, I'm sure of it, but we have to get him proper aid."

"I tried to ring for an ambulance, but he wouldn't let me," Freya said.

"No, they wouldn't have been able to help him. We know some people who might be able to."

"Who *are* you?" Freya repeated her question.

The girl looked torn as though she wanted to tell Freya everything but knew she couldn't. The man didn't reply and looked like he would rather not be there. "Look. Any moment now, my Aunt's going to come through that door, and she'll want to know why there are now three strangers in her house."

"We're here to help," the girl said. "We're friends of Enna's and we need to get him proper aid. You're clearly in danger too - we'd like you to come with us as we can help you."

Freya looked at the girl. Her eyes were as pleading as her words, and she looked honest and trustworthy. But looks could be deceiving. She had learnt that from a very young age. The girl stared back at her and Freya wished she could know what she was thinking.

Freya tried to stand up but felt so dizzy, she slumped back on the floor.

"I'll go to the police tomorrow morning and report the incident. We left them knocked out," she mumbled as she remembered more details, "they might still be there."

"They aren't." The man spoke this time, his low guttural voice sounded almost like a growl. "We checked. They'll be long gone by now, but they'll be more."

"More what?"

"We'll explain everything. But you need to come with us," the girl urged again.

"No," Freya replied without hesitating. "You clearly know Enna and that's fine. I accept that you know the best thing for him, but I don't know you. I've never seen either of you before. I'm not going anywhere with complete strangers."

"That is sensible," the girl said, her soothing voice sounding panicked, "but we're here to help you."

Freya looked at them both and then at Enna. What had happened that night that had made all these strange things happen? If they really *were* happening. It seemed more likely that she was imagining the weird events. Perhaps she should stop the job after school: it was clearly making her too tired and stressed.

"We can explain," the man grunted, bringing her thoughts back, "but you wouldn't believe it."

"That doesn't help, Elamra!" His companion glared at him.

"I'm sorry." He bowed his head quickly to her as though it was an embarrassment and turned back to Enna. Freya was about to speak when she was interrupted by a knock on the door. She tried to get up, but the girl stopped her and put a finger to her lips. She looked across at Elamra who nodded and sidled up to the door. Freya could hardly believe that a man that tall could make himself so quiet. Slowly, and quietly, he bent to look through the peephole for two seconds before he walked swiftly back to them.

"We have to leave," he whispered, "now."

"It'll just be my aunt," Freya looked from each of them to the door and back. When Elamra gave her an angry look and hissed for her to be quiet, she realised too late that she had spoken louder than she meant to. There was another knock at the door, more insistent this time and, in the flurry of activity, Freya wasn't sure what happened next.

Elamra nodded to his companion while he grabbed the unconscious Enna. As Freya was about to argue, she felt the girl pull her close. The door flew open and two men and a woman strode in, but Freya only had time to realise it was not her Auntie Jessie before there was a rush of air, something that felt like beating wings bashing against her face, and she fell onto something cold and wet.

"We made it," the girl gasped, the effort clearly tiring her. "I'm…sorry. You can go… home when we… confirm…it's safe to return."

Freya didn't say anything but looked up. She was too confused; she could not speak.

They had arrived in a garden and the cold, wet landing was short grass which was part of a neat lawn. It was dark of course, so Freya could not make out much of her surroundings, except that there were plenty of trees looming out of the shadows. To one side of her, something immense was cutting into the night sky and Freya, with puzzlement and a little relief, realised it was only a tall brick and stone wall, with high arched windows.

"Come on, Freya," the girl guided her, and Freya did not question how she knew her name. *People do know you in dreams,* she thought. They went through a small door that looked like the windows, like the sort of door you find at the side of a church. Once inside the building, Freya felt the firelight fill her with warmth and she relaxed a little. Then, they walked into a room that looked like a library. Its bookcases filled all walls except the outer one and were filled with ancient-looking books and bits of paper. A desk in the middle of the room was covered with blank scrolls. Along the outside wall, some sticks of fire were burning in their brackets, like in pictures of ancient castles she had seen on websites for homework.

Freya realised that Elamra and Enna had disappeared - probably through the door that was between some of the shelves, but the strange girl led her through another door on the opposite wall. Through this, they walked along a long corridor which came to a sharp turn. All along the walls were flaming torches and paintings of people - all looking stern and foreboding and quite similar to Freya's companion.

At the end of the corridor, they came to one of the largest rooms Freya had ever set foot in. She could fit the school gym hall four times into the gigantic space. The rafters that held up the roof seemed so far above their heads she couldn't make out any detail at all. Around the sides of the room were thick pillars that also supported the roof, and sculptured around the pillars out of red stone, were birds of all shapes and sizes.

Nothing was quite so striking, however, as the statue at the far end of the room. Stretched out, with the tips of his wings touching each side of the immense hall, was a bird made from the blackest stone Freya had ever seen. Its beak was open, and its black eye seemed to take in all its surroundings so that Freya was half surprised she did not see it move. Below the beak was a tufty kind of beard which made Freya realise that this must be a statue of a raven, probably the emblem of this house. She had never seen a raven in the wild before but recognized them from a visit her family had made to the Tower of London four years ago. They were tame then but this one was completely different.

Her companion seemed too tired to talk but hurried through a door to the side of the large bird and up a wide flight of stairs.

The upstairs looked far more comfortable, with lush carpets that were like cushions to Freya's sore feet. They were now in another corridor and the girl finally stopped outside a carved wooden door and pushed it open.

Inside was a large bedroom with two chapel-like windows at one side. It was like the sort of room you would find at a posh hotel - not the sort of hotels Freya had ever been to. Against one wall stood the grandest and most luxurious four poster bed Freya had ever seen and, once she had lain eyes on it, she began to feel unbearably sleepy.

"I'll leave you now," the girl whispered. She sounded like she needed sleep herself. "I think you will need some rest. We will explain everything in the morning."

Puzzled but too tired to argue, Freya walked over to the bed and fell on it. It was the softest bed she had ever been on and she felt her eyes droop close. Certain that all this had been a strange dream and she would wake up in her aunt's cold flat in the morning, she sighed contentedly and allowed herself to fall asleep.

CHAPTER FOUR
Accepting the Invitation

When Freya opened her eyes, the first thing she noticed was that it was a beautiful spring day. The sun was pouring onto her, warming her face as she realised she never got into bed properly last night. The second thing she noticed was that she wasn't in her own bed and she spent some time trying to remember where she was. All she could remember was the strange dream.

Her phone was vibrating in her pocket and she took it out to see why. *Low battery*, it read, and she only had time to see that there was only one bar of signal before it switched itself off. Any other time, she would have been annoyed and frustrated with her three-year-old phone, but she was too intrigued by her surroundings to really care.

She sat up, rubbed her tired eyes, and couldn't

help yawning. She did not jump when she saw a girl sitting smiling at her from the end of the bed, the girl's cheerful face making Freya more confused than frightened. Her puzzlement grew when she realised it was the person from her dream.

So, it wasn't a dream.

"You've slept well. Are you feeling okay?" The girl smiled as Freya simply nodded, feeling confused. "I realised that I never introduced myself last night. My name is Winifred, but you can call me Winnie."

"You seem to know my name," Freya said, and Winnie's smile grew. The permanent dimples on her face showed that Winnie smiled a lot. Freya edged away from her slightly as she remembered more of what had happened last night.

"We must have given you quite a fright," Winnie laughed. "I'm sorry for that."

"I thought it was a dream." Freya mumbled as she tried to remember as much as possible from the night before. "Where are my parents? Enna…there was a boy called Enna…" She trailed off as she remembered what had happened to him.

"He's in the infirmary at the moment." The smile slid from the girl's face. "He has the best help that is available. I don't doubt he will make a full recovery."

Although Winnie swore he would be fine, her

tone of voice made it clear that she did not believe her own words. Freya recognised the gentle-lie-tone that adults used when they talked. She wondered if they ever realised they were doing it, or if she might use it herself one day. There was silence for a few moments while both people tried to work out what the other was thinking.

"And my parents? My auntie?"

"Your aunt went home last night and had no idea that anything had happened," Winnie explained. "I'd like to explain everything to you, but let me just reassure you that when you go back home, your Mum and Dad will greet you like you've just been away at school. I promised your host that I would introduce you this morning. I think he will explain things. It's not really my place, to be honest."

Freya looked around her room, still puzzling about the little details Winnie had tried to explain. It was like a room in a castle, with the high arched windows letting in streams of light, and the heavy velvet curtains drawn back on the carved four poster bed which, Freya noticed, had the same detail she had seen on the pillars yesterday.

"Do you live here?" Freya asked as she looked around, Winnie following her gaze to every detail in the room.

"Yes. I've spent most of my life here," she smiled. "I was invited to train here by your host when I was very young."

"You keep saying 'host'. Who is it?"

"You should come downstairs and find out."

Freya reluctantly stood up but found that she felt refreshed after her deep sleep. Winnie waited outside until she was ready, and they walked down together, Freya looking around her in awe as daylight gave her a better view of all the wonders of the castle.

Winnie didn't speak as they went downstairs, and the people they saw stopped and stared at them as they walked past, which made Freya's fears rise to the surface as they approached a large wooden door.

When Winnie pushed the door open, Freya felt like she had walked onto the set of a film. It was the same hall that they had passed through the night before, with the same intricate carvings and the statue of the raven at the end. Below the statue were two large chairs that looked to be made from ebony, their sleek black carvings looked classy and smooth.

On one of the chairs sat a man. He was old, his beard turning from black to grey, and his hooded eyes stared at the two of them as they walked towards him. Beside him was a teenage boy who must have been about 14, sitting up straight. A silver crown was placed on his short black hair, looking so natural there that Freya wasn't entirely sure it wasn't part of him. Around his shoulders, he wore a robe-like coat with a fur lining. It looked like something you would find in a woman's clothes shop, but you could never have described him as feminine. Freya felt sure he would have been a hit with the girls in the High School.

She followed Winnie up to the two chairs and, when her guide bowed low, Freya did the same, slightly uncertain. There was a ripple of quiet laughter throughout the Great Hall and for the first time, Freya noticed that there were crowds of people gathered around the sides of the room.

"Well, well," the old man said, a hint of laughter evident in his voice, "so you're what all this trouble has been about."

"Trouble? I didn't cause any trouble. I just want to go home." Freya felt her face burn as she grew angry at this unfair accusation.

"My apologies," he said, now laughing outright. "My silly sense of humour."

At this, there were several loud guffaws throughout the hall, as if everyone was trying to be the one with the loudest laugh. The laughter stopped, though, when the old man raised his hand. The boy at his side, and Winnie, seemed to be the only ones who had not laughed at her, and Freya wished that the ground would open and swallow her as she felt countless pairs of eyes staring at the back of her head.

The young man leant to the side and whispered

something in the other's ear.

"You're right, my son." The old man nodded and turned to Freya again. "I think a little privacy is called for. If you'll accompany us, we will have a little walk in the gardens."

The old man said this as though there was no opportunity to refuse and Freya nodded, though her distrust was clear on her face. The old man got up from his chair and, standing, commanded even more authority. The young man followed his father's lead and walked up to her, bowing slightly. Freya, who had always been overshadowed by others and had nothing to make herself stand out from the crowd, was entirely taken aback by this.

They walked out of the large arched door and into the fragrant garden. In the daylight, it took Freya's breath away. The branches of trees bent towards the ground, laden with leaves. The garden looked more like it was summer than spring, with colourful flowers lining the paths and borders. Freya had never been very good at gardening and she could not remember the names of the plants, but she had always loved being outside.

"My name is Eanfrith," the old man said as they reached the garden, "and this is my son, Elialdor."

"And this is your house?" Freya looked back at the castle, its fairy-tale turrets reaching up into the sky.

"Yes, in a way," Eanfrith laughed. "I am, in effect, a king. But the house belongs to my tribe."

"You're what?" Freya stumbled over the words and could not help a little titter. Elialdor laughed too, although Freya wasn't sure if he was laughing at her or his father. For a moment, Eanfrith stood silent before he, too, started laughing.

"I suppose you want to know what is going on! And why the world you know has turned mad."

"Well…" Freya began stammering at the loss for words. "If you put it like that…yes."

"I don't blame you. You have a right to know." It was the first time she had heard Elialdor speak and his voice was smooth and rich.

"My son should tell you." The king took a step back to give centre-stage to the boy, who looked entirely used to this sudden burden of responsibility.

"My father is the leader, or king you might call it, of our small tribe. We live, as you can see, away from the hustle and bustle of the life you are used to." Elialdor smiled at her. "You see, humans, and indeed your good self, cannot understand us, or understand that we even exist."

"Right." Freya didn't know whether to laugh, but her heart sank as she realised they were going to make it all up. *Either that, or they're mad,* she thought. As these thoughts flickered through her mind, a grey-haired man came running towards them and bowed low. He looked so small against the two men he was grovelling before, it was embarrassingly amusing.

"My Lord." He bowed deeply again. "We have received news of Raedwald."

The king glared at the man and he glanced at Freya, a nervous glint in his eyes. One second later it was gone, and Eanfrith turned back to the small man and smiled.

"Thank you, Reve. My son, you must entertain our guest. Please forgive me, Freya, but I have my usual business to attend to. I fear it would bore you if I told you about it."

With a smile and a slight bow, he left Freya with the prince, who did not look taken aback at all. Elialdor continued with his lies as though his father was still there.

"You see, many years ago, the tribes were created to protect humans, who are unable to protect themselves. To do this, we were given gifts. Our most precious gift is long life. Some would call it immortality."

"What?" Freya may have sounded sarcastic and she realised too late that it was obvious how she was feeling.

"I don't blame you for not believing me. Many of your kind wouldn't, but I thought that perhaps you had seen enough of our world to convince you."

"I've been here one night," she corrected him.

"And, that night, you were knocked unconscious by things flying around your flat, without explanation, and you were brought here in seconds from your cold little Living Room. Yes, I was informed of what happened."

"I'm sorry," Freya interrupted him, "I can't believe you."

"You mean you won't believe me." He paused. "Very well but let me finish telling you the truth. We were supposed to protect humans, but it proved harder than expected, and things began to go wrong. We have all but failed because we began to quarrel amongst ourselves. We think, we hope, that you might be our salvation."

"Salvation?" Freya choked on the word. "This gets weirder and weirder. What do you mean?"

"We have become too… well… independent. Our advisers think we need to ask for help from the very people we are supposed to be helping. There have been signs. Omens, I suppose you would call them. They show us that you are the one to help us."

"Right." It was clear from Freya's voice that she was trying hard not to laugh. Elialdor seemed unsurprised by this and almost laughed himself.

"I know it's difficult to understand," he smiled. "I don't know what to say to help you believe us."

As he said it, a thin ray of light appeared from his hand. It turned from white into blue and, as it changed colour, it changed shape and moved as though it were a bird flying. Freya felt her mouth drop open as she realised it *was* a bird. It was larger than normal, but it was unmistakably a crow which, when it opened its translucent beak, made a low croak.

"I don't know how you did that," Freya whispered as her companion closed his hand and the light went. Elialdor just laughed. She had seen a magician perform a trick once before at a Christmas event - he had sent cards flying through the air to land on a man's head. There had been lots of laughter from the grown-ups, but she had been disappointed with it. This, however, could not be explained. A tiny thought appeared in her head that, perhaps, just perhaps, she should believe what the boy was saying.

"This world is full of strange things we can't quite explain but want to. Please forgive me for showing you in this way. Really, we can do a lot more than these tricks."

"I don't understand this place," Freya smiled but she didn't feel happy, only confused. She wanted the comfort of her parents, her home, just anything that was familiar. She wished Winnie was there, even though she hardly knew her. She seemed so kind and cheerful.

"You have only just arrived here. Stay here for a few days and I think you will begin to understand more."

"I need to go home. My auntie will be back," Freya said absentmindedly, as she looked around her at the beautiful gardens and windows of the castle.

"That can be sorted," Elialdor urged. "Your family will not realise you are gone until you return when it will be like nothing has happened. As for the flat, our people sorted all of that last night."

Freya laughed out of complete confusion but could find nothing to say.

Elialdor only smiled and led her through more of the gardens, which were bursting with unexpected beauty. Everywhere Freya looked, there was another plant she had not seen before, and she could not help running her hand along the branches of some of the trees. The leaves were wet as though it had been raining but the ground beneath their feet was dry and warm.

"You must have so many questions," Elialdor smiled. "Please, don't be afraid to ask anything."

"You live in such a beautiful place, Elialdor," Freya began, and the prince bowed his head in gratefulness of the compliment, "and you clearly have many people to command."

"We are lucky with that," he nodded. "The Crows are one of the most powerful tribes. Was there a question?"

"Well...why do you need my help?"

"Like I said, I believe we have become too

independent." Elialdor smiled but looked down at the floor.

Freya could remember her Mum telling her that, if people couldn't make eye contact, they were probably lying or, at least, hiding something.

"I have nothing to offer," Freya said, and shuffled, suddenly finding her feet very interesting. "I think you have the wrong person."

Freya found herself too embarrassed to stay there. She was aware of Elialdor watching her but didn't want to look up at his face in case he was angry with what she had said, or if he would agree they had made a mistake. Puzzled, she realised she wanted neither. She didn't actually want to leave this enchanted place yet. She felt his hand on her shoulder and raised her eyes to find herself looking into his gentle and patient face. Relief spread through her, making her heart beat faster and her fingers tingle.

"Your unwillingness to accept it confirms my point," Elialdor smiled and Freya felt a rush of frustrated annoyance mingle with the relief. "Please, give us a chance to persuade you to stay. I think you will like being here for a few days."

"I need to go home," she whispered, although something was urging her to accept the invitation. The more she saw of this beautiful place, the less she wanted to leave and the more she wanted this adventure.

"Stay for two days and I promise that you won't be disappointed. But it's your choice. You can leave at any moment." Elialdor smiled and Freya hesitated. The promise of adventure was almost too much to resist.

"I have work to do this afternoon," the prince continued, "but I've asked Winnie to keep you entertained while I'm busy. I think you made quite an impression on her."

Freya was unsure what this statement meant but something at the back of her mind, some niggling little opinion, told her that staying was the only option. Feeling like she, and the whole world, had gone mad, she nodded.

CHAPTER FIVE
Sea Eagles

Freya found Winnie's company surprisingly comfortable given that she had only met her last night and on stressful terms. She found that Winnie got the same excitement from being in the garden as she did, her dimples growing with wide grins each time she turned a corner in the enchanted garden. They talked about how strange it was that everything seemed more beautiful here than the place Freya was used to. Winnie was as interested to talk about 'humans' as Freya was to learn about her.

"Why do you have to go back to school?" she asked as they were wandering through the avenue of trees to the south of the castle. The trees led to a gatehouse where they seemed to be heading.

"Well...I want to be a doctor when I get older,

so I'm hoping to get into university, but I need to learn loads first. Besides, when I get older, I'll need a job to pay for bills and things," Freya said, remembering the stressed looks on her parents' faces when they opened official-looking letters.

"Don't you share all that cost?" Winnie asked, very interested.

"Share it? With who?"

"Well, the rest of your tribe," she said as though it was the simplest thing in the world. "Or family, I suppose."

"Oh. Well, I don't expect I'll stay with them when I go to university."

There was a silence and, when Freya turned to her companion to see what the matter was, she saw Winnie regarding her with a look of extreme pity.

"Oh, I'm so sorry. I had no idea." Winnie looked like she was on the verge of crying for her poor unfortunate friend.

"No, no," Freya laughed.

Freya felt that she could not explain it any better and was puzzled as to why Winnie thought it was such a terrible thing that she would no longer live with her parents.

"We live together here," Winnie explained, realising after a while that she might have confused her. "This is the main stronghold of the Crow tribe and we share everything. I assumed that, in your society, it would be the same."

"Do your parents live here too then?"

"No," Winnie whispered, suddenly quiet, "they are not here anymore, I'm afraid."

The moment the words had left Freya's mouth, she knew they were not well thought-out. Winnie's eyes filled with tears that made her usually cheerful face grow grey and Freya rebuked herself for so clearly causing her new friend pain. She whispered an apology, but Winnie just smiled.

"No, it's me who should apologise. I can't seem to put them behind me, even though I left them years ago. It is the one thing that will let me down in battle."

Her companion's words brought a new surprise to the conversation. In battle?

Freya looked up to realise that they had walked the length of the sheltered avenue and had reached the gatehouse. It looked as grand as the castle itself, and impenetrable. Winnie seemed to follow her thought process and was eager to divert the conversation.

"It has never been breached." She lifted her chin in pride. "Please, come inside. I'll introduce you to my old tutor."

As Freya walked through the thick, carved wooden door into a high-ceilinged but plain room, she was expecting to find an old man sitting inside, perhaps reading a book or sagely looking out one of the slit windows. She was not expecting a young man to throw a spear at them as they entered. Fortunately, Winnie caught it with astounding dexterity before it could cause any harm.

"Careful now, Elamra. The king would not be pleased if you caused any harm to his guest."

Elamra - the man who had thrown the spear - was a broad man with a square face. His features looked so perfect it was like they had been finely carved. He had a small beard and black hair, so black it shone. It was this that reminded Freya she had seen him before.

"You were there in the flat last night," she said, trying to piece the events of last night together again.

"Yes," Winnie nodded before Elamra could speak, "he helped me find you."

Elamra did not talk much and Freya grew annoyed at the man's abrupt rudeness. He would talk to Winnie, but his expression made it clear that he did not approve of Freya's presence.

"Elamra taught me everything I know," Winnie said, a hint of pride in her voice. "He is the best soldier we have."

"Your guest is finding this conversation tiring, Winifred." Elamra had clearly mistaken the look of distaste for him to be distaste for the topic.

"No, really," Freya's voice was clipped, "I'm really interested."

Winnie looked from Freya to Elamra with

uncertainty as neither spoke.

"She is the king's guest, Elamra." Winnie frowned at the man. "Remember that when you welcome her next time."

"Always considerate." The broad man smiled at Winnie and, at first Freya thought he was making fun of them both but then she realised there was a connection of mutual respect between the two. Elamra turned to her, making Freya feel a little threatened. "I apologise. I was never very good at small talk."

He bowed his head and, not wanting to appear rude, Freya did the same before Winnie led her out of the gatehouse. As they were walking back down the avenue, Winnie spoke again.

"I'm sorry about him. He was right when he said he's never good at talking. He is an exceptional fighter though."

"I didn't mean to be rude, but I think I might have offended him."

"No, no." Winnie smiled. "It isn't you. Elamra has…"

She trailed off and sighed. Seeing it was clearly upsetting, Freya did not push it, but Winnie seemed to want to talk.

"His mother was killed, oh many, many, years ago, by a human. Some stupid man shot her."

"That's awful!" Freya gasped, feeling suddenly guilty for her harsh opinion of the man.

"Yes, and it gets worse," Winnie sighed,

subdued. "His father couldn't handle it. He went and killed the person responsible."

Freya said nothing. She felt sorry for Elamra for losing his mother, wondering what she would feel if her Mum died. For a moment, her eyes prickled with the thought of such a pain, until she remembered what her friend had said about Elamra's father. Of course, his father must have been devastated but to go and murder someone else for it was barbaric…terrifying. Thinking back to the man she had just met, she wondered if he was capable of the same violence.

"Where is his dad now?" she asked finally, expecting her companion to say 'in prison'. Instead, Winnie looked at her, confused.

"He is dead," she said, as though it were the simplest thing in the world.

The statement was abrupt and so unexpected that, for a while, the two girls wandered along the gardens side by side, each stuck in their own thoughts.

The walled garden was full of surprises, with hidden doors here and there with lawns, rose gardens, rock gardens, and kitchen gardens that seemed to stretch on forever. It was an optical illusion that couldn't possibly be true.

Only when they walked back into the castle through an iron-studded door, Winnie finally spoke, mistaking Freya's silence as annoyance.

"I really cannot apologise enough for Elamra's

behaviour. I should have known how he would react."

"Please, don't." Freya shook her head, thinking of his terrible past. "I had no idea he had such a good reason for being like that."

Winnie smiled and did not bring up the subject again, preferring to show Freya even more delights of her home, her eyes glistening proudly as she watched her stunned expression.

Exploring the inside of the castle was almost as exciting as the grounds and Freya found she was lost instantly. She knew that, if she had to find her own way back to the garden door, she would be stuck. The castle was full of corridors, tiny rooms which didn't have any clear use, and larger rooms which were decorated with tapestries and armour. Light spilled into each of them through large glass windows. It was in an enormous conservatory that Winnie stopped her tour. The room seemed to be made of glass and looked out to the castle gardens, slightly shaded by ancient trees. Freya had never been anywhere so peaceful. She felt like she could sit here for hours simply listening to the sound of a waterfall, which was coming from a large water fountain in the centre of the floor.

"I thought I would bring you to see Enna." Winnie smiled and pointed to another door. Freya was sorry to be leaving this room but walked through the door to find herself in a larger room with a high ceiling. It seemed very quiet, even though there were several people walking around. Around the edge of the room there were several beds, like in the hospital ward she had been to with the school choir at Christmas.

"Where is he?" Freya looked around but couldn't see any familiar faces.

"Just over here." Winnie led her over to a bed next to the opposite door. An elderly man was standing at the foot of the bed and Freya felt a nervous smile slip over her face as she realised it was indeed Enna who was lying, unconscious, on the soft bed. *Enna*, she thought, *who had caused such havoc back at her flat*. Thinking back to last night seemed strange: it seemed so long ago, and so far away.

The old man looked up when the two approached. He looked like Enna, with the same hooked nose and sharp eyes, but he had wrinkles around his forehead which showed worry and concern, almost as if it had become a permanent feature.

"And you are?" The old man sounded as weary as he looked, so Freya understood his tone. Winnie, on the other hand, looked sharply across at him.

"I am Winifred, the king's captain. This is Freya, the king's guest." There was significant emphasis, Freya noticed, on 'king's guest'. The old man bowed his head slightly.

"I am sorry," he muttered. "I have other things on my mind. I did not mean to be rude."

Winnie bowed her head in return but said nothing. Through a need to change the subject, Freya looked at the boy on the bed, who was oblivious to all these words.

"Hasn't he woken up since last night?" she said, diverting the old man's attention.

"No," he sighed and turned back to Enna, "he has not."

"Do you mind me asking..." Freya began, looking from Winnie to the man. "But when he was unconscious in my flat, things started flying around the room. Why was that?"

The old man turned to Freya and regarded her with a sudden interest.

"So, he was with you?" he murmured and then laughed. "Their salvation? You're a child."

In response to his tone, Winnie shot him an angry glance, but he seemed to hardly notice. Between his laughter, he stared at Freya, who found herself backing away.

"That's enough," Winnie snapped. "She is the king's guest."

"As am I, captain," he mocked, his laughter stopping. "The king has invited me to stay until my son is recovered, so I advise you to tread carefully."

Winnie did not argue with him further but sat

on the edge of the bed and took Enna's hand in her own, smiling at the boy's peaceful face. A mischievous glint appeared on her now-twinkling face and she lifted by hand and kissed it once. His father's face turned red, but he said nothing.

"Freya," she whispered. "I must go and resume my duties, but you are free to wander around the castle and its grounds if you like."

"I'll stay here for a while, I think," she replied. "Thank you for helping me today."

Winnie bowed slightly and walked away in the direction they had come.

"He saved me." Freya looked up at the old man, who regarded her with significant interest. "He's your son?"

"Yes, he's my son." The man's tone was lighter, softer, than it had been when Winnie was there. "And our prince. I am the king of our tribe."

Freya smiled at this strange statement and, not really knowing how to address a king, bowed her head like Winnie had done. Feeling awkward, she turned back to Enna, who looked so peaceful.

"When I was called and told of what had happened, everything was chaos in here," the old man said. "Much like it was, I think, in your flat. The chaos is kept in control by my being here."

"So many things about today and last night I don't understand."

"I'll help you understand where I can." He

said, smiling. "My name is Eli. You are not in my tribe, so we shan't bother with any titles. What are your questions?"

Freya began to feel a little more relaxed as Eli's tone changed.

"What tribe is that?"

"Eagles. Sea eagles."

This made no sense to Freya, but Eli had said it like it was the simplest thing in the world, and she was worried she would sound stupid by asking him to explain further. Instead, she thought of more questions that were puzzling her.

"Why was it chaos in my flat, when Enna was wounded?"

"My dear son has never been steady in the skills he uses." Eli glanced at Freya to see if she had understood. She hadn't. "From a very young age, Enna has not been able to use his skills well. Sometimes he is too powerful, other times he cannot perform a simple task. And, when he is in this state, he will not have the same control of himself that he has learned."

Freya was unsure whether she was less or more confused than she had been before, but she was thankful to Eli for trying to explain.

"From what I understood from Enna, he is a son to be proud of," Freya whispered. "I owe him a lot."

For a moment, she thought she might have

seen Eli's eyes glistening and the old man turned his face away.

"My dear boy," he whispered. "He has never fitted in as I'd have hoped. My younger son would be a better heir to my throne, but tradition dictates the title must go to him. I worry about that day when it comes."

Freya did not have an answer for this but felt confused and a little upset on Enna's behalf, who she appreciated for his help the night before. The incident at the flat had scared her but she had reminded herself of how Enna had protected her in that alleyway, which now seemed a thousand miles away.

She didn't speak much more to Eli after that, feeling stung for the poor boy. The Eagle king seemed to have lost any interest in conversation too and stared at his son's body. After a few minutes of awkward silence, Freya stood up and whispered goodbye to both eagles, before turning back to the glass room. She was not aware of Eli watching her go with interest, his eyes burning into her back right up until she closed the door to the infirmary.

Freya tried to remember the way back to her room. For the first four times of trying, she wasn't sure where she had taken the wrong turn but each time she tried, she kept coming back to the glass room so must have been walking in circles. On her fifth time, she found her way to the Great

Hall which was empty of all but one individual who was sweeping the floor. Remembering the blur of the night before, she retraced her steps as best she could and finally found her way alone back to her room.

Curled up against the window, watching the evening sun slip behind the horizon, her eyes suddenly felt very heavy. By the time Winnie opened the door to see if Freya was okay, she was already fast asleep on the four-poster bed, unaware that the next two days would change everything.

CHAPTER SIX
A Macabre Threat

Freya was unsure what time it was when she woke up, but the sun was streaming in through the large window, creating sunbeams that fell on the cold fireplace. Realising she was alone in the room, she lay back again on the soft pillow and considered the events of the past day. She had been stunned yesterday morning to realise that it had not been a dream and a part of her had thought that, when she woke up this morning, she would be back at home. As opposed to her confusion yesterday, she was surprised to find that she was happy for the opportunity to spend another day in this strange, magical place. Her happiness faded, though, when she realised that tomorrow was Monday and she would have to return to school. On the other hand, her parents would be home. Although she was enchanted by her new surroundings, she had to admit that she missed her Mum and Dad.

With a certain amount of caution, mixed with the excitement, she got dressed and went downstairs in search of someone familiar. It must have been earlier than she had thought because there was not the same hustle and bustle as yesterday. Blurry-eyed people wandered around, doing their jobs and Freya felt a sudden need to find the large conservatory next to the hospital room. She wandered around the corridors and rooms, looking for anywhere familiar, until she finally stumbled across the glass room.

The early morning sun made the room into a greenhouse and some of the windows were opened slightly to let in the fresh morning breeze. The water feature in the middle of the room splashed happily over itself. With some time on her own in what was certainly her favourite room in the castle, Freya moved closer to the fountain. It was taller than she was, and the water spilled out of the stone branches on a stone tree. Beneath the branches were large birds, some sitting and others flying. Freya realised with astonishment that the birds that were flying were held up by nothing. She brushed her hand against them and felt the air, but there was no explanation. There was no invisible thread like she had seen on magic tricks. The water from the branches spilt onto the birds' backs and dripped from their wings into a small pool at the bottom. The grace of the water as it fell, and the illusion of the birds' flight, was mesmerizing and Freya didn't know how long she was standing there watching before she heard a voice behind her.

"It was a gift to my grandfather." Freya jumped around to see Prince Elialdor watching her, a smile catching his dark eyes as well as his mouth.

Unsure what to do or say, Freya bowed, but Elialdor laughed and walked over to her.

"Please. You're my father's guest. There is no need for you to bow. Indeed, it is I who should bow to you."

"I don't know what you mean," Freya murmured as Elialdor bowed low, feeling that he was somehow mocking her.

"I didn't mean any offense. I simply meant that guests matter more to my father than his own son. So, you are of more importance in this castle than I am." The prince did not sound angry or sad when he said this. "I'd like to talk to you." He pointed to a sofa, woven out of rushes with cushions covered in black feathers, and led Freya over to it. Feeling uncomfortable, she sat on the edge of the seat while he sat back opposite her.

"You live in a very beautiful house." Freya smiled, trying to find conversation. She looked around at the garden beyond the windows and rubbed her eyes as the sun shone into them. Elialdor looked suddenly concerned.

"You look tired." He sat up. "How are you feeling?"

"I'm fine," Freya said, a little taken aback. "It was a very confusing, exciting day yesterday."

Elialdor relaxed slightly but did not sit back on the comfortable chair and creases of concern formed on his forehead.

"I'm sorry I couldn't be with you yesterday, but Winnie said that you enjoyed exploring the castle and gardens."

"Yes, I loved the garden." Freya's mind turned to her encounter with Elamra yesterday. "I met some interesting people too."

"Winnie told me you'd met our famous Elamra," the prince laughed, his laughter sounding so genuine that Freya relaxed slightly. "You must know that he distrusts humans, but he is a good man."

"He certainly made an impression," Freya laughed but stopped and looked serious. "Winnie told me that his parents are both dead."

"Yes." The look was now mirrored on Elialdor's features. "It was a long time ago now, but I remember it clearly. But I'm sure when Elamra gets to know you, you will find him more polite."

"Well," Freya murmured, unsure how to approach the subject, "I have to get back to school tomorrow, so I'll probably have to leave today. I can't thank you enough for letting me stay, though."

Clearly, she hadn't handled it well, as Elialdor's face grew white, making a sharp contrast with his black hair. His mouth grew thin and his eyes held a look of worry. Freya apologised quietly but this seemed only to make things worse as the prince did not look angry, just very worried and unhappy.

"Stay for a few more days, I beg you." Elialdor's eyes showed that he really was begging. "There is still so much of this place that you haven't seen."

"Believe me when I say I would rather stay here than have to go back to school, but I miss my Mum and Dad. You're so lucky living in a place like this but I have to get back." She laughed, hoping it would make her companion feel better, but he still looked worried.

"Then you must make the most of today," he said at last. Freya smiled as her mixed feelings confused her. While she was relieved that Elialdor understood, and pleased she would see her family soon, she was ashamed at how disappointed she felt at leaving the enchanted place. Shamefully telling herself off for these feelings, she stood up from the sofa and the prince did the same.

"Besides," the prince added, "tonight, you will see our castle in all its splendour."

Freya asked why, puzzled at this strange

announcement, but Elialdor seemed to childishly enjoy keeping the secret, and continued to change the subject.

"I hope you'll allow me to show you more of our castle's treasures today. It's so early, I don't think many people will be up so we may as well make the most of it." Elialdor smiled and held out his hand to her. Cautiously, she took it and he grinned.

"Well, I see that this is your favourite room. It's mine too," the prince said, a slight hint of pride in his voice. "The fountain was a gift to my late grandfather, the king's father, from a good friend."

"Who?" Freya asked, admiring the beauty and excellence of the piece. When Elialdor did not answer, she looked at him expectantly.

"I'm sure you know now that there are several tribes, all with their own gifts. Well, we are the Crow tribe. This was a gift from the owl king."

"Owls?" Freya could not help a little laugh, "there are Owls too? Are they like you?"

"No," he said sharply, and she looked up in surprise. "They are nothing like us. And we are no longer good friends. In fact, it would probably be best if you didn't mention this to anyone."

The worry in the prince's voice made Freya agree to his request and they moved from the room into the cool garden. The sun was shining and there were no clouds, promising a beautiful summer-like day. For now, though, it was a morning with magical promise and potential. Everything was so still and quiet, Freya thought she could hear the plants growing.

"Ah, there's Elamra now," Elialdor smiled and led Freya over to where the large figure of Elamra sat, hunched over and watching the garden. After her encounter yesterday, Freya wanted to escape from meeting him again, but knew it would be rude. Elamra looked up at their approach and bowed his head to the prince.

"Something is happening," he said and Elialdor could not hide his look of concern from Freya.

"I hear you met our guest yesterday," he said, clearly trying to change the conversation. Elamra nodded and gave Freya a cold smile before he turned back to the wall of the garden. Freya could not see what was so special about it. It looked like an average garden wall, with latticed trellis which supported some purple flowers, just beginning to open out. She could not see beyond the wall but Elamra seemed to find something there interesting.

"Come and look," he said, getting to his feet and, without looking to see if they were following, he walked over to the gate-like door. Elialdor paused before he led Freya over to follow. Opening the door, Freya could see masses of parkland, with a lush green floor and ancient trees dotted here and there. Further over from the wall was a hedge of tall trees. Beyond that, she could see nothing.

Elialdor and Elamra, however, seemed to be able to see something lying on the grass, and they tentatively walked towards it. It was small, that's all Freya could tell from where she was standing. Bending down to look closer, she realised it was a small shrew. A small, dead shrew.

She looked up as Elamra pointed over somewhere else and Freya realised that it was another shrew. A little further along was a dead mouse, and she realised that there must have been about a hundred dead rodents scattered across the small bit of parkland.

"What is it that's done this?" Freya gasped. "A cat couldn't kill all of these!"

Elamra looked across at her, clearly wanting to say something and struggling not to. Elialdor shook his head.

"No, you're right." His brow was creased in worry. "This wasn't done by a cat." He glanced at Elamra, who nodded.

"Owls, then?" Freya questioned, remembering the conversation earlier. Elamra glanced back at her, the usual look of indifference replaced with interest.

"Yes." Elialdor gave Elamra a look which could only have meant for him to keep his mouth shut. "I must tell my father about this. It is clearly a message they are wanting to send. They just have such a cruel way of doing it. Poor things."

Without another word, Elialdor led Freya back through the garden door, with one brief glance back at the park. Elamra left the park too, slowly, watching them so that Freya could almost feel his gaze burning into her back. The prince was storming towards the castle faster than Freya could manage and she had to run to keep up. Elialdor would not slow down but kept glancing behind to ensure Freya was still there, eventually offering his hand and rushing towards the castle. His behaviour puzzled and frightened her. Surely she, having only just come here, could not be in danger from these Owls? Why would they be a threat to her?

The prince did not even stop when they were inside the castle but continued at his fast pace until he pushed open the door to the Great Hall. The hall was full of people again, gathering around the king, who was the only person Elialdor seemed to notice.

"I need to speak to you now, Father. Please." He made only a small effort to bow and Freya did the same, although she was slightly out of breath after their journey through the castle and grounds.

"What is this?" The king sounded angry and everyone in the room stared in silence. "Why are you dragging around my guest?"

Elialdor seemed to only just realise that he was still clutching Freya's hand. He let it drop. Unsure what to do, Freya remained rooted to the spot.

"Alone, please, Father." There was a note of begging in his voice - something that the king clearly noticed as his face relaxed and the anger was replaced with concern. He nodded, and everyone else got up and left silently.

"Stay here," Elialdor whispered to Freya. It would never have occurred to her to leave as she was too scared to do anything but stay.

"What is it, my son?" Eanfrith asked when the hall was all but deserted.

"A threat, Father." As Elialdor began to explain what had been found in the parkland, Eanfrith's face grew more and more worried and he kept glancing across at Freya, who was just staring at the floor.

"And our guest?" he asked when his son had finished. Freya looked up, realising he was talking about her.

"I was with Elialdor when he saw what had happened." She cleared her throat as her mouth felt suddenly dry. "I don't really understand it."

The king seemed satisfied with the answer and Freya could hear Elialdor let out a slight sigh of relief.

"Freya," the king smiled, "please. My son and I need to discuss some matters and I don't think you will be interested."

"One moment, Father." Elialdor stopped Freya as she moved towards the door. "Freya said she needed to leave today to get back to school tomorrow. I think given this new threat…"

"It will simply not be possible," the king nodded in agreement with what he guessed his son was about to say.

"No, wait," Freya felt her temper rising at the total disrespect for her. "I need to get home."

"I'm afraid that is out of the question." The king did not sound like he was going to put up with an argument. "You must remain here until we are sure you will be safe back home."

"Of course I'll be safe," Freya could hear her voice rising but seemed incapable of stopping herself. "This is your battle. I have nothing against these people, and they have nothing against me. I don't know what I'm doing here anyway! I really appreciate your hospitality, but I can't let it ruin my actual life."

Freya knew immediately that she had made a mistake. The king's face was hard to read but it held a look of anger, although it seemed to be directed more towards his son than her. Elialdor walked quickly over to her.

"Go to the glass room," he suggested, leading her towards the door. "I'll come and find you soon, but please just let me talk with my father and then I'll explain things to you." He said this in such a quiet voice, his father could not possibly have heard.

Freya nodded slowly and bowed to the king. She could almost remember the way to the glass room and only got lost once or twice, correcting her mistake almost immediately.

Sitting on the sofa, she looked at the fountain with the water spilling from its branches. It really was beautiful and a magnificent gift. *What had happened,* she thought to herself, *to make the Owls and Crows hate each other so much?*

It was the sound of water and the calming atmosphere it produced that made her so drowsy that she fell asleep.

She did not think she had been asleep very long when she felt a cool hand on her forehead and opened her eyes to look into the concerned face of Elialdor. Winnie, she realised, was there, also looking concerned. Freya tried to remember her dream, which had seemed so real, but all that she could remember was a shadow: a man with no face.

"How are you feeling?" the prince asked.

"I'm fine." Freya sat up. "I'm just tired."

Elialdor didn't look convinced but Winnie stopped him fussing.

"I believe you promised Freya an explanation," she prompted. The prince nodded but still looked distracted.

"I'm afraid the king is adamant that you will not leave the castle or its garden. You are not even allowed into the park, given that the Owls have clearly found a way to get past our first defences. He doesn't want me to talk to you about this, but I think you should know."

"And what about home?" Freya snapped. She had to admit that she would rather remain in the luxury of the castle than go back to school, but she had not missed her parents as much when she knew they'd be away. Now they were coming back home, she was concerned what they might think, despite Elialdor's insistence that they wouldn't notice.

"When you can return home, your parents will not even notice you have been gone," Winnie said but Freya was not about to believe her either. She didn't reply.

"The reason you will not be allowed outside the garden wall is because the Owls will now associate you with us. They realised we needed you before you came here. That was who attacked you in that alleyway before Enna stepped in."

"And it was an owl that caused all that..." Freya struggled for the right word.

"We believe they did that as a threat," Winnie sighed, "to show us that they have broken through our barriers. We don't know how they did it yet, but we'll find out soon. In the meantime, one of us - or Elamra - will make sure you're safe."

"Elamra?" Freya repeated. "I don't need looking after. I'm strong. And capable."

"I assure you." Freya jumped as she heard a low voice behind her, "I am perfectly capable of keeping you safe."

Perhaps she should have checked that it had just been the three of them in the room, but she felt angry that Elamra had been there without making himself known.

"He's right," Winnie beamed, "he is the best we have."

"Then surely he should be protecting the king?"

"And I will be," Elamra said, "when Winifred or the prince is with you."

There seemed to be no argument on the matter and Freya gave up the fight in favour of learning more about the Owls, telling herself that she would not be 'protected' and determined to lose her 'protector' at the first opportunity.

"And why have these Owls turned against you?" she asked. Elialdor looked down at his hands but it was Winnie who finally spoke.

"A long time ago when we were very young, there was a terrible misunderstanding. That's all you should know. Elialdor, I don't know what the king would do if he knew we'd been talking to his guest like this."

"He already suspects it, Winnie," Elialdor mumbled. Freya had a feeling there had been a severe argument between the prince and his father while she had been asleep.

"Then that's everything you need to know," Elamra commanded, "until the king decides it is right for you to learn more."

The others looked like they wanted to argue with him but said nothing. Elialdor looked up suddenly as if he just remembered something.

"The king is adamant that the ball is to go ahead, and that you will be his guest of honour." Elialdor smiled as though their conversation about enemies and Owls had not happened. Elamra gave a grunt of displeasure.

"Yes, Elamra," Winnie said in return, "the king wants to show the Owls that they can't stop us. It's important."

Freya smiled at the tone of Winnie's voice and tried to imagine anyone else speaking like this to the warrior.

"The ball is now tomorrow, Freya. Tomorrow evening." Elialdor smiled. "Through the day, there will be lots of people arriving from all over the country."

Elialdor seemed genuinely excited at the idea of this event and Freya couldn't deny that it would be a helpful distraction from the disturbing threat of today. Surely a party would be a welcome event?

CHAPTER SEVEN
The Harbinger of Death

Elialdor had been right: throughout the next day, a lot of strange people were arriving. They looked so funny Freya enjoyed watching their arrivals. It certainly made a welcome change from trying to make conversation with Elamra, whose job that morning had been to watch her every move, which was becoming even more irritating. At twelve years old, she felt certain she was old enough to look after herself and had tried to get rid of him twice before he had become wise to this.

That morning was the first time she had eaten there in the presence of other people. Elamra had refused to eat but had no problem watching her as she tried to be polite and take smaller mouthfuls. If he disapproved of something she did, he would make it known by a loud snort, and

Freya was finding it almost impossible to control her temper with the man.

"Where's Winnie?" She asked pointedly when he grunted a laugh at her gulping down a drink only to get hiccups from it.

"Winifred is greeting the guests. Some of her family are arriving today. I'll be with you until midday."

"Great!" Freya rolled her eyes.

So, she had watched everyone arrive from an upstairs window. She could not have made up such characters if she had tried. Some of them wore dazzling clothes of gold and red, while others preferred browns or greys. Some were over-confident in their greetings, while others were shy and subdued, speaking to the king in embarrassment at such surroundings. Despite this, Elamra did have his uses for Freya, as he explained who they were.

A group of quiet, beautiful people, dressed in flowing grey robes, were apparently the dove tribe. Another group, who seemed to ooze confidence and wore smart colourful clothes were the blue tits. Freya could not help a little giggle at their unfortunate name. At least 'Crows' sounded mysterious, and 'Doves' sounded graceful. Even Elamra found this amusing when Freya shared her thoughts with him. He seemed to like that Freya described them as mysterious and agreed that they were lucky, not only in their name, but also in their abilities and standing in the tribal community.

"Of course," he added, "being one of the most powerful tribes does have its difficulties. For instance, not many of the other tribes are locked in a centuries-long war."

"Centuries?" Freya turned to him. "I thought Elialdor said that it started when he was young."

"And how young do you think he is?" scoffed Elamra. His tone did not anger her this time though, as she was too curious and puzzled that the prince, who only looked slightly older than herself, could have been alive centuries ago.

"Look at that one," Freya said in wonder as she saw an elderly man walk up to the king and kiss his hand before putting his arms around him. He had wide eyes and looked like he had jewels studded into his face. His sleek sandy brown hair was matched by the cloak he wore, that flowed so naturally it seemed like water rippling on a stream.

"Ah," Elamra smiled, "the king's cousin. He is the lord of the 'Jays'. He's like an underking who is answerable to King Eanfrith."

"Because he's a Crow?"

"That's right," Elamra gave a slight laugh. "You're already getting used to our ways."

Freya had become so used to his rudeness that this mini-compliment was more than welcome. She didn't say much more for a while, the shock too much, until Elialdor came rushing in.

"I've been caught up in greeting people. I'm so sorry, Freya, Elamra. I should have been here sooner." The prince sounded out of breath.

"It is no trouble," Elamra smiled. "We have been watching people arrive and comparing the different tribes. It's been quite educational for her, I think."

The feeling of being complimented was replaced once more by a feeling of annoyance as Elamra spoke as though she was a small child.

Elamra left, bowing slightly and actually smiling at Freya, and Elialdor looked from one to the other with puzzlement and glee. When the large man left, the prince could not help but give a slight laugh but looked instantly apologetic when Freya glared across at him.

"So, you've made a bit of a break-through this morning?" He could not hide the laughter in his voice.

"Elamra is so patronising. I'm twelve, not four." Freya sounded grumpy. "But he's been very helpful in telling me who everyone is."

She turned back to the window in time to see Winnie rush forward and embrace two elderly people who, Freya thought, must have been her relatives.

"Why is Winnie here then? Is it usual for you people to leave home? Only, with such an immense place like this, it hardly seems necessary. She seemed so upset when I mentioned leaving my parents."

"Winnie is one of the best soldiers we have. Elamra trained her himself and she is an excellent captain. We could not bear to lose her." Elialdor stepped over to the window and smiled at Winnie's reunion.

"But she clearly misses her family," Freya whispered and Elialdor placed a gentle hand on her shoulder.

"We have all had to make sacrifices in this war. You and I included."

"Elamra said that the war had been happening for hundreds of years, but you said it began when you were young." Freya opted for one of the questions that had been the most confusing.

"Did he now?" Freya was unsure whether Elialdor sounded amused or annoyed. "Well, I'm sure you've realised by now that we're not exactly human."

"I'm not sure what would surprise me now, if anything," she mumbled, hoping her companion might explain this new puzzle.

"I told you that our most precious gift is immortality," Elialdor reminded her, "so centuries to you may only seem like fourteen years to me. It's a difficult concept, I know."

Freya did not answer. She believed more now than she had done before, but something in the back of her head told her that all this was impossible. Still, she had seen impossible things in the last couple of days.

"My father is looking forward to the ball tonight, and it promises to be quite the party. You'll love it, seeing all the different tribes."

"Tonight?" Freya stood up, a little taken aback. "I don't want to be rude, but I can't go to this ball thing. I've never been to a ball in my life."

"Oh, you'll love it." Elialdor did not sound like someone to be argued with. "You're never too young or too old to go to your first ball. Besides, the king says you are the guest of honour and you don't want to argue with him."

Freya laughed but she wasn't sure if it was a joke.

"Isn't dancing a necessity at these things?" she pointed out. "I've never danced and somehow I don't think I'll be very good at it."

"Our balls aren't like your average event," the prince laughed. "Each of the tribes have their own dance, more for everyone else's entertainment than their own. All you'll have to do is to look interested and impressed by each of them. I learned that from a very young age."

"Oh, right. Like two hundred years?" Freya laughed, as did Elialdor.

"Yes. Something like that."

When the prince suggested finding something more interesting to do, they wandered around the castle looking for a diversion. They got this by watching and meeting all kinds of different people who had come to honour the king at tonight's ball, but they eventually found themselves in the glass room, once more looking at the sculpture of the fountain.

"Tell me more about the Owls," Freya requested. She couldn't deny that the statue fascinated her. It was such a magnificent gift, it seemed tragic that the people who gifted it were now at war. Elialdor, standing behind her, placed his hands on her shoulders.

"Their king is a man called Raedwald. He commands perhaps more than even the Crows. Perhaps the most powerful of our kind." Elialdor spoke almost in a whisper. "It was him who killed my grandfather."

"The king?" Freya turned around to face him. The prince's face looked so sad, but proud all the same.

"Yes. But he was my grandfather too." He bowed his head. "Raedwald was angry with our tribe and wanted revenge. So, he killed him."

"Revenge for what?" Freya could not help but ask.

"He believed we committed a crime that we did not. The only way to prove our innocence was to find the truly guilty party: something we failed to do. So, we remain at war." Although Freya wanted to find out more on the matter, the look of pain on Elialdor's face stopped her from asking any more questions. She was struggling to piece together the fragments of information she had received, and each conversation made it more intriguing.

The prince offered to eat dinner with her and, in his words, she was doing him a favour as otherwise he would have had to eat with his uncles and aunts, which was clearly something he avoided where at all possible. Freya was glad of the company though and found that his friendship was becoming increasingly enjoyable. At the end of the meal of cold meats and surprisingly few vegetables, Freya had become even more comfortable with the prince. They talked all the time but, when Freya looked back on the conversation, she could not remember much of what had been said. They laughed about the mistakes Freya had made over the last couple of days, and the solemnity of Elamra. Elialdor was loyal to him but found him intimidating and amusing at the same time and they both shared a respect and affection for Winnie. Freya learned that, when she had to leave home to train in the castle, she had become terribly homesick and, being of a similar age, Elialdor had helped her through it. Elamra had always claimed that she was the best one he had ever trained. Freya struggled to imagine Winnie ever fighting anyone, but the prince quickly corrected her.

"I've never seen anyone so determined as

Winnie," he mused, a glint of respect in his tone, "and so ruthless in battle. Make no mistake, Freya, once the bloodlust takes hold, she is the most formidable force we have. That is why the king insisted on her leaving home to finish her training."

"Blood-lust?" Freya gulped and Elialdor nodded.

"It is something we all suffer from. Part of being a Crow, I'm afraid. Birds of prey are the same. Most civilised until our tempers are raised, and our instinct comes to the surface. There's nothing to fear though," he added, seeing the expression of her face, "Winnie is one of the kindest, noblest people I know. But do not underestimate bloodlust in battle. It may very well save your life."

Freya didn't answer. She refused to believe that Winnie who had done all in her power to help her feel at home, was a ruthless killer.

"And you?" she asked finally. "What about you?"

"I hope that you never have to see us in battle, Freya, but I fear that you will, no matter how hard my father tries to protect you."

"Maybe that's why I'm here," she wondered, still not understanding this strange place. "But I don't think I'd be much of an asset, although I've got pretty good at karate."

"Kara-tay?" Elialdor asked.

"Karate. It's like martial arts," Freya replied, but this caused more confusion. "It's like fighting with arms and legs. It's a sport but it's artistic too, and it's pretty good for self-defence. My mum insisted that I went when I was younger."

"That sounds interesting, Freya." Elialdor sounded surprised. "I'd like to learn this kara-tay. But, even without this, you have qualities that you cannot even know about. And perhaps it is best that you do not know."

They sat silently for a while, looking out of the glass wall at the stooping trees and listening to the water splashing off the fountain.

"Did you know," Elialdor murmured, breaking the silence, "crows have been persecuted for many years because people associate us with death, but owls are also seen as a bringer of death."

Freya did not answer. She had never come across that tradition before, although she knew that crows were considered bad luck.

"I suppose we are as bad as each other really," he sighed and leaned back on the sofa. Freya didn't argue with him as she wasn't sure what she thought. She had begun to trust Elialdor and Winnie but everyone else in the Crow tribe made her feel uneasy and she was frightened of them. The king and Elamra unnerved her. The discussion with the prince about bloodlust made her wonder if the Crows were the correct side to follow. She had never met someone from the Owl tribe but how bad could they be?

Her thoughts had taken her attention away from the prince and when she looked across, she thought he was asleep, but he sat up suddenly.

"What is it?" Freya asked, surprised at the sudden movement. The prince smiled at her but not before she had seen a spark of concern, almost fear, in his eyes.

"Nothing," he said, trying to be casual. "But, if you are to be ready for tonight, then you should start getting ready. I hear girls like to take hours over themselves when going to a party."

He laughed but, as he led her upstairs, she was unconvinced by his false, unconcerned looks.

"Ah," he exclaimed, almost excited when he opened the door to her room. "My father, I see, has foreseen your need for suitable clothes."

Hanging on the door of the large imposing wardrobe was a long, black dress studded with something that looked like sequins here and there, making it look like a starry sky. Freya could not help but gasp when she realised they were not sequins, but perfect tiny diamonds somehow attached to the velvet material. Elialdor laughed.

"Oh, how my father does love to show off to his guests!" He smiled at Freya's stunned face. "It's a matter of pride for him. Well, I think we'll be expected downstairs in about an hour and a half, so I'll come and meet you then."

With a slight bow, Elialdor left Freya alone in her room, confused and astonished. For a couple of minutes, she stood there, stunned, when there was a slight knock on the door. She went to open it, hoping it would be someone who could help, and was delighted when she saw Winnie standing there.

"Hello," Winnie smiled. "My grandparents are just settling in, so I thought I'd come and see how you were doing."

"Well, Elialdor said that I have an hour and a half to get ready, and then just left."

"Yes," Winnie nodded. "He had to go and check something for tonight. Apparently, there has been a development, but he wouldn't tell me what it was. No doubt it means that I will have to focus more on security tonight than my family."

Perhaps it was because she had spent a lot of yesterday with her, or she was becoming more used to these people, but Freya noticed disappointment in her friend's tone.

"He wouldn't tell me either," she said, trying to make her feel better, "and I have no idea what to do."

"Well," Winnie seemed to cheer up instantly, "I'll help you get ready."

Freya was grateful for this and the mood in the room lightened as the two of them laughed and talked about today. Winnie seemed genuinely glad to be back with her grandparents again and

Freya felt it was terrible for her to have been torn apart from them. Winnie would not hear this, however, as she insisted she was glad of the opportunity to fight for the tribe. It was a great honour, she had explained.

"And besides," she added, "I wouldn't have met Elialdor, or come to know Elamra so well."

"Elamra actually smiled at me today," Freya laughed, and Winnie joined in.

"I know he takes a bit of getting used to, but he is a good man." There was a fondness in Winnie's voice which confirmed her words.

Winnie spent the next hour getting Freya ready, which meant persuading her that she was going to have a great time and wouldn't stick out like a sore thumb. She appreciated Winnie's efforts but was unconvinced.

When they had finished, however, Freya could hardly recognise herself. She didn't look like the plain girl she was so used to seeing in the mirror but looked quite pretty. The dress fitted perfectly, and she was mesmerised by the glittering diamonds, which matched a necklace Winnie had lent her.

"Now, I have to run and see to myself," Winnie laughed and, after Freya had thanked her for spending so long with her, she ran off down the hall.

Waiting for Elialdor to come as he had promised and not wanting to go downstairs by herself, she went to look out of the window. The evening sun was casting long shadows on the lawns and something was gliding to and from some of the trees in the park.

A knock on the door brought Freya's attention back and she went to answer it.

"You look…" Elialdor trailed off. "Amazing."

Freya laughed, unsure of what to say and unsure whether to believe him. Without another word, he led her out of the room and down the stairs, which were now decorated with twining branches and petals, bringing the scent of the garden inside.

The Great Hall was decorated too and looked almost magical. The statue of the crow almost shone and there were spectacular bouquets of flowers under each of the tall windows, lit by too many candles to count.

The hall was full of people, all of whom turned to Elialdor as he entered and bowed low, all except the king, who stood with his face burning with pride.

"What was it that you had to sort before, when you left so suddenly?" Freya asked, concerned around so many strangers.

"Another threat," the prince whispered. "But you're safe with all these people. Don't worry."

Everyone in the room was so eager to meet her, she was overwhelmed with fascinated faces and, although Elialdor tried to keep at her side, he had other duties to do as well. The king was particularly gracious to Freya and asked her to sit with him for a time, something that the prince seemed incredibly proud of. The king hardly seemed willing to talk, however, and was content to watch the happenings of the room, greeting people who came up to him so that Elialdor saw the need and invited Freya to get a breath of fresh air.

"My father is not accustomed to such fine company," Elialdor laughed as he and Freya went outside to a balcony that overlooked the rose garden, now covered in twilight. He leant against the stone railing and glanced across at her. "My mother died when I was born, and I've never had any sisters, so he's much more used to the company of men."

"And he doesn't have to talk to the men?" Freya smiled and the prince laughed but stopped when a guard came out and whispered something to him that Freya couldn't make out. Elialdor looked intensely disappointed but nodded and thanked the guard, who walked away.

"Another development, I'm afraid," he sighed. "It seems they can't defend the castle without me, or so my father would have me believe. You can stay out here if you like. I know you're shy."

Freya watched him leave with regret, knowing that he and Winnie were the only two she felt comfortable with here, and Winnie was enjoying her time with her family - as she should.

And would it seem rude, Freya thought to herself, *if people realised she was avoiding them?* A little rude - after all the kind hospitality they had given her. Making up her mind, she turned to go back inside and make another attempt, but she crashed into someone so forcefully that she was knocked backwards and would have fallen onto the stone boundary if the person hadn't caught her in time.

"Thank you." Her voice shook as she turned to see who it was. She didn't recognise him, and he certainly didn't look like he was part of the Crow tribe, with his sandy brown hair coming to an unusually sharp widow's peak although he only looked like he was her age. His wide eyes looked very apologetic as he let her go.

"I'm so sorry," he sounded anxious, "I came out here because I saw you were on your own. You should never be on your own at a party like this."

"Thanks," Freya smiled, unsure. "Who are you?"

"Oh, I'm sorry. My name is Rald. I really didn't mean to startle you."

"Well, Rald, it should be me who's apologising. I should have looked where I was going." Freya smiled but started to walk inside before Rald stopped her.

"No. I won't let you apologise for anything."

"Well, it's getting quite cold," Freya said pointedly. "Shall we go inside?"

Rald nodded and followed her in through the oak door. Everything about him seemed nervous and he even seemed to be shaking when he closed the door behind him.

Without another look to see if the strange boy was following, Freya walked over to the king and stood next to him. Rald, she noticed, hung a little way behind.

Everyone seemed to be focusing on the centre of the room where seven people were gathered, all wearing flowing grey robes. Freya recognised them from earlier as being the dove tribe. Out of nowhere came floating music, soft ripples of a liquid tune and, as soon as the music started, the seven people began to dance gracefully, floating like the music. It was fascinating to watch and almost hypnotic: the way the robes swished and glided, and the decorated headdresses that the women wore shining in the candlelight. *Doves are the birds of peace,* Freya thought to herself, as she began to feel more peaceful with every second of the dance.

When the music and dancing stopped, Freya felt like she had just woken up. She wanted to shout for more so she could experience that blissful feeling of inner happiness again but, instead of a well-deserved applause, a shattering scream issued from one of the doves as her companion fell to the floor.

It took no time for the king to realise what was happening and he called his guards before the windows were shattered and clouds of ghostly white birds swooped into the hall. One headed towards the king, and Freya realised with confusion and fear, that it was a barn owl. With supreme strength, the king wielded his sword, which he had not yet taken out of its scabbard, and thrashed it towards the owl, who fell against the stone wall.

There were more screams as the Owls clawed the people in the hall, but the guards were already fighting them off. The king, although angry at the attack, seemed to be enjoying watching his men defeat the enemy so easily. His smile slipped, however, when the large door opposite burst open to allow in, not any birds, but several men, all of whom looked ready for the fight. At the head was a tall man with long, sleek white hair. The king's concern seemed infectious and Freya was terrified, not helped by hearing Elialdor shouting her name somewhere, almost screaming it, but she couldn't see him in the tangle of people.

She gasped as she felt herself being dragged backwards and breathed a sigh of relief when she realised it was the prince.

"You're alright?" she gasped as she checked him for wounds. He nodded but, without speaking, pulled her through a door and into the room behind the hall.

"Hide here," he panted, pushing her behind a tapestry. He sounded weary and frightened but went immediately to join the fight. Freya looked around her in desperation and realised there was a grill, like a small drain, near the bottom of the wall. Through this she could see the Great Hall, the back of the throne and the battle that was still sweeping through. She desperately tried to find anyone she recognised - Winnie, the prince, Elamra - but could not. In her worry, she did not hear the door being pushed open and was unaware of anyone entering the room until the tapestry was pulled back and someone gripped her hair, pulling her to her feet.

The man who had intruded had wild large eyes that made Freya want to scream, but she seemed to have lost her voice. He put his hand on her throat and all the self-defence she had learned suddenly left her. The panic caused her to forget everything, and she had no idea what to do.

"Stop!" a harsh voice shouted, and the man instantly let go of her. Freya fell to the floor, coughing and breathing raggedly. She looked up to see the man who had come through the doors to lead the attack. His pointed hairline and wild wide eyes were the same as her attacker. Everything about the man seemed pointy, even his short thin nose came to a definite point.

"You said kill everyone," the other man whined, almost begging the newcomer.

"And now I've said 'enough'," he hissed. "You don't want to kill this one, trust me. Now leave."

The attacker left the room, looking as though he had just been grounded.

"Let me apologise." The older man bowed his head and tried to help Freya stand up, but she knocked him off and staggered to her feet herself. "Please forgive him. He does get a little carried away with killing sometimes. It can be very useful, you understand, but also ever-so-slightly irritating. I do hope he didn't do any damage?"

Freya glared at the man, unsure what to say. Her heart was racing so much it was giving her a headache, and she had to concentrate so she didn't fall over. Swaying from side to side, she tried to keep her balance but, when she took a step back from the man, she fell sideways.

"Oh dear," he sighed, and helped her to her feet before she could shake him off again. "There's no need to be afraid. I'm not going to kill you. I simply wanted to offer you better hospitality. You accepted it from the Crows, why not now accept it from me?"

"I know who you are," Freya croaked, finding her voice. "Or what you are."

"Yes, yes." The man walked towards her, but Freya backed off again, this time keeping her balance. "I'm sure you've been told all about me."

He reached out suddenly and grabbed the collar of her dress, pushing her against the wall but, before he could speak, someone else pulled him backwards and Freya sat gasping on the floor again. With a feeling of surprise and triumph, she realised that it was Elamra who had somehow crept into the room and was now fighting the older man. His impressive strength and skill seemed to have been underestimated even by Winnie, and Freya could only feel glad that he had found them in time.

The fight before her seemed to be between two equals, however, and Elamra found himself triumphing only to be beaten down again. Feeling guilty that he should be beaten because of her, Freya rushed forwards, but was pushed backwards by Elamra as the other man moved towards her.

The next few moments seemed to happen so quickly; Freya could not stop it. The door opened and Winnie rushed in, taking in the scene before her. The split second that Elamra paused to see the newcomer was crucial, and the older man took his dagger and pulled him back with the blade against his neck but did not make any effort to hurt him. Elamra blinked in surprise and looked across at Winnie, who stood there entirely helpless, terrified to move in case the attacker hurt him. The older man stared straight at Freya and, for a moment, she thought he was about to kill Elamra. As Freya watched, both him and Elamra grew smaller and smaller, one of them white, the other black, until they resembled a barn owl and a small animal clutched in its murderous claws.

Before either Winnie or Freya could stop him, the owl flew with Elamra through the doorway and out of an open window. Whatever else happened that night, Freya was not able to see it, as the burning pain on her neck caused her eyes to cloud over and, without even knowing it, she collapsed on the floor.

CHAPTER EIGHT
Back Home

The following morning, Freya woke up early in her luxurious room. No one was in sight, so she wandered down the stairs, desperate to find Elialdor or Winnie, and get news of what had happened last night. The last thing she remembered was the owl flying away after transforming from a man and turning Elamra into a small animal - small enough to fit in his claws. Winnie had seen it, she remembered.

There were several people about, but it wasn't the same hustle and bustle of yesterday. Everyone was quiet and did not even spare a second glance for Freya, but instead deliberately scurried off down a different corridor. She didn't mind this but felt a growing unease in her stomach as she wondered where the prince and Winnie were. When she thought of it, she had no idea if they had been injured.

As she searched through the castle, she found herself lost countless times. She didn't want to ask any of the scurrying people, so she wandered through corridors and rooms until she found herself back in the Great Hall.

The hall was filled with people, but the king was not on his throne. Freya couldn't believe that anything could have happened to him, after seeing him in the battle. He was surely one of the strongest Crows. On the other hand, she could not help thinking, he would be the perfect target. Him and his son, she realised with worry.

Silently, she wandered through the now-familiar corridors to find herself in the glass room. The air in here was hot, but not stifling as the windows were opened slightly. She walked up to the fountain in the middle of the room and reached out to touch the water. As she felt the refreshing cold liquid on her hand, she remembered the Owls she had met the night before, and how intent they were on killing or harming the Crows. *Why did the Crows keep this fountain*, she thought to herself. Perhaps it was a reminder of better days, or a hope for the future.

She wondered if the war between them would ever stop. Perhaps two bloodthirsty tribes were a recipe for disaster, and yet Elialdor had said it was all due to some terrible misunderstanding. Surely, if this was the case, it would be easily solved by clearing up the mess. Perhaps that's what she was here for. The Crows seemed sure she was there for a reason, but only wanted to keep her 'safe' in the castle.

This thought brought her back to her home, and she wondered what her parents were doing, and if they did notice her absence. She could not bear to think they had noticed, as they would be so worried. What a strange world she had been brought into. What was perhaps stranger was that she had started to believe everything in this magical place as being real and not a trick at all.

Freya sat down on the woven sofa, her mind filled with concern. She must have searched through over a hundred rooms with no sign of either of her friends. She thought perhaps she should go through the door into the infirmary but was terrified to, in case her friends were in there.

As she sat there, her mind was split between her missing friends and her parents. She watched the water flow over the Crows' wings on the fountain and found the constant motion almost hypnotic. As she watched more and more, she found that her thoughts were growing fewer and fewer until she had an almost empty mind. The feeling of freedom from her own thoughts was thrillingly peaceful.

A sudden rush of air brought her from her peaceful state, and she turned to see that two people had entered the room from outside. She could not describe the jolt of relief when she recognised Elialdor and Winnie and, for a moment, she couldn't speak out of happiness. They saw her and rushed over, Winnie taking Freya's hands in her own, while Elialdor sat wearily on the chair opposite.

"What happened?" Freya asked, letting out a relieved sigh.

"We don't know how it happened." Elialdor rubbed his eyes. "My father has spent the day appeasing the other tribes, while Winnie and I have been testing our defences. I don't know who got the worst job."

"Winnie," Freya whispered, "Elamra. He…"

"I know." Winnie nodded and sat next to her. "I saw."

"Then you know it was my fault." Freya found that she was shaking.

"What?" Winnie smiled. "No, I saw that he was protecting you. It was not your fault."

"Why did they take him?" Freya replied. "I thought they were going to kill me?"

"Freya," Winnie said gently, "the tribes were created to protect mankind. If we kill a human, we lose our immortality and die. It's not your fault they took Elamra instead."

"No, it was my fault," the prince sighed. "I thought we could protect you, but we've brought you into this place. We have to show you how to protect yourself."

"We'd hope that you wouldn't be put in danger again," Winnie reminded the prince.

"But in case, Winnie, neither of us can protect her."

"I thought I could protect myself, but when it came to it, I just froze," Freya whispered, but Winnie took hold of her hand, her reassuring smile easing her.

"We can practise and practise, but in a real situation like last night, most people would have frozen."

"I have a suggestion," Elialdor spoke up, ignoring the situation before him. "I'd like to learn this kara-tay, and you should probably learn our methods of self-defence. We could swap. You could teach us, and we could teach you."

"I'd like that," Freya smiled. She liked the thought of teaching these century-old people something, and she was reasonably good at karate, already achieving her brown belt. "But I've been thinking: I have to see my parents."

"Why?" Elialdor asked, while Winnie looked understanding. "The king won't let you just yet. It's dangerous."

"Apparently being here is dangerous," Freya reminded him and realised too late that she may have been a bit harsh. For a minute, no one said anything. Winnie smiled at Freya, but she was sure that her thoughts were elsewhere. Elialdor studied his hands, twisting his long fingers through each other. The only sound was the fountain and Freya's mind was brought back to last night.

"Very well," Elialdor said at last, so quietly that Freya had to ask him to repeat himself. "We will take you home," he agreed. "But we can't tell my father, and you should return with us. Please."

Freya felt as though she could hug the boy before her, especially as he was risking so much, but instead simply smiled and thanked him.

"The king is preoccupied with the dove tribe at the moment," Winnie smiled. "We should go as soon as possible."

"How?" Elialdor asked. "Freya can't fly and being carried is most undignified. Can you manage to get us there and I'll bring us back?"

Winnie nodded but didn't look convinced. Freya remembered traveling here, and how tired Winnie had seemed afterwards, so she was not surprised by this uneasiness. She felt a pang of regret that she was putting her friends in such a difficult situation, but not so much to stop her from visiting her parents. She just wanted to see them, and to let them know she was okay.

"Are you ready?" Elialdor asked, not wanting to wait around for his father. Winnie nodded but said nothing. She smiled at Freya as if to show that she didn't mind doing this and took her hands tightly. Before Freya could thank her, everything went black and she could feel the same beating of wings against her that she remembered from the other night.

In a matter of seconds, Freya felt them land on concrete and found that she had closed her eyes to protect them from the beating wings. When she opened them, she realised they were just outside her flat and, although there were a couple of people walking down the street, they had not seen them arrive.

Elialdor looked around with a mixture of interest and suspicion and Freya realised that he had probably never been in such a crowded place. He must have been to towns before, but perhaps too many years ago. For Winnie, this seemed like a perfect distraction and she looked around in interest.

Realising that she must have left her house keys at the castle, she rang the doorbell to her own flat, feeling somewhat foolish. She heard Elialdor give a nervous cough but Winnie seemed more interested, having already been to this place.

There were distant footsteps from inside and the door opened. Elialdor smiled as pleasantly as he could as he saw a tall, thin man standing there. He could not look more different from Freya, with his thin face and black hair.

"Freya," he said, uncertain, "why aren't you at school?"

"Oh," Freya replied, unsure of what to say. "I wasn't feeling very well."

"And who are these people?" Her dad smiled at the unusual people. "And what are you wearing?"

Freya looked down at herself. It was true that she looked odd and out of place in the tunic like dress that Winnie had lent her, and she could not think of how to introduce her friends.

"Are you going to let us in, Dad?" she said, trying to sound confident. "Only, it's actually quite cold out here."

Her dad moved back to let her and her friends in, still looking puzzled. Freya led them in, worried in case they might say something that she would have to explain. They didn't. In fact, they remained remarkably quiet as she sat them down and her dad made them all a cup of tea. Elialdor bowed his head when he was offered the drink, which amused Freya's dad, although he said nothing.

"So, who are you then?"

Freya frowned at her dad's abrupt question.

"This is Winnie. She's a friend of mine. She showed me round the High School. You remember," Freya tried to sound convincing, realising with every word that it had been a bad idea to invite them inside. "And this is…" she paused, knowing that the name 'Elialdor' would just be too weird. "This is Fred."

The prince raised his eyes at his new name, and Freya gave him the briefest of looks before turning back to her dad.

"So, where's Mum?"

"You really aren't feeling well, are you?" Her dad laughed. "Tuesday is her work day, isn't it?"

"Oh," Freya nodded, "of course."

It had been a very bad idea to come here.

"How was your trip south?" Freya asked, trying to think of something to say.

"I'm sure you asked me that when we got back." Her dad laughed again, and Freya looked at her friends uncertainly. She had not been here when they had got back, she had been preparing for the party. Winnie and Elialdor did not seem to think anything of it.

"So I did," she murmured. "Well, thanks for the tea, Dad. I think we'll go upstairs and see if we can get any schoolwork done."

"You're not like normal kids, you know." Dad smiled as he cleared the cups away. Freya watched him go before she wandered upstairs with Elialdor and Winnie silently. Elialdor seemed intent on looking at some of the old photos that lined the walls, but Freya had too many questions that needed answering so she pulled him upstairs and closed the door.

"Okay. You need to tell me what's going on." She sat down on the bed, feeling the tears coming to her eyes. She wasn't sure why she was crying, but the tears started falling down her cheeks. Winnie sat next to her but did not say anything.

"Your parents, or your school friends, or anyone, will not notice you are gone until you return," Elialdor explained, kneeling in front of Freya. "If this was not the case, your parents would have become worried out of their minds when they realised you had gone. You have to understand that it is for the best."

"Perhaps for my parents," Freya sniffed, "but not for me. They didn't even notice I was gone. It's their trips to the lawyer - I know what it means. It means we won't be a family anymore...and now they're forgetting about me."

"No," Elialdor's voice was somehow firm and soft at the same time as he sat beside her. "Your family loves you. I can see it on your Dad's face."

Freya looked at him through her teary eyes. The shock of her Dad's attitude had knocked her confidence. She had expected them to be out-of-their-minds with worry but instead they acted as if nothing had happened. *Because,* she told herself, *as far as they know, nothing* has *happened.*

"We need your help, Freya," Winnie said, so quietly it was almost a whisper. "You saw last night what we are up against."

"I can't help you," Freya shook her head. "I'm sorry but I don't know why you think I can."

"Things, I'm sure, will become clearer to you,"

Elialdor sighed. "But we are fighting against an ever-growing force. Our advisers say…"

"Yes, you told me," she interrupted. "You didn't tell me why."

"It isn't often that a human is able to help us, Freya." Winnie held onto her hands. Her friend's hands felt cold and rough.

"Will you have us give up hope so easily?" Elialdor looked into Freya's eyes, swollen with tears. Freya looked at him: the picture of charm, as though he had walked straight out of a fairy-tale book. There would be very few, she thought, could refuse such a look of pleading in those dark eyes. Why then would he ask her to help? She knew that teenage boys preferred the company of other teenage boys, and rarely mixed with primary school children unless they were related and really had to.

"I suppose you have asked loads of others before me," she said, trying to tease out more truth. "What happened to them?"

"I have never known a human like you," he said, smiling. "After all these years, I think we have finally found our true salvation."

"That's that word again," Freya scoffed. "Tell me what you want me to do. I can't help you if I don't know what I'm supposed to do."

"Whatever comes to mind." Winnie spoke this time. "Perhaps we have been going about this wrong. Tell us how you would solve things.

Come back with us and help us. Why not come home when you're finished, and it will be like you had never been away."

Warning bells began to ring in Freya's mind. She wondered, if she did go with her friends, would she return home to find nothing had changed? Whatever was going to happen, she would have surely changed herself.

On the other hand, she had already seen what trouble the Crows were in. One of their number - their best soldier - had been taken because of her. And they had saved her life.

Wouldn't it be completely ungrateful to turn them away when they needed help?

Freya nodded slowly, wondering if she was making the right decision. Elialdor sighed and bowed his head but, when he raised it again, his face was the picture of relief. Winnie hugged Freya, causing her to almost fall off the bed with shock. Whatever she had agreed to had made her friends uncontrollably happy. Although she knew she should be pleased by this, it only made her more worried.

"And when I come back here," Freya asked, "my parents will not have realised I've been gone?"

"No," Winnie smiled. "No, it will be like you've been here all the time."

Elialdor stood up and held a hand out for Freya.

"We should go," he suggested, "my father will be looking for me. Freya, please, whatever he asks, don't tell him where we have just been."

When Freya had promised not to reveal their secret, Elialdor thanked her and, holding her close, made the room black out completely. This time, Freya kept her eyes open, but could see nothing except darkness. Again, she felt the wings beating against her and, in moments, they were back in the glass room. Elialdor glanced around but they were, fortunately, alone.

The light streaming in through the glass made Freya blink constantly after the complete blackness. She felt exhilarated to be back in this enchanted place, even though she was a long way from home. Although she felt sad that she hadn't seen her Mum at home, she told herself that, when she had helped the Crows like she agreed, she would return home and spend as much time as she possibly could with both her parents.

"Tomorrow," Elialdor brought her back to the present, "we'll start training. I would start today but I fear we have a lot more to do with the other tribes today. I look forward to what you have to teach us."

Winnie reluctantly left Freya in the glass room. Now they were back in the castle, she seemed to be melancholier and Freya felt a painful wave of guilt, realising it was because of Elamra's disappearance. She had no choice but to help the

Crows, Freya thought as she watched her friends leave to attend to their duties, when she had been the cause of all this worry and pain.

CHAPTER NINE
The Shadow

It was more difficult than Freya could have guessed. Each moment she thought she might just collapse from exhaustion, and each evening she went to her room too tired to get ready for bed, she had to remind herself of the reason for doing this. Her friends needed her help, and she needed to get Elamra back to the Crows.

The training seemed to have lifted Winnie's spirits, although Freya was almost certain this was an act and her friend was still devastated by Elamra's fate. *Perhaps*, Freya thought to herself, *if they only knew what had happened to him and whether he was even still alive, Winnie could get some peace of mind.*

When Elialdor and Winnie were not teaching her everything they knew about defence (only ever defence, not attack, as Freya was insistent that she didn't want to know how to attack) they insisted that Freya shared some of her knowledge about karate (or kara-tay, as Elialdor insisted on calling it). Teaching them the techniques she'd learned was almost as exhausting as learning new ones, but she enjoyed being able to teach her older friends

Although they were centuries older, when they were together, it seemed like there was only a few years between them. Elialdor and Winnie both acted as they looked - Elialdor about fourteen, and Winnie sixteen. There was no scorn, they were not trying to protect her at every opportunity, and they treated Freya like she was their age.

If Freya was not too tired by the end of the day, she would visit the infirmary to see Enna. There was no improvement in his condition and the nurse was growing tired of Eli watching his son. It was clear she was trying to control her anger, but the old man was relentless in his advice about his son's treatment, so the nurse was almost at her wit's end. Freya could understand this, especially as Eli delighted in telling everyone that his son had never fitted in and listed his many faults to any passer-by. As the week wore on, however, Freya grew more certain that this was a strange way of managing his grief as Enna's recovery became more and more uncertain.

Freya always felt sad and guilty after she had

been to the hospital, but she owed it to Enna. After all, the boy had saved her from the Owls, before she even knew that this whole extra world existed. She found the medical work fascinating. It was not old-fashioned, but it seemed like they used magic instead of science to heal, and she wondered if she would ever fulfil her dream of becoming a doctor. She tried to take in everything that the nurses and healers were doing, but knew that it would take her years to learn everything about their healing art. But, fascinating as the medicine was, it still wasn't working for Enna.

"That nurse will not allow Enna to wake," Eli grunted one night, loud enough for the harassed nurse to hear as she wandered past. She turned to them with such a cold stare, Freya shuddered.

"When he was brought in, two of my staff were blown off their feet by the force of his uncontrolled skill," the nurse said, her voice matching her icy stare. "It was your job to teach your son to control his abilities. I will keep him in the state of unconsciousness until I am certain we will all be safe."

Eli said nothing but scowled at the woman. Freya just stared at the unconscious man on the bed, who remained blissfully unaware of these unending arguments.

The seven nights of training found Freya sitting in the glass room, her favourite part of the castle, with Winnie and Elialdor. The last week had seen her become more and more comfortable around her two friends, and more settled now she knew her parents would not notice her absence. There had been times, particularly towards the end of the day, when she missed her parents but Elialdor and Winnie were good company. They were sitting together, each pre-occupied with their own thoughts and, like all good friends, happy just to be with each other.

Freya no longer wished her mobile would be charged, or that she could go on the computer to use the internet. She was becoming comfortable with all the castle had to offer, including the friendship of the two people sitting with her. Winnie had been more cheerful in the last couple of days and Freya was certain this had something to do with the talk of a rescue mission to recover the famous Crow warrior – Elamra. Elialdor – or Aldor as Winnie called him – had joyfully shared the news after a meeting with his father. He seemed certain that they would have Elamra back, but he just wasn't sure when.

The sun had been hidden behind dark clouds since the morning and the rain was hammering at the windows and on the roof of the conservatory, falling down the glass making the view distorted. Now it was evening but the garden birds didn't feel like singing when the weather was so dismal. Instead, the only sound was the flow of the water fountain.

Through the week, Freya could see a definite improvement in her defensive skills, although her impatient nature interfered with her success. Winnie was a natural at karate, the skill almost becoming one with her, and Freya was just ashamed that she couldn't teach the more advanced skills. Elialdor, on the other hand, was *not* a natural and it was quite amusing to see something he was not good at. He would go red-faced after being beaten by Winnie, and insisted it was because she was older than him.

"Were I born under a fighter's moon, like you were," he said with confidence, as he nursed his bruised pride, "I would have won hands up."

"Hands down." Freya corrected, but smiled at his attempted use of a saying she often used.

Freya was certainly learning and was much stronger than she had been a week ago. Her muscles ached with hard work, and from running around the castle grounds every morning. She was told to do this by Elialdor while he and Winnie went out every day 'on a hunt'. Whenever Freya asked to go with them, she was told that her time would be better spent getting fitter. Initially angry about this, she found the run around the castle to be restful and calming.

"Why should you not learn how to fly?" Winnie wondered aloud. Freya jumped awake from her thoughts, startled at how her friend seemed to have read them.

"You know very well why." Elialdor's voice was firm.

"That is just the only thing left to teach," came the reply. Freya looked from one to the other, completely lost as to what they were talking about. The prince looked at her, and she felt as though he could see right through her.

"When you first arrived, I showed you something to try and help you believe us," he began, glancing nervously at Winnie. "Can you remember?"

"Yes," Freya nodded, "you made a bird out of blue light."

"Would you like to learn how to do that?" Winnie asked. Freya didn't say anything.

"We don't know if you can, for certain," the prince shook his head. "But if you can, you will find it is the most powerful tool and defence you possess."

"A bird made out of blue light?" Freya laughed. Winnie gave a slight laugh and the prince just smiled.

"It's a symbol," he persisted. "It is only a fraction of our abilities once we have them trained."

"Is it as difficult as the training I'm doing at the moment?"

"More so, in many ways," Winnie sighed. "It requires mental strength, but not much physical strength."

"Then I might be able to manage it," Freya laughed, but the prince did not even smile.

"It can be dangerous," he mumbled, shaking his head. "I'm not sure."

"Come on, Aldor," Winnie said, exasperated. "Freya needs to defend herself with her mind as well as her body. You know she is capable."

Elialdor looked from Winnie to Freya - one determined, one confused - and back again. He stayed there for a few moments, while the only sound was the hammering of the rain on the glass, and the gentle fall of the fountain. Eventually, he nodded, although the look of concern did not leave his face.

"Close your eyes, Freya. It should help you concentrate," he said, and she immediately closed them. "Okay. Now, what do you see when you close your eyes?"

"Just a dark red light," she mumbled. Still with her eyes closed, she heard him sigh heavily. She was about to open her eyes again and say just how useless it was, when she saw something. It seemed like the red light was swirling and dancing to make patterns - patterns of things that didn't make any sense to her.

The light danced around behind her eyes and she felt transfixed by it. She heard Elialdor and Winnie murmuring together but didn't care what they were saying. She didn't care about the sound of the rain slashing against the roof. Eventually, all sound seemed to die away.

Freya found that she didn't have to concentrate on the shape anymore as it came into focus on its own accord. It was a silhouetted person and, as it seemed to come closer, Freya felt his stomach tingle with fear. Relentlessly, it moved forward. She felt panic begin to creep into her mind and she tried to open her eyes to dispel the vision, but it was like they had been glued closed.

"Why do you try and leave me?" the silhouette asked. Although the voice was gruff, there was a hint of disappointment and hurt. The pity that Freya could not help but feel persuaded her to stay here longer and see what the silhouette would say.

Being just a shadow, he had no features, and the lack of emotion was frightening. But there was still something about him that seemed familiar.

"Who are you?" She spoke without moving her mouth.

"I am you," the silhouette replied.

"What?"

The figure did not reply at first but moved closer so he was only a foot away from her face, and yet she still could not see any features.

"Your friends want you to learn to defend yourself," he said, his voice lighter than before. "I can help you in this."

"How?" she asked again, unsure if she wanted

the shadow's help. There was a slight laugh, but Freya could not see a smile.

"You have freed me. Not many people are able to do that. Now, together, we can unlock all of your abilities."

The warning grew in Freya's stomach and she wanted to return to her friends, to their honesty. As she stared at the featureless shadow, the fear grew until she threw out her hands to push him back, but they fell straight through him. The same laugh sounded again.

"You can't touch a shadow." It was mocking now. "And why do you want to dispel me? I can make you powerful."

In her mind, Freya took a step back, but the silhouette took a step towards her. There was a sigh.

"Leave then," he said, "but I will see you again. And now, to prove my friendship, I will give you a warning which may save your life. Do not trust the one who helps you."

"Do not...what?" Freya asked, and was surprised to find that she could now open her eyes and return to her friends and the castle.

Winnie was sitting next to her, and Elialdor was kneeling at her feet, their faces creased with worry. They both sighed as they realised Freya was back with them. Something wet was trickling down Freya's face and getting in her eyes. At first, she thought Winnie had put a wet flannel on her forehead but, when she raised her hand to remove it, she realised she had been sweating.

"I've never seen it happen so quickly," Elialdor whispered. "What did he say?"

"Who was he?" Freya asked, unable to remember the figure's exact words. "I was frightened."

"They can be a little intimidating at first, I know." Winnie squeezed Freya's hand in her own.

"But who was it?" she persisted.

"It was you," Elialdor said, echoing the shadow's words.

"I'm sure I don't sound or look like that."

"You're not used to it, Freya," Winnie said. "We, each of us, have a soul. What you saw was simply an embodiment of your soul. They have been called many things over the years - conscience, spirit guides - almost every culture has a name for it. Only a handful of people, though, listen to them, and very few humans can summon them. I've never seen one summoned so quickly."

"Can I trust it?" Freya could hear her voice shaking. "Is it good?"

"It isn't good, or bad. No one person is entirely good, or bad." Elialdor smiled. "But you can trust it for it cannot lie. But you must be careful - its motives are your deepest inner-most desires. Desires that even you don't know you have. And you may be concerned to discover what they are."

"I don't think I ever want to close my eyes again," she shuddered.

"It will help you defend yourself." Winnie clasped Freya's other hand. "It will guide you through learning your abilities - until you can command it as it now commands you."

"And what happens if I can't control it?"

There was a silence. Winnie looked at Elialdor, who stared back. Freya thought she could see a trickle of fear in their eyes.

"You're a strong person, Freya," the prince said at last, "you will control it."

The clever use of words chilled Freya. Neither of her friends had answered her question and it was clear they were keeping something from her - something that would happen to her if she lacked the mental strength to control this inside shadow.

"I don't want it anymore," she whispered, and Winnie looked at her with pity. "I think I've released something dangerous."

"You do not give yourself enough credit," her friend insisted, and did not release her grip on her hands. "You are strong enough for this, and we are here to help you, just like you've helped us."

"Now you have unlocked your shadow," Elialdor began, "a whole range of abilities will be opened for you. It's all about mental control."

After he spoke, Elialdor closed his eyes and, almost immediately, the glass room was filled with a blue light, cold and ethereal. The light in the room pulsed like a heartbeat, but Freya realised it wasn't a heartbeat, it was the sound of immense wings. Slowly, the blue light grew more and more intense as it caved in on itself, becoming smaller and brighter. When the light was only a metre across, Freya could make out the figure of a gigantic bird, which flapped its wings menacingly. Opening its beak, it made the unmistakable caw of a crow, but the feathers were not black - they were pure light.

Elialdor opened his eyes and the bird vanished. The room was back to normal, with the rain still hammering down on the glass.

"A being like that," Elialdor smiled, "could help save your life one day. It would have done whatever I had commanded."

Freya nodded, shell-shocked, but was becoming more and more uncertain. She found whatever lurked in her mind far scarier than the people who had taken Elamra.

The fear stayed with her until the end of the day. Although worn out after the days' events, she could not bring herself to close her eyes in case she saw the shadow again. Desperate for a way to divert her mind from sleep, she wandered through the dark castle until she came to the infirmary.

She was somewhat surprised to see that Eli was still awake, staring at his son's motionless body and shaking his head. Freya did not want to interrupt his thoughts, so she moved backwards towards the door, but Eli heard her and looked up.

"Don't leave on my account," he croaked. "Come and sit down."

She did so, sitting and watching Enna's chest rise and fall, and finding it surprisingly peaceful.

"I cannot move him," Eli sighed. "Your king will not allow me to take him home. Apparently, he must stay here until he is fully recovered."

"Why?" Freya felt a wave of pity for the old man. "Did he give a reason?"

"My son has never controlled his abilities well." Freya prepared herself for a round of abuse on Enna's part, so she was surprised by Eli's words. "It was my fault. You see, as king of the tribe, I could not give up as much of my time as I should have done."

"But you are staying with him now rather than returning to your people. That's what he needs."

"I've never really understood him," Eli said, softer than before. "He was always different."

"But you've stayed by him," she persisted, but the eagle king shook his head.

"I have a duty to my people, Human." He looked at her and she was shocked to see his eyes glistening with tears. It seemed so strange on the old man's face. "It is the curse of my position. My people come before my family. I will be satisfied now, knowing that you are here for my son. You have been a greater friend to him than the Crows."

"They are nursing him," Freya reminded him. "You cannot leave. Your son needs you."

"No," Eli shook his head, and the tears in his eyes fell down his weathered cheeks, "he does not need me. I have never been there for him."

Freya would have argued, but Eli rose decisively from his chair. The tears had gone now and were replaced with a look of firm acceptance.

"Now, I understand you will need your strength tomorrow," Eli bent down and laid a hand on Freya's shoulder. "Don't let your own abilities frighten you, Human. You have enough power to control it, and enough good in you to use it wisely."

"I'm scared to even close my eyes," Freya glanced at Enna, feeling jealous of his peacefulness.

Eli said nothing but laid both hands gently on Freya's head. At first, she didn't know what he was doing but, as the ripples of sleep washed uncontrollably over her, she felt both cross and grateful.

When Eli left the castle, Freya was fast asleep with her head on Enna's hand. The sea eagle murmured slightly, and his eyelids flickered. Somewhere in the room beyond, a window blew open, but Freya was too tired to notice.

CHAPTER TEN
On the Hunt

Freya woke up, startled, as someone laid a soft but firm hand on her shoulder. Sitting up, she grimaced as her neck and back were so stiff. She looked up into the stern eyes of the nurse that Eli had taken such a dislike to. Having just woken up, her brain seemed unwilling to give her the right words to say so she just mumbled an attempt at an apology. The nurse's face softened, but her mouth remained in a frown.

"I don't believe it is safe for you to be here at the moment," she said and nodded her head towards the unconscious man. "I think he is battling my blue light and may wake up at any moment."

"But that's a good thing, isn't it?" Freya was nervous about the nurse's tone of voice but could not help but feel excited about the opportunity to talk to the boy who had helped her, and to thank him.

Instead of replying, the nurse pulled Freya to her feet with surprising strength and guided her from the infirmary to the room beyond. The door creaked as she swung it open and, for a while, Freya was frozen in the doorway, unwilling to move any further.

The room looked like it may have once been an office, with a large desk and bookshelves lining the walls, but it seemed to have suffered from a terrible earthquake during the night. The books and papers that must have been on the shelves were scattered and torn all over the floor of the room, some of the pages crumpled and shredded so much as to be unreadable. Wax was splattered across the desk, probably from the candle that must have been blown out and fallen over. The windows had shattered and there was glass lining the floor. Freya stood and stared, reminding herself of the havoc Enna had caused before she had come here.

"He didn't mean to do this," she muttered, when she could finally make her voice work.

"That I don't doubt," the nurse's words were sharp but, Freya thought, somewhat deserved. "That poor boy has no control over his abilities. I don't blame him as much as his father. To think that he is the king of a great tribe!"

"He's gone." Freya turned to face her and was

surprised to find her startled by this news. "He left during the night."

The nurse did not speak for a while and surveyed the room before them, before she turned back to Enna, ushering Freya to do the same. Reaching the unconscious boy's bedside, she laid a hand on his forehead, almost tenderly.

"Poor boy," she whispered.

"I thought you didn't like Eli," Freya said, confused.

"I don't. I detest the man. But I think it is clear from last night that his son needs him here."

Freya didn't answer but considered Enna, only the same age as Elialdor. She remembered trying to stop Eli from leaving last night, trying to persuade him that his son needed him, and she could remember the tears in Eli's eyes. She realised that she agreed with the nurse: it was his father's presence that was keeping him calm.

"You should leave," the nurse turned to her. "I don't know when Enna will become dangerous and the king will not be happy if his guest is injured. I can only say it is fortunate there is no one else in the infirmary at the moment. Now, go. Come back later if you must, but make sure you don't stay here on your own."

Freya did not have any choice but to leave as the nurse pulled her towards the door to the glass room and, with a tiny smile of apology, closed the door in her face. Freya stood there, stunned, but knowing the nurse would do everything in her power to help Enna. And surely it was good that he was waking up?

She turned around to face the fountain, watching the water spill over the statues in mid-air. With a feeling a fear, she remembered the events of yesterday, and why she had been afraid to go to sleep. Would she become like Enna if she didn't control her new ability? What would the king think if he knew that his son and Winnie had opened the door to this terrible power within her?

The sun had risen, but the reds and oranges of the sunrise were still splattered across the sky, and the light beamed into the conservatory, falling on the fountain and causing one of the crows to look red, as though it were covered in blood. Elamra was Freya's first thought and she felt her stomach turn. She took a step closer to the fountain and reached out a hand to touch the red crow. She was only inches away from its head when the door opened, and she spun around to see Winnie walk in. Freya turned nervously back to the crow, worried that Winnie might come to the same conclusion, but the sun had slipped behind a cloud and the red light had gone.

"Is something the matter?" Winnie asked, confused. "It's quite early. I didn't think you would be here."

"I slept in the infirmary last night. No," she

began when Winnie looked worried, "it's not like that. I fell asleep watching Enna."

"It's a credit to you that you show such an interest in him." Winnie sat down on one of the woven chairs.

"He helped me," Freya reminded her. "He is in a coma because of me."

"Forgive me," Winnie smiled. "We Crows look after our own but are very wary about everyone else."

"What about me?"

Winnie turned to her and her smile deepened.

"You are one of us," she said. "That's becoming clearer with each day. Do you still miss home, Freya?"

"Yes, but not as much now I know they won't be worried about me." Freya looked at her friend, who was staring outside wistfully.

"I come here when I need to think, Freya," Winnie sighed. "But I'm glad you're here. When I'm alone with my own thoughts, things become very dark and clouded. This has always been my favourite place in the castle, ever since I came here."

"How do you stop yourself from missing your parents?" Freya asked, and was surprised to see Winnie's shoulders shaking.

"I don't. It reminds me of who I am." Winnie looked up, her face red with tears. "I used to talk things through with Elamra. I love Aldor dearly, but it was his father's laws which meant I had to leave my family."

"Can't you return to them now?" Freya asked. "Surely you've given enough already?"

"We're at war." Winnie whispered. "I can't leave them now. And now Elamra has been taken. I need to get him back, but whatever the king is planning, he won't let me take part. He knows I'm too fond of Elamra."

"Have you spoken to Elialdor about it?"

Winnie nodded but said nothing. She had been so comforting to Freya when she'd needed it but now the tables had turned, Freya could not think of anything to say. She placed her hand on Winnie's own and she clasped it, as though all Winnie's pain could flow through into her, just so she could save her from suffering.

"What a pair we make!" Winnie laughed, wiping the tears away from her face. "Both taken from our homes into a place we don't really understand, but which is necessary."

The door opened and they both turned to see the prince enter. He stopped suddenly as he realised that Freya was with Winnie.

"Let me guess," Freya said, with a look of tired annoyance. "My time would be better spent exploring the castle grounds, but not going into the parkland beyond the gardens?"

"No," Elialdor smiled and glanced over his shoulder. "I was going to invite you to come with us this morning."

Winnie looked up, startled, and glanced at the door. Freya didn't speak.

"Have you checked this with your father?" she asked. Elialdor tutted in annoyance.

"You're beginning to sound like Elamra." As the prince mentioned his name, Freya looked up at her companion, but her face did not even twitch. Winnie looked at Freya who smiled sympathetically, but she could not deny that she would love to do as the prince said: to go with them on a hunt.

"It's too dangerous," Winnie argued. "Don't you care about her?"

"She proved yesterday that she has strength my father doesn't know about." Freya had to strain her ears to hear what the prince was saying. "She can handle herself."

"She can't fly," Winnie insisted.

"Then we help her." It was clear that, now Elialdor had thought about it all night, there would be no dissuading him. When his mind was made up, that was final.

"If I told your father, what would he say?" Winnie frowned.

"You wouldn't do that." The prince looked somewhat frightened by this suggestion. Winnie stood up but said nothing. Instead, she pointed to the door leading into the castle. With only a slight acknowledgment to Freya, they stepped through and, although she could not see them, Freya could hear raised voices. For the first time that week, Freya felt as though she were centuries younger. It stung her that her friends had left specifically to talk about her while she couldn't take part in the conversation.

Nosiness and hurt got the better of Freya and she stood up to go and listen at the door but, as soon as she was on her feet, the door opened and Winnie and the prince came in, both looking slightly sulky.

"It's up to you, Freya," the prince conceded. "Do you want to come with us?"

Freya looked from one to the other. She wanted to leave the castle grounds so much, but she was worried about letting Winnie down. Eventually, she nodded and, as the prince looked pleased, Winnie smiled sadly. Freya almost wished she had told her how stupid and foolish she was being. She felt more guilty given her friend's calm acceptance.

Half an hour later found them on the roof of the castle, in a part where there was no one around to see them. Freya got the distinct impression that Elialdor was terrified of his father finding out he had disobeyed him. He kept glancing behind him and wouldn't talk at all as they made their way towards the roof.

"Why are you so eager for me to have this opportunity?" Freya whispered when they reached the top of the castle.

"I know how annoying my father can be when he tries to protect you," Elialdor smiled. "I'm trying to save you that. If he knows that you can handle yourself, he might let you go home more often."

Freya said nothing but smiled gratefully. It was, she had to admit, becoming claustrophobic being cooped up inside the grounds. As they looked over the battlements, however, Freya wanted to change her mind. She hadn't realised just how high the building was but, when she looked down the many feet to the ground, she was almost sick with fear and she swayed as her head started spinning. It only stopped when she felt a firm hand on her shoulder and looked up at the prince, who smiled sympathetically.

"Don't worry," he whispered. "We won't let you fall. As long as you stay with us, you'll be safe."

Freya looked across at Winnie, who nodded although there was still a slight look of concern in her eyes.

"To fly," she began, "we need to transform into our other selves. You'll need help with this because you've never done it before, so don't panic."

The definite panicky tone in the "don't panic" certainly didn't help but, before Freya could reply, she felt a strange tingly feeling in her stomach. At first, she dismissed it as her fear of heights kicking in again but, when she looked down, she could see her body and legs transforming. They were growing smaller and thinner, and she was aware that her head was doing the same. The tingling feeling continued throughout her body as, instead of her clothes, she realised she was growing feathers - jet black, shining feathers. Her initial reaction was to be horrified, and terrified that she would remain like this for the rest of her life, but she had to admit that the sleek feathers were rather beautiful.

Looking around for her friends, she saw that they too had transformed: one into a jackdaw, and the other into a magnificent raven. They were both staring at her.

"This is how you hunt?" Freya asked, and was surprised to find her voice hadn't changed at all.

"Yes. This is how we fly." When the raven spoke, Freya realised it was Elialdor. "It may take a while for you to get used to it, so we'll help you to begin with."

The raven hopped onto the battlements, and the jackdaw followed. Freya reluctantly tried to jump on the wall and was surprised to find she could manage it.

She gasped as she looked beneath her at the steep fall.

"Just trust us," Winnie whispered, and this reassurance encouraged Freya to follow the two birds by stepping off the battlements. For a moment, Freya was sure that she was falling through mid-air, but she felt her arms stretch out without her thinking about it. The wind whipped past her feathers as she soared on. It seemed that her wings had a mind of their own and, as she watched her friends glide gracefully up and down the wind, she realised it was their 'magic' that was keeping her in the air.

She could not describe the feeling of flying. It was entirely different from being in an aeroplane, and she wondered if this is what it felt like to go parachuting. Looking down, she realised they had passed the castle border and were into the parkland. It looked so strange from up high: the green blanket of grass dotted here and there with the majestic trees that only looked like wide bushes from the sky.

Soaring on the wind was so beautiful that she wanted to open her mouth and shout it out. Instead, she giggled, as she experimented by turning left and right and finding the whole experience thrilling.

Through her elated mind, she thought she could hear Winnie and Elialdor shouting her name and she turned to find them. They were only slightly ahead but Freya felt an apprehensive wave wash over her as she saw they were flying into a storm. The clouds had gathered in one place and grown dark and angry.

She saw her friends trying to turn back, but the wind was now at their backs and, however hard they tried, they had to fly into the storm.

The experience turned from thrilling to terrifying as they were battered by the wind and the rain that hammered down on them. Elialdor's voice came to Freya in fragments so she could not make out what he was trying to say, only the note of panic in his voice.

They circled lower and lower to escape the clouds, but a flash of something brighter than light knocked Freya backwards and she found her wings had stopped working and she was falling with more and more speed towards the ground.

She must have called out to her friends, but she couldn't remember the last few seconds, which seemed to last for hours. She was barely conscious when she felt something grab her around her waist, and needle-sharp claws cut into her chest.

When she woke up, Freya hadn't even realised she had lost consciousness. She was lying on a hard, rocky ground and it took her a few moments to realise that she was back to her human form. Feeling suddenly grateful that she no longer had wings, she looked around to try and find her friends and was surprised by a sharp pain in her chest.

"I'm sorry about that," a voice spoke behind

her, and she spun around, grimacing as the pain sharpened. The boy looked familiar, but Freya could not place where she had seen him before. He looked to be her age and his face looked incredibly smooth, with wide eyes that watched her intently.

"Who are you?" Freya tried not to sound annoyed, but the pain in her chest and the disappointment at not seeing her friends was clear.

"We met at the castle." The man did not seem surprised that Freya had not remembered him, but he had a tone of sad acceptance. Although it had not been long ago, so much had happened that it took a few moments for Freya to remember where she had seen him.

"Rald," she whispered, smiling. The man nodded and, as Freya tried to stand up, he moved over to help her.

"I'm sorry about your wounds." He pointed to her chest and Freya noticed there were six patches of deep red blood. "When I caught you as you fell, I may have dug in a little too hard."

"You caught me?" Freya asked. "Did you see my friends?"

Rald shook his head and looked at the ground. They were standing on a rocky ledge at the side of an inland cliff, but the storm seemed to have faded and everything was calm. They were above an expanse of woodland and trees could be heard rustling in the peaceful breeze.

"What are you then?" Freya asked the awkward boy before her. "You're certainly not a Crow."

"No," he laughed, "but you wouldn't believe me if I told you."

Freya watched her companion closer. His widow's peak, the smooth sandy hair, the long fingernails. What really gave it away, though, was his delicate poise, like a cat watching a small bird. She could not believe she hadn't realised sooner.

"You're an Owl!" It was more of a statement than a question but Rald nodded. Looking around, Freya realised there was no way off the small rocky ledge and, without her friends, she had no hope of turning into a crow. Rald took a step towards her.

"Stay where you are," Freya demanded. "What did you do to my friends? Where are they?"

"I didn't realise you were with them," Rald pleaded. "When I saw you falling, I had to help you."

"But you're an Owl." Freya could not help the disgust in her voice. Rald simply nodded.

"If my father knew I was with you..." He trailed off and left Freya confused as to what he was going to say.

"You were after my friends?" Freya froze. Should she then be glad that her friends were nowhere to be seen? Rald nodded again.

"It was a task my father knew I would not be able to do." He frowned. "But I couldn't let you die."

Freya didn't speak. All she had heard and seen of the Owls confirmed they were a race not to be trusted, and even one to hate. But Rald seemed so like Elialdor in many ways: eager for his father's approval but disagreeing with him. Perhaps Rald was not like the others?

"What happened to Elamra?" she asked, although she was frightened of the answer. She had never warmed to the Crow, but he meant a lot to Winnie and she could not imagine telling her friend that Elamra was dead. Rald didn't answer. He took a step forward and looked like he was about to explain, when he suddenly looked up. Freya followed his gaze and saw five large Owls swooping down on them. When she turned back to Rald, it was clearly too late.

"I'm sorry," he pleaded and, before Freya could anticipate his move, he had formed a blue owl in the palm of his hand, as Elialdor had done with the crow, and swung the light at her. Freya was aware of nothing else, apart from a silhouette walking away from her as she closed her eyes.

CHAPTER ELEVEN
A Reckless Rescue Plan

"You did what?" The king's voice was calm, but his eyes flashed with anger. Elialdor and Winnie stood before his throne, their heads bowed. They both looked like they had been in a fight, their clothes torn, and their hair knotted and wild.

They had just returned from their hunt and, on realising that Freya had been lost in the storm, had resolved to tell Eanfrith together as soon as they returned. Winnie could only expect the worst, knowing that Freya did not have the power to fly without their aid, and could not bear to think of her lying dead somewhere because of them. Elialdor was grieving too, but he did not show it as clearly as Winnie, whose tears were streaming down her face so fast they were falling on the ornate floor. Eanfrith seemed unconcerned about any display of remorse.

"She has been asking for days to come with us on a hunt," Elialdor mumbled. "I didn't foresee the danger."

"No," Eanfrith snarled, "but I did. And I warned you not to take her beyond the castle gardens. Did you think I was saying this frivolously?!"

He had been speaking so quietly that, when he shouted the last sentence, the prince took a step back, and Winnie looked up, her face red and swollen with tears. They said nothing.

"I think, perhaps, you ought to leave us alone." As the king spoke, Elialdor looked up, hoping that his father was speaking to him and Winnie, but he was addressing the rest of the room, who had fallen silent when they had arrived and were now listening intently. As soon as the king addressed them, however, they left without a second glance, no doubt to gather round the door to hear what was happening.

"We're sorry," Winnie sobbed. Eanfrith turned to her and Winnie looked again at the floor, finding the gaze too much, and started crying again.

"I've not seen you like this since you arrived here, Winifred, so I believe you're sorry," he growled, before he raised his voice. "But what good is an apology to me when you have already cost someone's life?"

"We can't do anymore," Elialdor snapped. "What do you expect us to do? You think you're mourning Freya? You hardly knew her. It was Winnie and I who were her friends."

"Such good friends you caused her death." Eanfrith's voice was back to being calm which, in many ways, was scarier than his shouting. "I fear for this tribe when I am gone, Elialdor, for their leader will be selfish and reckless with other lives."

The prince looked as if his father had mortally wounded him. He could say nothing, but the words stung deeper than he had realised he could feel.

"We could not be more sorry," Winnie sobbed.

"That is not good enough." The force of his last statement seemed to propel the king off the throne so that he was now standing in front of her. The look on his face made Elialdor concerned he might do something terrible, but Winnie didn't flinch, although she shook with crying and her breath was ragged. The king did not seem sympathetic but walked forwards so he was standing just in front of his son.

"Do you not understand what you have done?" he whispered so that, although the people crowded around the door wouldn't be able to hear, his anger seemed to vibrate around the high-ceiling hall. "As well as killing an innocent girl, who was only here because we persuaded her, she was also a human! I am cursed with only one heir, Elialdor, and you have thrown your life away so carelessly."

"I do care!" the prince shouted, even though his father was only inches away. The king's face turned red with anger and he struck his son so hard across the cheek that Elialdor fell to the floor.

"Stop it," Winnie sobbed. "It's punishment enough knowing Freya is dead."

As she spoke, Winnie staggered backwards as though there was a sudden gust of wind. She rubbed her eyes as she realised that her vision was going blurred, but this only cut out her vision altogether. Elialdor seemed to be suffering a similar affliction and the king watched on in interest, although his face was still red with fury.

Winnie's vision started to come back gradually, but she realised she was no longer in the Great Hall. Though utterly confused, she felt her heart leap as she saw Freya sitting up against a wall. She did not appear to know she was there and looked even worse than Winnie and the prince. There was a cut at the side of her face and wounds on her chest that could not have happened in her fall.

Relief at seeing her friend alive gradually subsided as Winnie looked around her at the whitewashed walls, the thin window through which only a little light could pour, and the thick iron door.

She gasped as she felt herself being pulled back to the Great Hall and realised that she was now lying on the floor, having collapsed under the force of the vision. Glancing across at Elialdor, it was clear that he had seen the same, as he looked at Winnie with a mixture of worry and relief.

"What is it? What did your shadow show you?" the king asked, expecting the worst. Winnie bowed her head, knowing how the king would react to the news.

"Freya is alive," Elialdor said eventually, taking the burden on himself. The king raised his eyebrows. It was clear by the prince's fear and sadness that there was more to tell.

"Indeed?" he asked. "And?"

"And she is in Listgard," Winnie mumbled, but it was clear that Eanfrith had heard. Instead of being angry, his face turned pale and he staggered back. Elialdor was immediately on his feet and moved over to support his father, who shook him away.

"It would be better if she had died," he whispered, before standing up straight and turning to the two people before him. "You know what to do. This is your mistake. You must go and retrieve her."

"Into Listgard?" Winnie asked. "To Raedwald?"

"Poor girl," the king gasped and allowed his

son to help him over to the throne. "What have we brought on her?"

"Freya is braver than most humans," Elialdor whispered, trying unsuccessfully to hide his own worry.

The king would not speak but nodded. With the dismissive wave of his hand, it became clear that he was not going to address them further.

Although reluctant to leave the king in such a state, the two of them concluded that it was perhaps better to escape before his wrath returned. Without a word, they walked out of the Great Hall towards the smaller door to avoid everyone. They walked on in silence, through the corridors, until they found themselves in the glass room. Although this place was usually peaceful, not even the soothing flow of the fountain or the sun streaming into the room could soothe their worry. Nervously, they sat down together and considered their best options.

"She is a human," Elialdor said at last. "Raedwald will not kill her. He will not risk losing his immortality."

"Don't put it past him," Winnie's voice shook. "He may not kill her himself but I'm sure he has thought of a way to get rid of her. He would rather that than let her return to us."

"So, we go and fetch her back," Elialdor said. "If it's just me and you, we stand a better chance than a whole army."

"In Listgard?" Winnie looked at him doubtfully. "Even if we do get past their defences unseen, we would never get out again. You know Raedwald wants to kill you."

"I won't leave Freya there!" Elialdor snapped.

"Neither will I. But I will go in there alone. I'm disposable."

"Don't ever describe yourself as that again!" It was clear that the prince's temper was rising, possibly because of his painful cheek, but his father's harsh words had cut deeper than any physical wound. Winnie said nothing. Although she was one of the most accomplished fighters in the tribe, she could see herself shaking at the thought of entering the enemy's stronghold. Although it had been the prince who insisted they take Freya on the hunt, Winnie had to take some of the blame for not putting her foot down. She would rather face Raedwald and all his warriors than allow her good friend to come to any further harm.

CHAPTER TWELVE
Listgard

Freya was surprised to find that the room she was in was filled with light. She had woken disorientated and, for a while, could not remember why she was there. The walls were whitewashed so, although there was only a tiny window, the sunlight beamed through and bounced off the walls. It was only a small room and a large iron door took up most of one wall.

She got shakily to her feet and tried the door, but it was locked. It was only then that she had remembered the encounter with Rald when she had realised that he was an Owl. This, then, must be where the Owls lived. Intrigue slipped into her fear and she went to the window to see what it was like outside.

Through the window, she could see that the room overlooked a courtyard, surrounded by tall buildings. Beyond the gates at the far end of the courtyard, Freya could make out fields. It was much wilder than the Crows' castle but there was a charm to it. The castle she had come to know so well was more like a stately home, whereas this was a self-enclosed country, with everything people would ever need.

She turned back from the window and looked around the pokey room. There was nothing here to distract her from her concerned thoughts, so she thought of the attack when Elamra had been taken, and then how she had almost been killed. But she was a human: surely the Owls would not throw away their immortality just to kill one person. This did not comfort her though as she remembered the attack on the castle. Whoever these Owls were, they were brutal and unmerciful.

She did not know how long she just sat there, growing more and more hungry but knowing that, even if she was given some food, she wouldn't be able to eat anything. As she sat there, she thought back over the last two weeks. She couldn't believe that two weeks ago she was still at school, and she wondered what all her school-friends were doing now. No doubt they had all forgotten her existence as her parents had done and, while she sat here with a very uncertain future, she realised that the only people who could help her were her new friends Elialdor and

Winnie. But there was no way of them knowing where she was, and whether they were still alive.

She rested her head on the whitewashed wall and closed her eyes in despair. As soon as she did, she knew that it was a mistake.

In her mind's eye, she could see someone walking towards her. She could not make out any features on the person as he was just a silhouette. Trying to open her eyes again, she was frightened but unsurprised to find that she could not.

"Hello again," the shadow's voice rang in her head. Freya didn't reply. "You've found yourself in an interesting situation, haven't you?"

"Yes, thank you for that," she snapped. "I thought you were here to protect me."

"I'm here to guide you," the silhouette corrected.

"Then guide me out of this." There was a bitter but pleading tone in her voice. The shadow stood there silently. If it had eyes, Freya was certain they would be staring straight at her as it considered the request.

"No," it said after a while, and Freya felt a wave of anger and disappointment. "You must help yourself."

"But you are me. You're a part of me," Freya snapped. "The part of me I don't like to think about."

The shadow laughed, and its facelessness froze Freya in fear.

"Then reach out to me." The laughter had died away and the shadow's voice almost sounded pleading. "Reach out your mind to touch your soul. Send me to your friends."

"How do I do that?" Freya asked, all anger and fear fading away and replaced by excitement that she could contact her friends from this place.

"Empty your mind."

Freya did as the shadow asked but found this cliché much harder than it sounded.

"Now, think about your friends. You really have to thrust your mind onto them."

"Easier said than done," Freya mumbled.

"I will help you," it sighed. Freya felt her mind being dragged towards her two friends. She saw their faces: Winnie had clearly been crying and Elialdor looked both hurt and worried. She found herself imagining them both standing in front of her. When she opened her mouth to speak, however, the vision cut out and she opened her eyes to find herself entirely alone. Her friends were not there, and her shadow had disappeared.

The feeling of emptiness grew within her and tears stabbed at her eyes as she wondered if she would ever get home again and see her parents, and if they would ever find out what had happened to her.

Although frightened by what might be coming, she was grateful when she finally heard a key in the lock. The thick door opened and Rald came into the room, looking apologetic yet determined. He closed the door behind him, and Freya looked expectantly across, refusing to get to her feet.

"I'm sorry about this," he mumbled. "I meant to let you go once you'd recovered, but my brother came."

"Your brother?" Freya sniggered. "Oh great - there's more of you." This comment did not seem to bother Rald much, and he looked as apologetic as ever.

"I failed in my attempt to bring the prince here, and you are the only thing soothing my father's anger."

"You were trying to get Elialdor?" Freya laughed. "He would have killed you before you brought him here."

"I imagine that is probably what my father was hoping for," Rald snapped, leaving Freya stunned. He pulled her to her feet and, without a second word or glance, dragged her out of the room. For a few moments, Freya wondered about making a run for it as the weak grip on her arm was hardly enough to stop her. She considered that, as the corridors in the Crow castle were teeming with people, this one would be too, and any crazy attempt at escape would be ridiculous. She would just have to wait and hope she wasn't killed in the meantime. She was glad the Owls hadn't got to the prince or Winnie, but a tiny part of her would have preferred this to having her own life threatened. Immediately after thinking this, she shook her head at her selfishness, realising she cared too much for Elialdor and Winnie to let that happen.

She had been right. The corridors were full of people, all of whom looked either angry or intrigued, and Freya held her head high as she walked past them, determined not to show any weakness.

Nevertheless, the walk seemed unbearably long, and she was grateful when they stopped. Freya looked around her to take in her surroundings. She was in a room similar to the Crows' Great Hall, but the walls had been painted white and, instead of the black statue of a raven, there hung an immense sculpture of a barn owl, its wings stretching from one side of the room to the other. Its beady eyes stared at Freya as she entered, and it took a few moments for her to prise her gaze off it. Below it were two thrones, occupied by two men.

One of them was young, though older than Freya. He looked critically at both her and Rald, and a mocking smile was fixed on the smooth face. Next to him was the man Freya recognised from the fight. This must be Raedwald: the Owl that she had heard so much about, and the man who had taken Elamra.

"Ah." Raedwald leant forward on the throne. "We meet again."

Freya didn't reply. She did not know what to say to ensure Raedwald did not have the satisfaction of knowing how afraid she was.

"What a great accomplishment for my otherwise disappointing brother," the younger man sneered, and Freya felt Rald's grip on her arm tighten. Raedwald held his hand up and the other man sat back on the throne, still glaring at Freya and Rald.

"That's enough, Ranald," the older man corrected. "Rald knows that he failed in his initial task of bringing the prince to me, as we knew he would."

"He almost let the girl go too," Ranald laughed. "If I hadn't arrived, I think she would not be standing in front of us now. And a poor substitute she is as well."

"I can leave if you're disappointed." Freya's sarcastic tone was almost a match for Ranald's, and Rald sniggered. Raedwald looked at her, seemingly impressed.

"Well, you have a bit of fight in you after all," he laughed. "After your performance back at your castle, I thought my dear brothers had chosen something of a fool."

Freya didn't mind the harsh comments, but the murderous look that Ranald was giving her made her a little uneasy. *I'm a human*, she thought to herself, *he wouldn't dare kill me.*

"Wouldn't he?" A voice spoke in her head and

she tried to push it to the back of her mind but knew she was unable to do so. As Freya was concentrating on not listening to the shadow, Raedwald stood up and walked slowly over to her. She did not realise he had moved until he was standing right in front of her and the grip on her arm tightened, although Freya was certain this was more out of nervousness of Raedwald than a worry she might run.

"I'm fascinated, I admit," Raedwald whispered. "You can hear him, can't you?"

"Hear who?" Freya snapped.

"You know, don't you?" the man before her laughed. "And I thought you were just a weak human."

"I'm a human, but not weak," Freya said, although she did not entirely believe her own words.

"My pagan brothers cannot show you everything you deserve to know," Raedwald said. "A human who can hear their shadow can become more powerful than the rest of their kind, and so your friends are holding you back."

"What are you trying to say?" Freya stared straight into Raedwald's yellowish eyes.

"The Crows are powerful, I grant you. But my people can teach you far more than you would have learned with them."

"Oh, I see," Freya laughed. "You think that because your son failed to bring Elialdor to you,

you have to make the best of a bad situation. If you can show that you converted a friend of the Crows, that gives you the upper hand, doesn't it?"

Raedwald lifted his hands and clapped. He gave a slight laugh and, as Freya glanced at Ranald, she saw he still had an evil look.

"That intelligence does not belong with my brothers," he laughed. "Come and sit down for a while."

Raedwald led her over to a row of leather chairs at the side of the room and sat down next to her, taking her hands in his own. Rald watched on, looking almost afraid but reluctant to leave the room.

"You must be exhausted," Raedwald smiled. "Not many humans can boast about hunting with Crows, growing wings and flying with no help."

"Not very well, I heard," Ranald laughed. "As soon as she was separated from her friends, she fell to the ground. She would have been killed if my pathetic little brother hadn't rescued her instead of doing his duty."

"Enough," Raedwald commanded. "That's no way to treat our guest, my son. Put aside your differences for one moment."

"It won't work," Freya laughed. "I know what you're like. I don't want to be associated with you, even if that does mean I'm held back."

"Listen to her," Ranald laughed. "Stupid girl.

She's already loyal to her pagan friends, even though she hardly knows them."

"Perhaps you need to know them a little better?" Raedwald whispered, a smile beginning to spread across his face. "You are ever loyal to them, but do you know what they are capable of? Do you know what they would have done to you without a moment's thought?"

"I'm sure you will tell me." Freya's voice sounded cold, but her cheeks burned with a mixture of anger and fear.

"Do you know why humans are so sought after by us?" Freya shook her head at the Owl's question. "Only a certain type of human, you understand. You see, we live apart from human society for many reasons. Perhaps most importantly, it is because humans simply cannot live with us. If they spend more than a few days with us at one time, we simply drain their energy. It's not deliberate, you understand. It is one of the crueller aspects of the power we have been blessed with. So, were you to survive living with your Crow friends, you would be something quite unique. Something quite special. A very powerful friend."

"But I did survive," Freya whispered. "So, what are you trying to prove?"

"That your friends had no idea how far your abilities stretched. For all they knew, you could have died. Not such a true friendship after all, is it?"

"You're guessing," she laughed. "You have no idea what they knew, do you. You think this changes things? It's only made my beliefs stronger."

Before Raedwald could answer, Freya pulled her hands away from his and struck him across the chest so sharply he started spluttering. Ranald was on his feet in an instant, but the Owl king held up his hand to stop him. Rald stayed where he was, looking around each person in the room.

Standing up, Freya glared down at the angry king who, rising to his feet, stood a foot and a half taller than her. She may have made a mistake, she told herself, but almost instantly a voice sounded in her head that this was what she was meant to do. Using a move that Winnie had taught her, she used her elbow to hit into his chest and her foot to trip him up. Her intention was to run away but, looking more angry than in pain, he reached out a claw-like hand and grabbed hold of her throat. With one hand, he lifted her off the ground, so all she could do was try to prise his hands away.

"Perhaps I was wrong about you," Raedwald whispered, but his voice sounded more like a hiss. "You would not make a good ally. You're too unruly. But you cause a slight problem for me."

As he spoke, he threw her backwards. She lay

coughing on the tiles, trying to ignore the burning pains on her neck and her back where she had hit the hard floor.

"You're a human." Raedwald now spoke with bitter distaste. "If I kill you, I die. And you are simply not worth it. On the other hand, I do have someone who may wish to see you."

Without taking his eyes from Freya, he motioned to his eldest son. Ranald walked over to the door behind them and opened it. Freya turned to see what was happening and her heart leapt as she recognised the large frame of Elamra. Her first thought was of how happy Winnie would be knowing he was alive, but the smile slipped as she watched the Crow walk into the room like a robot awaiting orders. His eyes were red and glazed over, and his face paler than Freya remembered. He did not even glance at her but looked straight ahead. Freya turned back to the Owl king, who smiled down at her.

"I will not kill you," he laughed, "but I may as well kill two birds with one stone, as it were."

Ranald laughed but Rald rushed over so he was standing between his father and Freya, who painfully got to her feet.

"Father," Rald was pleading, "this is a mistake. She may still be useful."

"Silence, boy," Raedwald snapped. "If you had brought the prince to me like I asked, instead of this useless, pathetic human girl, then she would not be in this situation."

"If you give the orders for the Crow to kill her," Rald begun a different tactic, "the blue light may still charge you for her death. You may die."

Raedwald looked at his son with distaste. Freya gasped when the king drew his short sword and rested it on his son's shoulder, dangerously close to his neck.

"Then you give the order, my son," the king sniggered. "You were always a disappointment to me. To your race. Give the orders and, for once, do something useful with your life."

As Rald had his back to Freya, she could not see his expression, but he was shaking and spluttering. It was clear he was crying. Raedwald, a warrior through and through, was not sympathetic but rather found this display of emotion disgusting. He dragged his son towards him and turned him around to face Freya, holding the short sword across his chest.

"My younger son, you see," the king began, "lacks the courage, the valour, and the strength to be part of our race."

"He has the compassion worthy of a better race," Freya snapped.

"Give the order," Raedwald growled, addressing Rald but staring at Freya. For a moment, she was unsure whether he would accept such a threat. His eyes were red with crying and he looked apologetically at Freya.

"Kill her," he sobbed, and Elamra, who up until now had been staring straight ahead, turned towards Freya. She may have thought he was frightening back at the castle but now, knowing his orders, he looked larger, more menacing and colder than she had thought possible, even for him.

"Stop this," Freya whispered, but Elamra began walking towards her. He held out his hand, palm upwards, and a blue light swirled around it. Freya was reminded of Elialdor back in the glass room, making the room throb with ethereal light, but now she saw how dangerous it could be. The light gathered to form a wooden handle, and two large curved blades facing in opposite directions. As the light faded away, Freya realised that he was now carrying a battle-axe and was ready to use it.

"Rald," Freya begged, "stop him. You don't want to die!"

Rald would have, perhaps, obeyed her, but it was clear that Raedwald was ready to kill him anyway if he stopped Elamra. The Crow warrior kept advancing and Freya backed away, although she knew that at some point soon, she would have to fight back. As she took another step back, she felt the back of her leg against one of the leather chairs and realised she would now have to defend herself.

Although she tried to remember everything

Winnie and Elialdor had taught her this week, it seemed to flood from her mind when faced with this real situation. Now Elamra was only feet away from her and she could remember nothing of how to defend herself. In the second it took for the Crow to swing the axe towards her, she gathered enough strength of mind to fall to the ground and roll over to safety. The safety was short lived, however, as Elamra at once knew what she was doing and lifted her by the back of her clothes.

As he was about to swing the axe again, he paused and the redness in his eyes cleared slightly.

"Elamra," Freya whispered, in the hope of waking him from his trance. His mouth opened but, before he could speak, Freya heard a relentless chanting. She glanced across at Raedwald who was talking in a strange language. The more he spoke, the redder Elamra's eyes became and, closing his mouth, he dropped the axe and placed his other hand on Freya's throat.

She was not entirely sure what happened next. The pressure the Crow was putting on her neck assured her that she only had seconds to act. Gathering all the strength that was quickly draining from her, she lunged her legs forwards and kicked Elamra. He seemed not to feel any pain, but dropped her to the floor, where she lay gasping, having thought that she would never be able to breathe again.

"Elamra," she croaked, "think of your parents. Don't go the same way as your father."

It was no use reasoning with him anymore. Whatever Raedwald had done, it was no longer Elamra who picked up the axe as Freya lay on the ground. In pain and exhausted, she closed her eyes and awaited what was to come, with more courage than she thought she was capable of.

She was vaguely aware of someone walking towards her, but she was too exhausted to listen to the shadow's remarks now. Slipping into unconsciousness, her last thought was of her parents, hoping they would never remember her only to never see her again.

Rald froze as he watched the Crow raise his axe to strike Freya. He wanted to cry out but was afraid of what his father might do. He had never chosen to be cursed with cowardice, and he hated himself for it but, even when he saw Freya lying helpless on the floor, he could not call the Crow off. If he killed her, it was only possible that he would die from giving the order. If he stopped it now, however, his father would almost certainly kill him there and then.

As Elamra brought the axe down onto Freya, she raised her hand to stop him. But it didn't look like her hand. It was surrounded by the blue light that swirled and twisted around her skin. As the axe hit her hand, it smashed into three different pieces and Raedwald released his son to use his own blue light to block one of the pieces from flying into his head.

Freya rose to her feet, but Rald saw that now her entire body was covered it blue light and, when she opened her eyes, a blue fire was lit in her pupils. He was about to call Elamra back, when Freya put her hand out and the Crow warrior went flying backwards.

Without a moment's thought, Elamra returned the gesture by sending a flash of blue light, something like a lightning bolt, towards Freya, but the girl met it instinctively and seemed to hold it in her hand for a moment before crushing it like it was a bit of scrap paper.

Intrigued and horrified, Rald watched as the new Freya turned her wrath on his father, sending a jet of watery light towards him. As Raedwald watched the light, he had no time to block it and the force of it landing on his chest sent him skidding backwards as far as the throne.

Ranald, angry at this, moved forward, but Freya threw him back to his father with frightening ease. She then turned back to Elamra, who just stood and watched her. Rald thought she was about to attack again, but the light was growing dimmer and dimmer until eventually the fire in her eyes was extinguished. Freya fell back on the floor, gasping for breath, and Elamra advanced once more.

"Enough," Rald was surprised at how commanding he sounded. "That's enough. Leave her."

Elamra did as he was told and stared ahead of him, dropping his arms at his side. Rald rushed over to the girl's side and supported her head.

"What happened?" she mumbled, but Rald could not bring himself to tell her what she had done. Knowledge of power may not be such a great thing, he thought to himself, as he considered his father and brother, who both lay unconscious at the foot of their thrones.

The door to the hall was smashed open, causing Rald to look up, startled, as Elialdor and Winnie entered, swords drawn and red, as though they had already slain many people. Elamra did not even look when they entered but kept staring straight ahead. Winnie noticed him and, in surprise, dropped her sword.

Dashing over, her gleeful face turned grey as she realised that he was not himself. Following her thoughts, Elialdor hurried over to Rald and put his sword under his chin.

"No," gasped Freya, who was still only semi-conscious. "No, don't. I think he saved my life."

The prince turned to Freya and helped her to her feet, allowing her to lean against him as otherwise she would certainly have fallen.

"What have you done to him?" Winnie demanded of Rald, who put his hands up, trying to show that he had meant no harm.

"It wasn't him," Freya whispered, but Winnie looked unconvinced. On seeing her friend grab hold of the Owl's collar, Freya pointed towards the two bodies near the thrones. "It was them."

Winnie wandered over to the two Owls warily.

"We should take them back with us," she said. "The king would be overjoyed to have his adversary safely locked away."

Rald watched on, unsure of what to do or say, realising he was now only alive because Freya insisted on it. Elialdor could not move over to the Owls but wanted to support Freya and would not leave her with Rald.

"Come away, Winnie," Elialdor hissed at her. "We need to get out before they call the rest of the guard."

Winnie hardly seemed to notice.

"We have to get Elamra and Freya out of here," Elialdor snapped. The use of her friends' names called Winnie back to reality. She looked around at Elamra, who was staring blankly at nothing, and at Freya, who needed support just to stand up. The Crow captain nodded slowly and rejoined them.

CHAPTER THIRTEEN
Waking Up

"Wait!" Freya put her hand out to stop Elialdor from leaving. "If we leave Rald here, his dad will kill him."

"No, I'll be fine," the Owl said quickly, preferring to take his chances with his own family rather than his enemy.

"Elialdor," Freya insisted, but the prince shook his head and pulled Freya towards the door.

"He wants to stay, Freya," he said as they made their way out of the hall. "Let him stay with his kind."

"They'll kill him." Freya's exhaustion meant that all control of her emotions had melted away and she found herself sobbing heavily. Winnie looked on as she dragged the unaware Elamra behind her. Freya thought she looked slightly annoyed at her eagerness to help the Owls, but she said nothing.

"No," Elialdor whispered. "It was lucky we reached this far into Listgard unharmed. If we take Rald with us, we lose any chance we have to escape unnoticed."

Although Freya could not stop thinking about what Raedwald would do to his son when he recovered, she could not lead her friends into danger again, so she went with Elialdor from the giant room. Elamra was quite willing to follow Winnie, although he was still staring straight ahead and made no acknowledgment of them.

The first person they encountered seemed to be a nobleman, with a haughty look and straight-backed stance. It took him a few moments to realise that these conspicuous strangers were not Owls, but mortal enemies. The seconds it took him to recognise this, however, was costly. Elialdor, ensuring that Freya could just about stand up herself, hit him on the back of the head with the hilt of his sword and awkwardly hid his body in a small closet-type room that full of hanging poultry and game.

"He'll be fine when he wakes up," he said when he saw Freya's disapproving face.

Without another word, he let Freya lean on him again as he encouraged her out of the corridor. The room they had just entered must have been a state room, with its splendid carpets and curtains and the elegant fireplace at one side. Fortunately, there was no-one there and Winnie pulled Elamra forwards before closing the door carefully. As she started moving again, she bumped into Elialdor who had stopped and was staring at the door opposite. He turned to Winnie and gave her a slight smile, as though trying to reassure himself of something. Winnie shook her head, seeing his expression.

"I know what you're thinking, and it would be suicide," she hissed. The prince led the almost-asleep-Freya over to a large ottoman and sat her down on it.

"The castle is full of people, Winnie," he insisted. "It would be suicide to take the front door."

"I didn't say we had to take the front door. We could go by the workshop and in through the kitchen like we did earlier. The Owls take so many slaves from other tribes, they would hardly notice us."

"Oh yes," The prince replied sarcastically, pointing to Elamra and Freya. "Yes, they wouldn't spare us a second glance, would they."

"So, you want to fly out of here?" Winnie laughed, and the prince anxiously gestured that she should keep her voice down. "And what would our dear hosts do then? When they see four Crows flying over their castle?"

"Two," he corrected. "There's no chance these two would be able to fly out of here."

"So, as well as dodging arrows and goodness knows what else, you want to carry one each. You, as a raven, may find that easy. But I cannot carry a raven on my own."

Without a word, Elialdor flicked some blue light in the direction of their two unaware friends who, without even noticing, started to change shape until they were both about the size of a sparrow.

"Where did you learn that?" It was clear from her voice that Winnie was annoyed and intrigued at the same time.

"A rather obliging wren princess," he smiled, but Winnie stared at him disapprovingly. "Shall we go?"

Winnie walked over to the window and ducked out of sight.

"You could have picked a better window," she snapped. "This one overlooks the battlements. We were supposed to take Freya back safely, not get her killed in the process."

Elialdor looked out towards the battlements. There were only four people patrolling this part and, without a glance at Winnie, he opened the window a few inches.

"Are we going, or are we staying here?" Without another word from either of them, the prince transformed once more into a sleek black raven. Hopping a few steps over to where the tiny Freya was lying asleep, he carefully picked her up and flew back to the window. When he was resting on the narrow windowsill, he glanced back at Winnie to make sure she was following with Elamra, before he dived out.

The exhilaration of flying never dulled for Elialdor, but this time, it was mingled with worry as he glanced down to see if the guards had spotted them. Winnie was following, the smaller jackdaw dwarfed by the raven.

Soaring over the battlements, Elialdor breathed a sigh of relief which was brought to a swift end by a call from Winnie. Looking over his shoulder, he saw two of the Owls who had been on the battlements were now flying close behind. The two left at the castle had clearly alerted more of the guard as Elialdor could see more of them piling onto the battlements.

Unwilling to admit defeat, he called over to Winnie to keep going as they dived fast towards the ground. There was a group of trees a little further away, and Elialdor hoped they might be able to escape in there. By the time he got there, however, his wings felt like they would seize up if he continued any further. He had never flown so fast before and, when he looked across to find his friend, he saw that she had collapsed in a heap on the floor, back to her usual form. Elialdor followed her example, feeling they would stand a better chance fighting their pursuers but, when he looked into the sky for them, he found they were startlingly alone. The Owls had, for some unknown reason, abandoned the chase and returned.

They had flown much further than Elialdor had realised and, although the land around here was all very flat, there was no sign of the castle. Although he hated to admit it, he had no idea where they had ended up. He was lost.

Trying to ignore the absolute exhaustion, he mustered enough strength to transform Freya and Elamra back into their usual selves, knowing he could never tell Elamra how small he had been. He laughed at the thought, which brought Winnie's attention back to him. On seeing her friends back to normal, she crawled over to Freya and put her hand an inch from Freya's mouth.

"Thank the heavens," she whispered, "she survived the flight."

Although Freya was barely conscious, Winnie hugged her tightly, letting out all the emotions that had been buried inside during their brief, dangerous time in Listgard.

"I thought you died when you fell," she sobbed. She had only known Freya a little while, but the human was the one person who she felt she could really talk to without being judged. She had brought a refreshing view of the world, with her human experience, and Winnie hugged her sisterly friend even tighter as she realised the amount of grief that she had bottled up inside for her. Freya closed her eyes, exhausted, without hearing Winnie's words.

When Winnie had recovered her senses after being so relieved, she crawled over to Elamra, who was laying on the soft mossy grass, his eyes open but staring straight up into the sky.

"This requires a strong magic," Elialdor whispered, joining her. "I don't know how we will do this."

"Leave it to me," Winnie said, but the prince laid a firm hand on her arm.

"We're both weak enough from exhaustion." He shook his head. "Leave it a while."

"I've seen this before," she replied. "He won't live long without his commander. We have to get him out of this trance before it's too late."

"Raedwald must have laid some protection over him. I don't know how dangerous it will be. Let me do this."

"No." Her voice was quiet but firm.

Before Elialdor was able to stop her, she bent over Elamra, who did not seem to notice her. Whispering words so quiet they were almost silent, the blue light swirled its way around her hand. She placed the hand first on Elamra's head and then on his chest, whispering all the time.

Nothing happened.

The whispering became louder and more frantic. Winnie could not make out the words herself, even though they came from her mouth.

As the whispering grew, so did the light, and she pressed hard on the left side of his chest.

Elamra gasped, as though he was taking his first breath but, as he breathed in, there was a piercing scream: so loud and relentless, Elialdor fell back onto the grass. Winnie continued, through sheer will, to press down with the light-covered hand. The piercing sound only grew louder as Elamra began to breathe more and more. The red light in his eyes was ebbing away, but he was very pale.

Elialdor could not handle the sound anymore. He writhed on the ground trying to block out the noise which was piercing his skull and vibrating around his entire body. All he wanted to do was stop the noise and the need to do this gave him the strength to get to his feet. Still, the noise weighed him down so he could hardly move his muscles, dragging his feet along the floor towards Elamra. Through the need to stop the screaming, Elialdor managed to draw his sword. The sound having taken control of his senses, all the prince wanted to do was end the terrible noise.

The whispering grew even more frantic as Winnie saw the look on the prince's face, and she stretched out her spare hand towards him. A jet of light knocked him backwards and he continued to writhe on the ground, trying to resist the urge to stop Elamra.

Winnie was still leaning over Elamra but, although the colour was returning to his cheeks, it was draining from her. She would not be stopped, however, and pressed ever harder on Elamra's chest.

Out of the corner of her eye, she saw the prince rise to his feet again and reach for his sword. Knowing she did not have the strength to stop him again, she focused all her energy on the man before her, willing him to wake up and break the enchantment.

She was aware of a terrible pain in her head, but she gathered every tiny piece of power she had left within her to finish saying the words and place a hand over Elamra's head.

The sound was becoming more and more penetrating, and the effort more and more draining, until she collapsed on Elamra's still body.

The prince reached the pair of them and, not knowing what he was doing, was about to raise his sword to stop the noise, but the piercing sound stopped so abruptly Elialdor felt he had been lifted off his feet. Winnie raised her head from Elamra's chest, and the prince knelt beside her.

"You look absolutely dreadful." He ran his hand over her cheek.

"Thanks," she laughed, but was too weak and started gasping for air.

"Stay still, and don't speak," the prince sighed. Winnie had smeared blood around her nose, which the prince wiped away, but there were still bloodstains on her clothes which he could do nothing about. She looked as pale as Elamra had done but, above all this, she seemed surprisingly contented as she looked at the peaceful bodies of Elamra and Freya.

"You need to sleep, and you need food, but I'm a little reluctant to leave you here."

"Go," Winnie whispered. "I will be fine. Go and fetch us some food."

Elialdor hesitated. Glancing at Elamra and Freya, it was clear they would not be able to help in the event of an attack. He looked back at Winnie and saw the dark rings around her eyes, mixed with the paleness of her usually rosy skin, and the traces of blood on her face. No, she wouldn't be able to fight back if someone attacked, but she also wouldn't last much longer without food. Looking back at his three friends again, he reluctantly flew off in search of something that may bring all their strength back.

Winnie collapsed on the ground and watched the clouds above them, her breath rasping and painful. Closing her eyes, she could still see the clouds: thick and white, sheltering her from the sun. She could not even move her little finger as she lay there, hoping that no one crossed their path as they would be entirely defenceless. Her mind focused on Elialdor and she wondered if he had managed to find something to eat. She thought about the castle, and of the king, and of her family. The memories came flooding back to her, the wonderful times and the moment when she was called away from them, and when her parents were gone.

The exhaustion and relief caused her to sob uncontrollably as she lay there, utterly defenceless. She had no energy and felt as though she would never be able to move again. She could see her parents' faces so clearly, she thought that she might be able to touch them but, instead of reaching out to them, it was her mother who held out her hand to take Winnie's. She felt surprised that she could feel the warmth of her mother's touch, even though this was in her mind. The older woman pulled her forwards and the effort of moving brought Winnie back to her senses.

She gazed up, expecting to see her parents, but she looked straight into the face of Elamra. Seeing she was awake, he squeezed her hand even tighter and, with his spare hand, brushed the stray hair out of her eyes.

"You're awake," she whispered. Elamra nodded and smiled, an expression so unfamiliar on his features.

"And I have you to thank for it." The smile deepened.

"I thought you wouldn't remember anything

from your trance."

"That was the worst part of the curse." The smile slipped. "I was aware of everything I was doing but I could not stop myself. I attacked the human girl."

Winnie glanced across at Freya, who was lying peacefully on the grass.

"She is fine," Winnie smiled.

"She is more than fine," Elamra began, but was interrupted by the prince returning, carrying dinner.

"Glad to see you're back to normal." He grinned at Elamra, but the serious concern was back on the man's face. "And you too, Winnie. I hear you make an amazing rabbit stew."

"At home," she laughed. "Surrounded by everything we might need. You can tell you're a prince. A stew takes a lot more than the meat."

"Sorry." The prince looked slightly downcast. "I'm usually the one to do the hunting. I leave the cooking to my father's servants."

"The women, you mean," Winnie rebuked him and leaned on Elamra for support.

"You've been talking to Freya, haven't you?" the prince looked annoyed.

"Pass them here," Winnie sighed and took them from Elialdor, who seemed instantly happier at being saved the ordeal of cooking. "See to Freya. She hasn't woken up yet."

The prince wandered over to Freya's calm

form, thinking what a shame it was to wake her up after her experience. Crouching down to put a hand on her shoulder, he paused and, without thinking, ran his hand through her hair instead. Her experience in Listgard had certainly taken its toll on her and she didn't move. Looking back at his companions to see if they were watching, he turned back as he caught a glimpse of something. Freya's eyes had opened but they did not belong to her. There was no emotion hidden within them: they just looked straight up at the prince. For a terrible moment, he thought she might be dead and, in his fear, he cried out. The others came rushing over to him but, as they did, Freya leapt to her feet with surprising agility and lunged herself at Elamra. It was everything the broad man could do to dodge her blows but, when he saw the fire that was now alight in her eyes, he ducked as a flash of something like lightning was aimed at his face. Instead, it landed a little way behind him, scorching the ground and leaving the grass black and smoking.

Seeing this, the prince ran behind her and was about to knock her unconscious to save them all when Winnie leapt in front of Freya and gestured him to stop. Elialdor stopped and looked horrified as the other Freya turned towards Winnie slowly.

Winnie never spoke but took hold of her friend's hands and looked deep into the eyes which were alight with blue fire. For a moment, she thought the other Freya would send the blue lightning directly at her, but she kept looking into her eyes and held her hands close.

Slowly, the blue fire began to die away, and Freya stumbled forward. Falling onto her knees, she stayed there, gasping as though she could not breathe. Winnie knelt beside her and whispered her name.

Freya looked up almost immediately. The blank expression and the fire had gone completely, and she looked like she was back to normal.

"Elialdor," Winnie whispered as she held her friend's hands, "fighting is not always the answer. See, Freya is back with us."

"We made it out," Freya smiled as though nothing had happened between Listgard and the forest.

"Yes," Winnie nodded, hugging Freya tightly.

"Oh, my heart's racing like mad." Freya clutched her chest. "I must have been dreaming."

"What did you dream about?" Elamra walked forwards and crouched in front of her.

"I can't remember, but it was the best rest I have had in a while. Now I've woken up, though, I feel like I've run a marathon. But you're awake," she smiled, "and you're not trying to kill me. That's good!"

"Yes," Elamra mumbled, "it's excellent."

Freya looked around her friends, from the two beside her to the prince, who was standing a couple of metres away. Looking from one to the other, her brow creased in concern.

"What's the matter?" she demanded. "What happened?"

Winnie sighed and was about to answer but, before she could speak, Elamra interrupted.

"It was harder waking me up than they had thought. Raedwald was thorough in his enchantments. I'm sorry - I think the noise must have woken you up."

"No," Freya smiled, suspecting nothing. "I'm pleased you're awake, and we're out of Listgard."

"Have some rest," Winnie whispered. "We can eat soon. I think we all need a good meal."

Cooking at the castle, or even on a planned hunt was one thing, but cooking when she had no tools, no seasoning, and actually nothing apart from what the prince had brought back, was completely different.

"Typical," she muttered while she prepared the meal. "It hardly occurred to him to gather something other than meat."

"Is this what we're having?" Freya came to join Winnie. There was something hesitant about her friend, Freya thought, and a kind of nervousness in her smile as she looked up. Thinking this was only because of their recent escape, Freya felt guilty that her friends had been put in such a dangerous situation because of her.

"I've never had rabbit before." Although she did not mean to hurt anyone's feelings, she could not hide the disgust in her voice as she watched Winnie prepare the poor dinner. Her friend did not seem offended.

"It is what Elialdor came back with. At the moment, I would eat anything."

"So, what is it? Rabbit stew?"

"No," Winnie sighed. "For that, you need a bit more than rabbit and more rabbit. We'll just eat this on its own and then head back to the castle. The king will be very pleased to see that you're well."

"We aren't his favourite people at the moment." The prince smiled as he joined them. "He was angry we had placed you in danger. Don't worry," he added when he saw the look on Freya's face, "he wasn't angry with you. He blamed us entirely."

Although Freya was not pleased that her friends had taken the blame, she felt relieved that Eanfrith was not angry with her. When he had mentioned his father's name, the prince had looked weary and worried. He had instinctively brushed his hand over his own cheek, and Freya was reminded of her vision while she had been at Listgard. She wondered what the king's anger would be like and was certain that he was harsher than any adult she knew. Elialdor looked worse than if he had just been grounded.

After the fire was lit, cooking seemed to take forever and, although Freya had always thought she'd never eat rabbit, her stomach started rumbling when she could smell it. Eventually, they were all sitting around the fire, eating over-cooked meat but just pleased to have something to stop the hunger.

"I prefer your stew, to be honest," Elamra said casually. Winnie's face reddened with anger which Freya could understand completely and, on seeing it, they continued eating in silence.

At the end of the meal, during which Freya really wished someone would break the silence, they felt revived enough to begin the journey back to the castle. Not one of them was entirely sure where they had ended up and therefore how far they were from home but circling around a little over the area gave them a confident idea of which way they should be heading.

Flying was as exhilarating as Freya remembered. Her strength seemed to be returning to her now she was in the air, feeling the air whistling past her head and watching her friends' graceful forms flying around her.

CHAPTER FOURTEEN
Uncontrollable Power

Although flying was amazing and Freya would never forget how much she loved it, she was relieved to see the towers of the castle looming ahead. They were flying over parkland, dotted here and there with trees, and Freya was amazed to see how green the land was: a rich, deep green. She was unsure whether it was entirely natural or if it just looked different from the air.

As she flew onto the battlements and turned back into her human self, her arms felt so heavy and achy she struggled to raise them as Winnie embraced her.

"Back to safety," she whispered. Her friend's warmth humbled her and the relief in her voice was mirrored by the thankfulness Freya felt at reaching the castle without any trouble.

"We should go to my father," the prince

mumbled. Although she was sure he was feeling the same relief, Freya noticed an uncertain step in Elialdor as they made their way towards the Great Hall. He and Elamra wandered ahead, talking quietly and arguing about something. Freya could not make it out, however, as Winnie would not stop talking.

"I'm not sure the king will allow us to take you on a hunt again," she began, "but you'll be much safer inside the castle walls."

"I'm not concerned about it, to be honest," Freya smiled, trying to reassure her friend so she would stop talking and allow her to listen to the heated conversation ahead.

"No, you beat Raedwald. That is quite amazing! Wait until we tell the king!"

"No, it wasn't me. It was Rald."

"Well, I'm not sure what he'd make of that. Perhaps we can reach out to him. He might help us in the future."

Freya stopped walking and, for the first time, stopped trying to listen to the other conversation.

"You weren't interested in talking to him before." She did not mean to sound harsh, but her friend's hypocrisy astounded her. "You left him to his father. We don't even know if he is still alive."

"You..." Winnie trailed off.

"I'm sorry, but if I were Rald, I would not help you."

"No, you should not be sorry," Winnie sighed. "I should be sorry. I did not realise you had feelings for him. If I had seen, I would, of course, have-"

"I don't have feelings for him!" Freya laughed, although she knew she sounded more hysterical. The sudden noise made Elamra and Elialdor look around and walk back to them with concerned looks on their faces. Freya hardly noticed. "Not like you're thinking anyway. But Rald saved my life and we left him to die. It's not feelings like that! It's morals!"

"What's this?" the prince whispered to Winnie when he had reached them.

"Nothing," Freya snapped and begun walking towards the Great Hall.

"Wait," Winnie shouted after her. Her voice was tired, and it was this that made Freya halt. "I'm sorry. I didn't realise what it would mean to you. I didn't think about it."

Winnie walked up to her and took her hands, clinging to them tightly. The others stood back a little way, seeing this display of emotion to be beyond their control and understanding.

"I have been brought up to see all Owls as my enemy. I thought that, when Rald had helped you, he must have an hidden motive. I did not understand that, perhaps, he wasn't like the rest of them."

"You can't assume they're all the same," Freya

mumbled, feeling foolish about her outburst but knowing that it had to be said.

"No, I can't," Winnie nodded, "but I do. This is why we need you, Freya. We need you to be with us so you can bring a little humanity into our lives."

Freya did not know what to say. She would have been angry, but Winnie had actually agreed with her. She had not expected that. She must have looked so stupid just standing there, unable to speak and feeling firm in her belief but unhappy she got so angry with her friends.

"We will tell my father of Rald's noble actions," Elialdor said, "and speak to him of a rescue attempt."

"King Eanfrith would never agree," Elamra stated. "Can you really see him risking a Crow's life to save an Owl?"

"Perhaps this is just the sort of thing we should be doing," the prince said, not taking his eyes from Freya. "We'll go and see."

Freya felt a mixture of awkwardness and fear as they made their way further into the castle. She was unsure how the king would react to her request, and whether he would, indeed, risk a rescue mission for an Owl. Something in the back of her mind warned her against her friends, although they had helped her twice now. What Raedwald had said about them was still stuck in her mind.

Had they known, she wondered, *that she might have died from spending too much time in their company?*

They reached the large door in silence. Whatever intriguing conversation the prince and Elamra had been deeply involved in had reached an abrupt end, so Freya had no hope of seeing what had made them so lively. Winnie did not speak, either, and Freya was worried that she had caused offence with her harsh words. After Winnie's help and, above all, her friendship, she could not bear to think she had caused her pain.

The door to the hall was opened from the inside and the four of them were reluctant to enter the crowded room. At the sight of them, the congregated Crows parted to form a path to the throne. On the throne sat Eanfrith, looking splendid but stern.

Giving a nervous cough, Elialdor took a step forward and took hold of Freya's hand. Elamra and Winnie followed together, their heads held high and proud. Freya was unsure why the prince should have been nervous, but his grip on her hand tightened as they got closer to his father. She held tight to his hand to show her support, trying to banish the distrustful thoughts from her suspicious mind.

Reaching the throne, Elialdor bowed deeply and Freya did the same, before looking up to see a strange look on Eanfrith's face. It was something between anger and pride and the mixture left his mouth set in its permanent frown and his brow creased.

"Father," Elialdor whispered, "we brought Freya back safely. She was unharmed."

"I'm impressed, my son." Eanfrith stood up and immediately everyone else in the room bowed low. "After such harsh words and actions, to follow my orders shows real dedication."

"I wanted to follow your orders, of course," the prince could not stop himself from speaking despite the sharp sideways look from Winnie, "but I was desperate to save my friend. I would have gone even if you had not given the order."

Keeping her eyes lowered, Freya noticed a tone of resentment in the prince's voice when he addressed his father. Glancing up again, she saw that the king's expression had not changed, but perhaps his eyes looked angrier. Then, out of the blue, the king began to laugh. At this, the crowd looked up in puzzlement but, seeing their liege in merriment, they also started laughing.

"My son," he said when he had controlled his laughter, "there is something of your mother in you."

Elialdor was so surprised at the sudden mention of his mother, he stood up from his bow, but Eanfrith hardly seemed to notice.

"I'm proud of you, my son," the king smiled. "Go. You look like you need some rest and you have certainly deserved some. You too, Freya. You have shown immense courage in these past days. You will fit in well here."

Freya did not have the heart, given the king's mood, to announce that she had no intention of staying. She bowed and follow Elialdor out of the room. The crowd bowed their heads at their prince, which was a definite improvement on a few moments ago.

As they turned, however, they stopped as they noticed a man in the crowd who did not fit in. His sandy coloured hair, with its widow's peak, and his pointed features betrayed him as an Owl. Before Freya could even shout out, Elialdor had pushed her backwards so she fell to the floor and, drawing his sword, began to advance through the crowd.

The others had noticed what was happening by this time and, seeing the cause of the distress, quickly dispersed to be as far away from the Owl as possible while remaining in the room at a vague attempt at courage.

"Stop," the Owl demanded, and the prince obeyed, lowering his sword. Looking to see what had made the prince obey, Freya saw that the Owl was holding a flame in his hand without it burning him. In the other hand, he held a globe of blue light. It must be bad, she thought. Strange blue lights in this place were usually followed by something weird happening.

The crowd were beginning to come back to their senses and some of them had also drawn swords, while Winnie and Elamra shouted at them to lower them.

"You light that," Elialdor's voice trembled, "and you die too."

"I'm willing to make the ultimate sacrifice for my king," the Owl snapped, and the flame was placed closer to the blue light.

"Stop!" King Eanfrith demanded, but the Owl just looked at him with disgust.

"This is a noble ending," he laughed.

Whatever happened next, Freya did not know. Feeling an uncontrollable desire to close her eyes and wait for the end, she obeyed, but instantly knew that it was a mistake. The shadow, that seemed to be coming more and more frequently, was there waiting for her. Without a word, it came closer, until Freya passed out through a sudden surge of sleepiness.

Winnie moved forward, but Elamra pulled her back. Shaking herself free, she approached the Owl, so she stood between him and the king.

"You think you can protect him?" the Owl laughed. "This little creation of mine will destroy everything in this building. Simply standing between me and your beloved leader serves no purpose."

"Stop!" the prince shouted as the flame came closer to the light but, seeing the look of triumph on the enemy's face, dived backwards to cover Freya from the destruction, knowing it was only a vain hope of saving her life.

To his surprise, he found that he had just hit the floor. Freya was not where she had been. Looking around but knowing that the sudden silence was a bad sign, he saw her. She was standing up straight, with her arm outstretched towards the Owl.

The Owl, it seemed, was so fascinated that their destruction seemed to have been paused. Standing up and walking over to her, the prince realised it was no longer Freya who stood there. Her face held the same lack of expression as before and her eyes burned with a blue fire that left Elialdor speechless. In the palm of her outstretched hand burned a similar blue fire, and the prince realised that the Owl was now desperately trying to move the flame towards the blue orb. Whatever Freya was doing, it meant that the man's muscles were frozen.

"Freya," he whispered, seeing the extent of her power. Her name seemed to have no effect and the prince saw the blank, cold expression on his friend's face.

"Freya!" Winnie gasped, and the prince looked around to see the Owl lying on the ground. "Freya!"

The king held up his hand to stop Winnie from breaking the trance, but she paid no attention.

Winnie leapt forward to seize Freya by the shoulders but was thrown back as Freya turned to her. She fell motionless on the floor.

Freya turned back to the Owl, who was awake with his eyes fixed on her, but unmoving. Freya now held both hands out towards him and the blue orb in his hand seemed to grow and grow until it was the size of a football. She did not seem content with this, however, and continued to focus all her energy on the man before her.

The orb grew, until Elialdor could not see the man's face, although he was grateful for this, as the sight of the man sickened him. The light throbbed as it grew brighter and bigger until it was the same size as the Owl.

Only when the Owl was completely covered by it did Freya lift her hands above her head, as though directing some unseen energy above her. Bringing her arms down again and holding them out towards the Owl, the light grew so intense that the prince and the other people in the room had to shield their eyes.

Unable to see, Elialdor gasped as he heard a loud explosion and assumed that, somehow, the Owl had succeeded and the castle was destroyed, while he had managed to survive. Feeling that the light had gone, the prince looked to where the Owl had been, only to discover that it was just a pile of ash. Everyone else had been untouched.

CHAPTER FIFTEEN
The Frightening Truth

Freya blinked. Her head throbbed and she felt like she was apart from her body. She tried to twitch her fingers, but they felt numb.

"Lie still," Winnie's voice whispered close by her, and she tried to focus. Her friend was sitting on a small stool next to the bed where Freya was lying. Once things had come into focus, she felt a lot better, although her head still felt like it might explode.

"What happened?" Freya mumbled, sitting up. "There was a man. He was going to blow us all up."

"He didn't," Winnie smiled.

"Why?" Freya tried to remember, but something was blocking her memory.

"How are you feeling?" Freya knew Winnie was deliberately changing the subject.

"Fine. I'm fine." She got up from the bed before her friend could stop her. Her head was spinning, but she felt like she needed to find out what had happened. She needed to find the prince, perhaps he would tell her.

Almost as though he had heard her thoughts, the door opened and Elialdor came into the room, followed by his father. Both of them looked worried which filled Freya with concern, wondering if the intruder had managed to do some damage after all.

"What happened?" she repeated.

"We've been talking." The prince took Freya's hands in his own. "It's clear that Raedwald will not give up. We have made him so angry - angrier, I think, than he's been in a long time. He's never been willing to sacrifice one of his own before. We need to resolve this."

"How?" Winnie interrupted.

"We are going to do what we couldn't before. We are going to find Edweth's killer. Edweth's true killer."

"That was over a thousand years ago." Winnie shook her head. "It's impossible."

"I think it's clear that it was someone from one of the tribes. They will likely still be alive. I need you to find them." It was the king who spoke this time, his voice stern and determined.

"But," Winnie bowed her head as she turned to Eanfrith, "you can't mean to take Freya with us.

We have to keep her safe."

"I think it's clear that our guest can look after herself."

Freya watched all this in confusion. She agreed that the best way to appease Raedwald was to find his wife's killer and bring them to justice, but she wasn't ready for such a task. From what she had heard, whoever this murderer was, he must have been strong and powerful. She could not fight someone like that. By the look on her face, a mixture of anger and dismay, Winnie seemed to agree.

"I'd like to help. Really, I would," Freya smiled, "but I couldn't win against someone like that."

The king smiled, but his expression showed that he was not going to change his mind.

"Gather your strength," he said, before walking out of the room, leaving his son to clear up the flow of abuse that would surely come.

"Aldor, are you insane?" Winnie hissed. "You can't agree to this."

"I agree that we have to put a stop to Raedwald before he puts a permanent stop to us."

"And, of course, you would defend your father!" Winnie snapped, giving no consideration to how she was challenging the king and prince at the same time.

"Because I actually happen to agree with him!" It was clear that the prince was a match for her rage any day.

"Stop it!" Freya snapped. "Both of you. We need to come up with an idea that won't get us all killed."

"I don't want you facing Edweth's killer, whoever it is," Winnie sighed.

"But you had no problems with killing me by keeping me here." Now Freya was getting angry, she couldn't stop the rush of emotions pouring onto her friends. "Raedwald told me what happened to humans who spent too long in your company. How were you to know that it wouldn't happen to me?"

"Freya!" Winnie sounded astonished, but Freya wasn't sure if that was because of her harsh words, or that she had been found out.

"No." Freya moved over to the door and put her hand up to show she did not want to be followed. They obeyed, stunned, and she wandered through the corridors alone. Her head was still aching as she made her way to the only place she could think of.

She had thought of the glass room during her brief imprisonment in Listgard and, as she pushed the door open and felt the hot air greet her, she let out a sigh of relief. Wandering over to the fountain, she ran her hand through the water and at once felt more relaxed.

Thinking over what she had said to her friends, she screwed up her eyes as if that would help her forget. Perhaps out of a need to take her mind off it, or because it seemed like such a long time since she'd been there, she wandered through the doors to the infirmary.

She had forgotten that Eli had left his son and was surprised to find he was not sitting by the bedside, his wrinkled face in his hands. However, this was nothing compared to her surprise when she saw that Enna was no longer lying on the bed. He was sitting up with his bright eyes wide open and looked as if he might leap out of bed at a second's notice.

Freya paused. She didn't think Enna had seen her and she was unsure about approaching the now-conscious boy. She had been so used to just sitting by his bed without him noticing, that she did not know if she could actually communicate with him.

Turning to go, she grimaced and stopped as someone said her name. She turned to see Enna's eagle eyes looking straight into hers. His mouth was turned up in a smile and he seemed as calm as before. Tentatively, Freya walked over to him and sat down at the edge of the hospital bed.

"I know you kept me company when I was asleep." Enna's voice was kind but there was an edge to it that made Freya nervous. It wasn't gruff, but it sounded like it could change character without warning.

"You helped me," was all that Freya could think of to say. "Your father was here too."

Enna looked down at his hands, which were clasped together above the quilt. Freya felt like she might have intruded on something she had no business with.

"I'm sorry," she said as she got up to leave, but Enna laid a gentle hand on her arm. Looking back, she saw that he wasn't angry, or even upset, but accepting. The smile had returned, although it wasn't as broad as it had been.

"Please sit with me for a while." The tone of Enna's plea was impossible to refuse. "I'm out of place. The nurses don't like having me here."

Freya smiled, knowing it was Enna's unpredictability that the Crows disliked, and he had no control over that.

"Now you're awake," she grinned, "you can get out of the hospital. Come for a walk with me."

Enna glanced around as if he feared something.

"They won't notice," Freya laughed, seeing that there were no nurses around. "Please, I need some company."

Uncertainly, Enna got out of the bed and put on the cloak which had been draped over the bedside table. He seemed a little unsure on his feet, so Freya allowed him to lean against her as she guided him out of the hospital room. Once outside, Enna drew in a deep breath and let out a sigh, ecstatic at being outdoors.

"You seem different, you know," he said as they wandered beneath the large ash trees.

"You only met me for a few brief moments," Freya laughed, but Enna seemed serious.

"I can get the measure of people relatively quickly. There's something different about you. Something's changed."

Freya didn't speak but gestured to the luxurious garden around her.

"It's more than that." Her companion shook his head. "It's something…"

"Darker?" Freya finished off the sentence as Enna trailed off. He made no attempt to disagree or reassure her.

"What happened?" he asked. Before Freya could face the question, she sat down on an seat carved out of stone, with something that resembled a crow as chair arms.

"I've seen things, Enna," she whispered, and the eagle looked intently at her. "There are things I'd never thought possible. But they are. I've always known there was this darker side to me, but I managed to hide it. Now I'm not sure I can."

"You know how I saw this in you?" Enna sat next to her. "It's what I feel inside of me all the time."

"There is this…shadow."

"That shows you how to do things? To protect yourself?" Freya nodded at Enna's question. "It is the same for all of us. Some are just more inclined than others."

"How do I stop it?" Freya could not help the

tears that welled up in her eyes. It wasn't sadness, it was fear and desperation.

"You can't," Enna replied. "It's part of you."

Freya looked angrily at Enna. If he was so unwilling to help her, there was no point to this conversation.

"You learn to control it," Enna sighed, "but it takes time, years, to become successful. I still struggle, but only when I am not entirely in control of my actions. Like when I'm unconscious. Yes," he added when Freya looked up, "I'm very well aware of the damage I did when I wasn't in control."

"I had a strange dream last night." Freya whispered, almost too afraid to confide in the eagle. "There was a man in the castle that wanted to hurt us. I dreamt I killed him."

Enna looked hard at her and, for a few moments, remained silent.

"Not a dream," he said at last. "That's what happened to me to begin with. I would remember my actions in dreams. That was until I realised that they were memories."

"My friends knew," she sighed. "They were trying to protect me. The king said it was clear I could protect myself."

As everything became clear, Freya stood up and ran her hands through her scruffy hair, closing her eyes to block the tears. Instantly, she realised her mistake and forced them open as the shadow began to form. Enna was looking at her with nothing but sympathy.

"Tell me how to control it," Freya sighed, though her tone was demanding.

"I am not the best teacher, although I want you to succeed." Enna smiled. "Look what happened when I was not in control. This…" He trailed off, trying to find the right word. "This condition. It is not uncommon in the tribes. There's one person here who I think is better suited to be your teacher."

"Who?" Freya waited eagerly. "Wait, in the tribes?"

"I'm intrigued too. Perhaps it is the same reason why you are not affected by our company."

Freya paused as she considered it. Perhaps she had more in common with these people than she had first thought.

"Who can teach me to control my shadow?" she whispered, desperation replacing the puzzlement.

"The head of the guard," Enna explained. "Elamra, I believe they call him."

"No," Freya said. She couldn't bear the thought of that impossible man teaching her. "No, there must be someone else."

"You've already taken a dislike to him?" Enna laughed. "From what I heard, he also saved your life. Elamra is darker than you know. He has a very dark side to him, which is only emphasised by his past. He has learned to control his shadow, and he will be able to show you how."

Freya sat back down beside the eagle. She had no choice: either she could swallow her pride and ask the irritating man to teach her, or she could put her friends in danger.

"Any tips?" she laughed and, without realising what she was doing, rested her head on Enna's shoulder. The eagle seemed happy about the strange act of affection.

"What I have found useful, though not always possible, is to put energy into some other activity. It tires you, and you lack the energy to use your shadow to its full effect."

Their conversation was cut short by an angry voice behind them.

"I've been looking for you," the snappy voice shouted. Freya turned around to see one of the nurses from the hospital. Her face was red, but Freya wasn't sure if it was because of anger or the gusts of wind.

"I'm sorry." Enna sounded resigned to the fact he was being told off. "I needed some fresh air."

"You need rest." The nurse reached them and looked surprisingly intimidating standing over them.

"It was my fault. I'm sorry." Freya felt she needed to stand up for the eagle who had just helped her once again.

"I should think so," the nurse snapped, turning on her. "The king may give you certain privileges, but they stop when you reach the doors of my hospital. Understood?"

There was no arguing with the snappishness, so Enna stood up and was pulled away by the angry woman. He looked around at Freya, giving her a look of resigned annoyance at being dragged inside.

She watched them go, feeling more and more lonely the further they went, until they disappeared completely through the garden entrance. She felt the eagle understood the fear she felt, far more than her friends did.

She didn't know how long she had been there, gradually getting colder and colder until she felt a warm hand on her shoulder. She turned around to see Winnie. Without a word, Freya moved along the bench so Winnie could sit down.

"You're getting cold," Winnie sighed. "It's not as warm as it has been."

Freya nodded.

"I'm sorry," her friend whispered. "We should have told you, but we would never have let you come to any harm."

"How did you know I wouldn't be affected?"

"We didn't," Winnie sighed. "But you would have gone home if there was a slightest sign of anything wrong." Freya thought back to the times when the prince had showed concern if she had looked tired or out of breath.

"I want to go home now," Freya sniffed. Her friend said nothing for a while but took her hand and held it tightly.

"We are going to put a stop to this war," she said eventually. "We leave today, and we would like you to come with us."

"We?"

"Me, Elialdor, and Elamra."

Freya paused. The last couple of weeks had seen her develop into someone that her parents may not even recognise.

"On one condition," she said. "Elamra teaches me how to control myself."

"What do you mean?" Winnie whispered.

"I know what I did." Freya looked at her friend. "Don't pretend. I'm dangerous. I need to be able to control myself. Enna told me that Elamra was the best one for it."

"He's right." Winnie nodded, but she didn't look happy. "Elamra will help you. But, Freya," she paused. "Don't ever think that you have changed. You have prospered, that's all. You're a good person - better than the rest of us. You're compassionate and kind."

Freya said nothing. However much anger she felt towards her, her friend's presence was comforting. She believed they would not have let any harm come to her. Even more importantly, she would be taught to control herself and would no longer be a danger to the people around her.

CHAPTER SIXTEEN
Rald's Punishment

Freya realised, as she soared away from the castle's safety, that she was becoming addicted to flying. The rush of the wind past her face, the strange view of the trees and buildings on the ground, and the possible dangers flowed through her and urged her on. She felt like she could shout out to her companions in sheer joy. Her worries and hurts had been left behind at the castle and it felt so good to be flying again.

They must have flown several miles before they touched the mossy ground for a rest. Freya had no idea where they were headed. How could you catch a murderer from hundreds of years ago? Where could you start? She had remained quiet, embarrassed about her outburst earlier, and still upset that the people she had thought were her friends had knowingly put her in harm's way. This was nothing, however, compared to the fear that she would lose control and hurt those around her. However angry she was, she could not stop caring about them. Especially Winnie. She had kept close to Freya, keeping an eye on her, and was always there whenever she needed someone, even when her own feelings must have been tearing her apart.

When Winnie had finished warming what she had prepared for their meal, she handed Freya a plate and came to sit next to her. Elamra and Elialdor sat opposite, staring into the dying flames.

Freya looked down at the plate and smiled as she realised it was rabbit stew.

"I thought you should know what proper rabbit stew tastes like," she grinned. Freya could not help a slight smile and she bowed her head, unwilling to let her friend see. It clearly hadn't worked as Winnie's own smile deepened.

"Have you asked Elamra yet?" Freya whispered. Winnie looked across at the broad man.

"She told me," Elamra said. "I appreciate that you want to control it. It's not easy."

"Which is why I need someone who has succeeded," Freya persisted.

"Yes," he nodded slowly, "I accept. We will start soon, but first we have this task. That must be my priority."

"No." Freya was almost desperate. "I need to start as soon as possible. What if I hurt one of you? I'm not going to take that risk."

"We're willing to take it," Elialdor said, with his head bowed so he could not make eye contact. "My father told me that we need to help you, but only after Edweth's killer is found."

"Why?" Freya felt her cheeks start burning and her heart race faster. "I'm going to put you in danger."

"Does it not occur to you that it's worth taking that risk?" Elamra demanded. His voice was restless, but his face kept inexplicably calm.

"I've never seen anyone with more power inside them," the prince whispered, raising his head, meaning Freya could now see his face. While hers was red with anger, Elialdor's was white. He looked frightened. "We need you to harness that power. You think you cannot defeat a great warrior like Edweth's murderer, but you're wrong. You're the only one who can."

"No. I'm not using it," Freya snapped. "It's not how I want to be."

Was this why they were delaying helping her? They were willing to put themselves in danger so they could use her unpredictable, dangerous power? This was insane!

"Don't think of it as a burden, Freya," Winnie said. Freya was unsure whether she didn't want the others to hear, or if her throat could not bring itself to speak the words, but her voice was not much more than a whisper. "No human has ever been able to access the power within them. You can. This is a gift."

"You don't really believe that, do you?" Freya knew her friend well enough to know she was only saying it to make her feel better.

"From the moment you came into our company, I knew there was something special in you," Winnie smiled. "You have the strength to control it, you just need the self-belief. But, please, we need your help."

Freya didn't know if it was her pleading tone of voice, or the desperate words, but she felt a sudden pang of guilt about how she was treating her friend. She had endured these problems for a matter of days. Her friends had endured them for years. Centuries.

"I want to help you," she said finally, taking a mouthful of the rabbit stew, feeling like she needed the strength. "I'm just worried about what I might do in the meantime. I had no control over myself last night. I killed that man."

"It was the only man you've ever killed," Elamra nodded. "I'd be worried if you didn't feel like you do. Understand this, though. Raedwald will know you killed his soldier. He will be after you now. Before, he was just curious. Now, you are an enemy."

"Help me." Freya felt as though she had just

drunk icy water.

"We will." It was the prince and Winnie who spoke together. Elamra just smiled and nodded.

"And, until I can control it," Freya said with determination, "I will not risk using my shadow."

Somehow, she felt that, with her friends' support, she could achieve anything. They sat around the circle without saying anything, each having their own opinion on whether Freya should use her dangerous power.

"How are we going to find this murderer?" Freya asked, eager to change the subject in case her feelings about it changed.

"Simple," the prince smiled, clearly relieved of this change of topic. "We ask the victim."

"That is no simple matter." Winnie's grave look did not comfort Freya.

"But she's dead." Freya looked from one to the other, completely confused.

"Raedwald was stupid enough to make a vow at her grave," the prince smiled. "She won't rest until that vow is fulfilled."

"So, she's...what...a ghost?"

"That's precisely what she is," Elialdor nodded. "We just have to get her to tell us who killed her."

"She's not going to speak to us," Winnie sighed. "She was your grandfather's enemy, Elialdor, whatever their past may have been. She hates you. She hates us."

"My father told me of a way to ensure her cooperation." There was a mischievous, almost childish, look on the prince's face. The others waited expectantly for him to detail his plan. "She will speak to her son."

"So, what?" Winnie laughed. "You're going to kidnap Ranald? We'd never succeed."

"No, Winifred," Elamra agreed. "We take Rald."

"You're in on this?" Winnie laughed. Freya could not help but agree with her. The plan sounded absurd, and a lot more terrifying than she had expected.

"We don't even know if he's alive." She bowed her head. "His father could have killed him for helping us."

"Raedwald is a monster," the prince nodded his head, "but not that much. He would not murder his own son. He'll have thought of some other punishment for him."

"How will we know where to find him?" Winnie still sounded doubtful.

"He goes riding every day," the prince said it as though it was the most obvious thing in the world, before he laughed. "It seems he's not as good at flying as the rest of his family. He'll be a sitting duck."

"So, when are we going to do this?" Winnie shook her head.

"Erm…in about seven minutes." The prince looked entirely relaxed as he leaned back and laid down on the grass.

Winnie stood up quickly and looked down at Elialdor with worry and disgust. Still looking as though she might throw soil at him, she hurriedly tidied away their belongings, but could not extinguish the dying fire.

"Don't worry about it," the prince laughed. "It's really quite simple. Every day, Rald leaves Listgard with another one of that foul clan. The only real threat is the other Owl. Rald is a weak, pathetic thing - he poses no threat."

"He saved my life," Freya corrected him, and the prince sat up and looked at her.

"That was, I admit, noble. But, make no mistake, he is a weak-willed coward."

"I won't believe you."

The prince sighed and laid back down. Winnie gave Freya a look of sympathy and was about to speak but stopped suddenly. Whatever she had heard, Elamra must have heard too as he looked even more alert than usual.

Gradually, Freya heard talking coming closer. They seemed to be coming towards them and, when she looked, Elialdor had a look of triumph plastered on his face. She would not, she told herself, allow any harm to come to the man who saved her life. She would not forget his actions, even if her friends did.

When the voices grew louder and louder, Elialdor and Elamra leapt to their feet and backed away into the trees, hiding themselves. Freya was not sure whether they had transformed into birds, but there was no sign of them. Winnie pulled Freya in the opposite direction and they hid together behind a hedge, full of thorns and insects.

They were hidden just in time and, as the prince had predicted, Rald came into the clearing with a woman. The stranger had long brown hair which seemed to shine in the light, as though she was wearing a thousand diamonds in it. They weren't riding, but walking. The woman's chin was held high with haughty dignity, while Rald hung his head.

The woman stopped suddenly and raised her hand to stop the young man. He obeyed and looked up in surprise. Her proud gaze scanned the clearing and Freya was sure she looked straight at her. Perhaps she did, as she drew a long, thin sword and pushed Rald backwards.

"So, you reached out to your friends, did you, you foul traitor?" she scorned. Rald shook his head, stunned at the action, but the woman pointed her sword towards him.

"You're insane," he laughed, when he had gathered enough composure to challenge her.

"You're pathetic," she sneered. "A burden on your father."

Her attention was directed away from the young prince by the sound of snapping twigs, and Elialdor, clearly realising that he had been found out, rushed out from the trees. The lady was too quick for him, though, and raised her sword to parry with astonishing agility. She looked almost frightened when she realised who it was, until the fear was replaced with a look of utter triumph.

"What will your father say, princeling?" she laughed. "When I send word to him that his son has fallen?"

Her haughty merriment was cut short when Elamra stepped out of the trees. He had no weapon but simply stared at the woman. This strange action seemed to unnerve the Owl more than the sword in the prince's hand.

On seeing the second man, Rald began to back away in the direction of Listgard.

"Stay there." Elamra commanded and, without knowing why, Rald obeyed. The fear on the woman's face was now more evident. She had expected the Owl prince to run away and was certain now that something was stopping his feet from moving. She looked fearfully at Elamra, her face growing whiter and the lights in her hair dulled to a dark grey.

"Bijojo," she gasped, and started to back away from him. Rald looked up and the same fear was clear on his features, but he could not move.

"No," Winnie whispered. Freya looked at her in confusion, but she was staring intently at the scene through the thick bush. The Owl woman had clearly heard, as she glanced behind her to where they were hiding, but quickly looked back at Elamra. The prince took a step back, which only frightened her more.

In utter confusion, Freya stood up and moved from behind the bush, Winnie following her. Now she could see clearly, she realised that Elamra no longer looked like himself. There was a blue light shining in his eyes, which seemed to radiate from the rest of his face. He raised his hand and, without warning, the woman flew backwards onto the bush with a piercing scream. Elamra walked towards where she had fallen, and the woman tried to hide herself in the thick gorse bush. Freya looked on in dismay as the deep scratches from the thorns did not seem to bother her as much as the man that was advancing closer.

"Ne! Ne! Prašau!" she screamed. Her haughtiness had vanished completely and was replaced with a sort of madness stemming from her terror.

Freya felt slightly afraid when she looked at Elamra to see that there was no sympathy on his face at all. The only emotion was a minor annoyance from the woman's terrible screams. Almost as a reaction to this, he raised both his hands and seemed to be holding the strange blue light. The screams stopped immediately, and Freya realised the woman could barely breathe.

"Stop it," Freya snapped, but the man paid her no attention. Meanwhile, the woman lay silent on the ground, bringing desperate tears to Freya's eyes. She rushed forwards to stop Elamra, but the prince stopped her, holding her back.

Winnie rushed forwards and the prince let her go to Elamra. She whispered his name again and again until a flicker of Elamra returned to his face. She persevered, turning the man's face round to look into his eyes. Freya thought that Winnie might have succeeded but, without warning, Elamra let out a terrible sound, more like a roar than a human noise, and threw Winnie backwards towards the trees, her long black hair flying everywhere.

Her hair seemed to cover her entire body and Freya realised that in that split second while she was in the air, she had transformed into the black body of a jackdaw. Flapping her wings madly, Winnie fell to the ground.

Freya rushed over to her and let out a sigh of relief as she helped her sit up. Her remarkable quick thinking and skill had meant she had missed the tree by a fraction. Looking up with a sudden anger at Elamra, she was about to let her shadow deal with him but stopped and remembered her vow not to use the terrifying power.

Winnie's actions seemed to have worked. Elamra was standing shaking on his feet until he finally stumbled backwards and sat on the grass. From behind, Freya could not make out his features, but he lifted his hands towards his forehead, and ran one hand through his hair.

The woman, meanwhile, was lying on the ground, gasping for breath. Whatever Elamra had done, he had stopped, but she would not raise a hand against him now for fear he might try again to kill her and, this time, complete the job.

The prince looked with sympathy at Elamra as he sat on the ground, before he walked purposefully towards Rald. Whether it was fear or shock at Elamra, or a mere desire not to return to Listgard, the young Owl remained silent as the prince tied his wrists together and pulled him over to Winnie.

"Are you alright?" Elialdor asked her. "That was a very noble thing you did."

"If you'd have let me stop Elamra, Winnie wouldn't have been hurt," Freya snapped, astounded at the prince's hypocrisy.

"If you had tried, you would have been killed." Elialdor looked annoyed at the accusation. "Winnie can handle herself."

Freya didn't really know what to say against this unfair statement. Winnie was out-of-breath from her ordeal, but she wandered over to Elamra and whispered something to him. The man was still visibly shaking.

"That is what I'm like, isn't it?" Freya whispered, as she considered Elamra's uncontrolled anger. "What was it that woman called him?"

"Bijojo," Rald whispered. His voice was shaking as much as Elamra's whole body. "In her language, it means 'the feared', or 'the dreaded'."

"Why?" Freya realised the question was a bit pointless after what she had just witnessed but she was surprised there was a name for it. Rald would not answer but looked at the ground.

"Sit," the prince snapped at the Owl, and Rald willingly sat opposite Freya. Elialdor glanced across at the other two, and the woman who was now unconscious on the ground and sat down next to him.

"My father has grown tired of your grudges," Elialdor said.

"Grudge?" Rald scoffed, with surprising confidence. "You killed my mother."

"No, you foolish boy," the prince addressed him as though he was much younger, even though they were a similar age. He seemed to be growing more impatient. "We did not."

Rald said nothing but looked scornfully at the Crow. Freya did not know what to do, trapped between a centuries-old dispute, and not feeling qualified to intervene.

"If you do not believe me, we can prove it to you. You're going to help us."

"My father would kill me if I helped you," Rald snapped.

"You helped me," Freya smiled. "You saved my life."

"And I've paid a price for it," the Owl replied and smiled at her. "But I would do it again if it meant you could live."

"Enough," Elialdor snapped, but Freya leaned forward and laid her hand on Rald's arm. He relaxed at the touch, but the prince looked on in distaste.

"What was the price?" Freya whispered. "You look tired."

"I'm leaving." Rald gestured towards the unconscious woman. "When my father realised I had helped you, and even called off the Owl's pursuit, he sent word to Europe. To her tribe."

"You called off the Owls? When we left Listgard?" Freya asked, open-mouthed.

"Yes, I knew they would catch you, and kill you. And being an Owl prince does have its advantages, but my father was so angry when he found out. Tomorrow I leave for her realm in Europe."

"Tomorrow, you will be in front of my father." The prince looked triumphant at what Rald had said. "Thank goodness he is not so harsh in justice."

Freya could not understand the two princes. They were, she thought, more alike than either one would have admitted. Elialdor seemed to be unable to stand their company and, getting to his feet, walked towards Winnie and Elamra. Freya looked at Rald, who seemed thinner and paler, even though it had only been a day since she had last seen him.

"A new place can't be so bad," Freya smiled, trying to comfort the frightened boy.

"When her family finds out that I helped the Crows," Rald looked straight into Freya's eyes, "they will kill me. My father has sentenced me to death. He just couldn't do it himself."

"This world I stumbled on..." Freya shook her head as tears welled in her eyes.

"You didn't stumble across it." Rald gave a slight laugh.

"Then why am I here?" Freya surprised herself at the bluntness of the question, but the Owl did not seem concerned.

"They did not tell you?" he laughed again. "Well, legend has it that a human who can withstand our society will bring about great change and prosperity."

This time, Freya laughed. Change and prosperity?

"They must have got the wrong person," she smiled but Rald was serious.

"You are not affected by our company, are you?" He smiled as Freya stared.

"How did they know I wouldn't be?"

"That, I don't know. I'm sorry." Freya wasn't expecting an answer to her question but she still felt disappointed by the lack of information. It made no sense to her why she, of all people, would be the one unaffected in this strange world.

Glancing across at Elialdor in search of an answer, she realised that he was looking straight at her, his dark eyes staring unblinkingly into her own. After a moment, he got to his feet, walked over to them, and pulled the Owl prince up so he was standing. They were the same height but Elialdor seemed to tower over him.

"We should leave now for your mother's grave." He talked with distaste. "It isn't far from here, and when your friend finally comes to her senses, she will alert Raedwald."

Rald did not argue as they transformed into their bird forms. Elamra, certainly the largest and strongest of the four, took Rald to make sure he didn't try to escape. Without asking permission, Elialdor had used his blue light to make the barn owl as small as a wren. Although Freya was almost certain that he wouldn't run away, the others refused to believe her.

Together, they began the silent journey to Edweth's grave.

CHAPTER SEVENTEEN
The Restless Dead

The promise that the grave was not far away kept Freya going as they flew over the trees, her wings aching with the amount of flying they had done today. Only once did they see people below, who stared at them, astounded perhaps at the sight of two ravens with a rook and a jackdaw.

It wasn't long before they touched the ground again, but it was getting dark and there was a strange blueish light in the sky, showing the quick coming of night. Transforming into her human self again, Freya rubbed her painful arms and looked around her.

She stopped. In front of her was an immense building, towering into the sky. In the twilight, it looked foreboding, although Winnie assured her that this was a holy place. As they walked through the archway in a courtyard, Freya looked up to see the shadowy statues staring down at her, and felt her stomach churn, their stone unseeing gaze meeting hers.

"My father built this in memory of my mother," Rald whispered. "I've never been here."

"You've never visited your mother's grave?" Winnie sounded surprised, but Elialdor scoffed.

"Not since she was moved," Rald sighed. "My father moved her from her original grave as it was thought too pagan."

"Pagan?" Freya felt her stomach churn again, as though it was turning inside out.

"A boat burial, as was the custom when she died."

Freya remained silent. She had read about these things, and had studied them at school, but now she knew someone who had witnessed one, it all seemed scarily close. As they walked into the grassy courtyard, she looked around for a grave or a tomb but could not see one. With a feeling of dread, she saw her friends move towards the small door at the bottom of one of the towers, but her mind was distracted as the prince spoke.

"When your father murdered my grandfather," he began, "we buried him in the same way. Raedwald never forgave the Crows for burying him like that. He exhumed Edweth's body and buried her in a hidden chamber. In here." Elialdor whispered something and the door swung open.

The tower was dark, so the only light was the blue ethereal beam coming from the prince's hand. Inside the tower were steep stone steps going around in a tight spiral. Struggling in the dark, Freya took hold of Rald's shoulder. He seemed remarkably confident on his feet, even though his hands were tied. Behind Freya, Winnie kept a watchful eye in case anyone was following them. The thought that someone *might* be following them into this claustrophobic staircase frightened Freya more than she wanted to admit.

They stopped suddenly and Freya peered up to see why. The prince ushered all of them onto a thin hallway. They only just managed to fit on altogether and, when their shuffling had died down and everything was silent, Elialdor held up his hand.

Freya strained her ears and realised why they had to be silent. So quietly it could have easily been her imagination, she heard low singing. It wasn't like anything she had heard before. It was sorrowful as it drifted up the stairs, somehow creating a warm and chilling feeling at the same time. Freya could have listened to it for longer, but the hairs on the back of her neck started standing up as she realised the singing was coming gradually closer.

As it came closer, it grew louder, and she realised that she had heard it before. It was a sound she associated with Christmas, although this was monotonous and sad.

As it drew ever closer, and grew even louder, she realised that it wasn't as relaxing as she had first thought. The deep notes, and the complete lack of emotion in the singing, was now threatening. She glanced across at Winnie and her fear grew stronger as she realised that she, too, was scared.

"Who are they?" she whispered, her head spinning.

"Men charged to guard Edweth's tomb," Elialdor explained, his voice shaking. "When they were alive, they were the monks in this abbey - also tribesmen. They were paid handsomely by Raedwald many years ago to keep his wife safe."

"And they will honour that pledge," Rald stated.

"They are dead, I guess?" Freya's heart was beating fast.

"Yes," the prince nodded. He, too, looked concerned. "They died of a mysterious disease shortly after their bargain. On the exact same day."

"Mysterious?" Winnie gave a whispered laugh. "Raedwald killed them to ensure they would guard her until Judgement Day. They must know we are here to find her."

"I hadn't thought of this." Elialdor ran his hand

through his black hair, before he hurried over to the door on one end of the small landing and whispered the same words as he had done outside. The door creaked open to allow the five of them into a spacious room.

As they entered, something dived at Freya's head and she gave a short shriek. Elamra glared at her in the darkness and Freya felt incredibly foolish as she realised it was only a bat that had been resting on the rafters. It must have been curious enough to investigate the newcomers.

Elialdor closed the door quickly and re-locked it with the same blue light. Turning back to his companions, his face was as grey as the stone walls.

"That won't stop them," Elamra stated with surprising calmness.

"I know," Elialdor hissed. "Hide."

At this, Winnie pulled Freya into an alcove in the stone wall. Rald followed quickly.

The alcove was not much of a hiding place, but it offered some protection on three sides. Pushing Freya to the back, and then Rald, Winnie stood in front so she would be the first thing anyone would see as they entered the room. Elamra and Elialdor had gone to the side of the room where there was the most shadow, their swords drawn.

What use would swords be, Freya wondered, *against people who are already dead?*

The singing continued and they could now

hear heavy footsteps ascending the stairs. Slow. Purposeful.

Then, just as Freya thought they must have reached the door and were about to burst into the room, the singing stopped. She realised then that the silence was far worse than the ancient ghostly singing. They seemed to be waiting there for hours, and Freya was beginning to think that they had left, perhaps content that they would never find Edweth's grave to disturb her.

"What's happening?" she whispered into Rald's ear. The Owl simply shook his head.

After what seemed like a lifetime, there came three more terrifying sounds.

Knock. Knock. Knock.

Freya could feel Rald's back straighten with fear.

Nothing happened and nobody moved from their pathetic hiding places.

Knock. Knock. Knock.

Perhaps they will go if we don't make a sound, Freya thought to herself. *Maybe they'll realise we're only here to do good.*

Knock. Knock. Knock.

At the final knock, the door creaked open as though it had been left ajar.

The darkness in the hall meant that Freya, or even Winnie at the front of the column, could not make out anything other than several shapes. The singing began again, louder as it came into the room.

Eight figures entered and the darkness seemed to gather around them so their features could not be distinguished. They seemed to be robed and, as they drew nearer, a sickening smell of rotten meat filled the close air, making Freya cover her nose and mouth with her cupped hand.

For a moment they did not move but stood there, singing their menacing chant. Rald's breathing became more ragged and Freya's heart was beating so fast, she thought it was pounding in her throat.

The darkness seemed to disperse, and a strange moonlight filled the room. Unable to help herself, Freya looked over Rald's and Winnie's shoulders and saw that there were 8 monks, dressed in black robes, holding their hands together as though their robes were muffs.

As the one at the centre raised his head to look straight at Winnie, Freya was almost sick. This was where the smell was coming from. The monk's eyes were sunken into his head, the skin around them tightened back to make the eyes look larger and more inhuman. Once, there must have been a nose, but not anymore, and its face was so gaunt as to be almost skull shaped. The most frightening part, however, was the way in which its mouth had shrivelled away, revealing a set of crooked teeth beneath its non-existent lips. The whole face was covered in red blotches that looked painful, but the thing before them did not seem to feel it.

The monk did not speak but moved one hand out of his robe - a smooth but red hand - and pointed a long finger towards Winnie. Instantly, she bent over as though she was in terrible pain. Freya pushed past Rald and knelt in front of Winnie, who hardly seemed to notice her.

A cry from the side of the room made Freya jump and the monks all turned their faces towards it. Elamra and Elialdor rushed forwards, swords drawn, but with one sweeping movement of his arm, the monk sent them flying towards the stone wall.

Freya stared at them and the ghostly monk slowly turned his face towards her.

She thought she had been frightened before, but it was nothing compared to the utter dread that gripped her entire body. She could not take her eyes off the face, and she felt her legs and arms stiffen so she stumbled over onto the cold floor.

From where she lay, she could still see the monk, and it stared at her until finally it decided to move towards her. Slowly, it held out a pointed finger and Freya could do nothing but wait for the terrible pain to follow.

There were several minutes, it seemed, until Freya felt herself being kicked from behind as someone fell over her.

This painful shock brought her to her senses, and she sat up to find that Rald had stumbled over her and now knelt in front of her, putting his arms out to shield her as much as he could. From the side of the room, something stirred, and Freya realised that Elamra and the prince were stumbling to their feet, but it was Rald who, once again, had saved her.

The monk paused as he watched this display of strange loyalty but, after a moment's thought, seemed content to take his wrath out on the Owl prince. The hand pointed towards him and, in an instant, Rald gasped as though he had just been stabbed. After a few moments, he let out an ear-shattering scream, which resonated from the cold walls, and seemed to last forever. Freya pulled at him to move him out of the way of the monk, but he pushed her back, still shielding her from the spectre.

Gasping, Rald opened his mouth to issue another terrible sound, but collapsed on the floor, his eyes staring upwards to the ceiling. Freya thought the monk smiled but it was so difficult to see on such a distorted face. Slowly and purposefully, it turned its face towards her.

CHAPTER EIGHTEEN
Neither Enemy nor Friend

"Enough!"

Freya waited for the pain to start but it never came.

"That's enough!" It was a woman's commanding voice, but it was not one Freya recognised. It did not even sound remotely familiar. Hardly daring, she raised her head to see. Behind the monks that now turned to face the newcomer, was a tall woman, dressed in a flowing robe. There was something strange about her. Her robe stirred around her as though there was a breeze but the air in the room was still and close.

The monks no longer seemed to notice Freya or her companions and were fixed on the tall lady. She moved forwards and they parted before her, turning around so they were still staring. She was only the same height as the monks, but her presence made it so she towered above them. She walked forwards, her cold stare transfixed on Rald, until she raised her head and looked straight at Freya. Her face was unnaturally white, as was the hair that rippled down her back. Freya could not help a cold, numb feeling grip her stomach as she met her gaze.

"You are neither my kind, nor my enemy." Her cold voice gripped Freya. "Yet you brought my son here, to this place of danger. You foolish, silly girl."

Freya thought the accusation was a little unfair, especially as she had been the only one to speak up for Rald, but the realisation that this was Rald's mother gripped her throat and she was unable to speak. Now she knew she was seeing a dead person, she realised that across the woman's neck was a deep cut which no longer bled.

Freya breathed a sigh of relief as Edweth released her from her cold stare and looked down at Rald. There was a flicker of something different on her face, something that may once have been love but the coldness had frozen it out of her. There was shuffling at the side of the room and Elamra and Elialdor emerged from the shadows. The prince clutched his side and his face held a look of annoyance and pain. Edweth turned to them and scowled.

"You, on the other hand," she began, "are my

enemies. What do you mean by bringing my son into danger?"

Winnie murmured slightly, which brought Edweth's attention back to Freya.

"Perhaps I was mistaken," she spat. "Perhaps you are my enemy after all."

"I hope I'm no-one's enemy." Freya was surprised that she could now speak. "I don't mean anyone any harm. I only want peace for my friends."

"And to gain it you would put my youngest in peril?"

"Your husband did that," Freya argued, standing up but still feeling unsurprisingly shaky.

"Raedwald?" Edweth's stern look faltered and she opened her mouth a little. Freya felt sure that this was the closest to surprise and shock that Edweth was capable of.

"Rald saved me." Freya pushed forwards. "And for that, his father was going to kill him."

"You are lying. My husband would never harm anything of mine."

"Perhaps he has lost sight of a lot of things since you've been dead." Freya did not care that what she said sounded cruel and harsh. The monks advanced slowly but, turning to them, Edweth pointed to the door.

"Away," she snarled. "You think I cannot handle this group of children myself? I have no need of you here."

One by one, the silent monks walked towards the door but, before walking through it, they simply melted away. Freya was sure that they were still in the room, hiding, and waiting until their mistress needed them. Elialdor rushed forwards, but one look from Edweth sent him stumbling backward.

"We need you to tell us who killed you!" Freya snapped as Edweth towered over the prince. She turned back to Freya as she spoke.

It was not Freya's words that softened her gaze, however, but Rald began to murmur and blinked his eyes open. Edweth advanced towards him, a slight look of fear on her face, as though her presence would somehow damage her son further.

Rald first saw Freya, who glanced at the young Owl. Seeing the look of concern on her face, and puzzled as to why he was lying on the floor, he sat up. Any previous knowledge of the night's actions seemed to have been erased from his memory and he looked around the room as though he had no idea where they were.

When his eyes rested on Edweth, however, he stared, his mouth dropping open involuntarily. Freya was astonished to see that the harsh look from the Owl queen was replaced by something that might have been a smile. Edweth's eyes glowed with something like happiness, but her mouth remained perfectly straight. Rald stared at her, as though she would disappear if he took his eyes away.

"What have they done to you?" Edweth spoke, this time with a tenderness that seemed odd coming from such a cold woman. "You look worn out and thin."

"Over a thousand years since I last saw you," Rald struggled to keep his voice steady, "and you say I look thin?"

He stood up shakily, but all the colour had drained from his face and he looked like he was about to fall over again. Freya supported him but Edweth wafted her away and gripped her son's arms. Rald shivered.

"You left me," he whispered.

"I had no choice, my son." Edweth now sounded like she was pleading. "I did not want to leave you."

"You were always so strong," Rald gulped back his tears. "You could not have been killed."

"I underestimated him." The pleading in Edweth's voice grew as Rald moved his eyes away. She seemed to think it was because of her son's anger but Freya was certain it was because he didn't want her to see him cry, as the tears ran down his cheeks faster than Freya had thought possible.

She could almost see Elamra and Elialdor prick up their ears as she sensed they may be getting close to an answer.

"Father thinks that the Crows killed you." Rald looked at the stone floor.

"I wish they had!" Edweth laughed, sounding desperate for Rald's attention.

"They didn't?" Rald looked up again into his mother's eyes. Edweth sighed as though a great pain had just stopped.

"No." The queen looked ashamed. "That would have been a noble ending, fighting my enemy. No."

"Then who did?" Rald gripped his mother's icy hand but now did not notice the cold. "Father has been at war with the Crows for centuries because of this terrible misunderstanding."

"You should not have come here." She seemed to become distracted and tried to pull away from her son's grip, but he was stronger than she had thought. "I don't know what your father would do if he knew you were with these idiots."

"He would kill me," Rald declared, braver than he had thought possible. "He was going to. Just...through someone else."

"Leave," she gasped suddenly. "I will deal with these fools. If they come into my resting place, they should have realised the consequences."

"No," Rald snapped. "I won't let you harm them. They are not my friends - but they are not my enemies either. Tell us, please. Tell us who killed you."

"It is so long ago now," Edweth murmured, "I forget the name. Terrible though it is that I should forget his name, it was my son."

There was silence. Freya looked from Edweth and Rald, to her friends. It could not be Rald who killed her as she seemed so joyful to see him, besides he was only a child at the time. It could only, therefore, be Ranald - Rald's angry, vengeful older brother.

Trying to focus her mind, Freya checked that Winnie was fine. She was breathing heavily as though in a deep sleep. Looking up, she noticed that the scene had not changed: Rald still clutched his mother's hands, looking at her with utter confusion and trying to decide whether to believe her. The two Crows looked at each other and back at the tall woman. Elialdor looked as stunned as Rald, but Elamra looked angrier. His brow had creased, and his eyes flashed in the half-light, creating a formidable sight. Freya was unsure whether this was because of the truth about Edweth's murder, or that he had just seen Winnie unconscious.

"We must go," Elialdor demanded. Elamra nodded, his face growing gradually paler, concerning Freya.

"You go," Rald answered. "I will stay here."

"You think we'd let you?" Elamra growled. "You're coming with us so you can tell everyone what we've heard."

"You think they'll believe us?" The prince agreed. Edweth spun around, her angry face glaring at the two Crows.

"They better," she snarled. "My son is staying here with me."

"Rald," Freya begged, placing a warm hand on his arm. Rald jumped and shivered at the change in temperature. "Your father will know you have come here. He will come for you."

"My mother will protect me." Rald turned to Edweth, who looked back at him, her gaze turning from anger to sadness.

"Those monks will obey Raedwald more than me," she gasped as the realization dawned on her. "The girl is right."

"No." Rald said firmly. "I'm staying here. Over a thousand years has passed since I lost you. I am not losing you again."

"You won't," her voice almost sounded gentle. "You know where to find me."

Freya took a step back as the woman turned towards her, but she realised she could no longer move beneath the icy glare.

"You will protect him." There was no space for a question in Edweth's tone. "You are not a Crow. At least," she paused, "not entirely. You will look after him."

"Once the king realises that he helped us, he won't be in any danger from the Crows." Freya did not want to commit to anything with Edweth.

"You will look after him," she demanded and Freya, unwilling to say anything out loud in case she was forced to break her promise, bowed her head. Fortunately, the Owl queen seemed to take this as an acceptance of the task.

"Rald," Freya urged, "come with us."

"Go, my son." Edweth leaned forward and kissed Rald on his forehead. He closed his eyes, trying to save the moment. "Go with them."

Rald still seemed reluctant to leave his mother but Freya tugged him away towards the door. He refused to take his eyes off her, and she seemed to share his feelings.

"Winnie," Freya mumbled, as she knew she could not carry her friend's body all the way back to the castle. There was no need however, as Elamra, still struggling to contain his anger, walked over to her and picked her up easily. Glancing across at him, Freya hoped that he would not let his anger get out of control again. The prince seemed to share her concerns and pulled him out of the chapel door. He pushed Freya out of the door next and she tried hard to direct Rald's attention away from his mother. It was only when they turned the corner and he could no longer see her that he turned around to look where he was going.

They made no noise as they descended the tricky stairs, and there was no sound anywhere in the abbey. Freya felt certain that Edweth's guardians, and perhaps the queen herself, were watching them, but there was no sign of them.

After the closeness of the abbey, Freya raised her head and relished the feeling of the breeze on her face. She breathed in gulps of air, trying to dispel the foul smell of decay from her senses.

As she stepped forward, Freya gasped as she bumped into Elamra, and she looked up to see why he had stopped so suddenly. She let out a sigh of frustration as she realised there were about thirty people watching them, all congregated in the courtyard before them. *It's one dangerous situation after another*, Freya thought with annoyance.

She felt a tingle of fear when she realised that it was Raedwald who stood in the centre of the gathering. At his side was his eldest son, Ranald, who looked as nasty as ever, and yet surprisingly calm given that he must know they now knew Edweth's murderer.

On seeing his father, or perhaps his brother, Rald froze and his face become the same colour as his mother's.

"I thought you might have made it here," Raedwald smiled. "My son sent for you, did he?"

"No. To think that we would be beckoned by an Owl!" Elamra sniggered and Freya was sure she saw something blue light up in his eyes. "Your son is our prisoner."

"I feel certain you would not have come out of there alive if that were the case. I was rather hoping you would not." Raedwald took a step towards them and, looking up at the dark windows on the abbey, smiled slightly.

"We met your wife." Freya let go of Rald and stepped in front of Elamra, hoping he would calm down. "She told us who murdered her."

"I know who murdered her," Raedwald spat, taking another step towards her.

"Do you?" Freya tried to keep her voice steady but found it irritatingly difficult. "I believe you are wrong."

Raedwald did not just take a step towards her this time but strode up quickly so he was towering over her.

"I may not know who struck the blow, but I know who gave the orders. His grandfather." Raedwald nodded to Elialdor, who moved forward so he was standing next to Freya.

"So, you had him killed? Because of your misunderstanding?" Rald stated.

"No, idiot boy," Raedwald smiled, "I did not have him killed. I killed him myself. I stabbed him as he tried to convince me that he was innocent."

"You were mistaken." Elialdor's voice was now shaking but Freya was sure that this was anger, not fear.

"Then who was it?" Raedwald smiled, seeing

the effect of his confession.

"Your son," Freya snapped, trying to lure the attention back to her to save Elialdor the embarrassment. "Ranald killed her. Edweth told us."

Raedwald looked for a moment back to his eldest son, who was about to speak, his face glowing white with anger. He made a move towards them, but the king raised his hand and he came to a halt. Turning his attention back to Freya, he swung the back of his raised hand towards her head so quickly, she had no choice but to take the blow. Stumbling backwards, she felt Raedwald's grip pulling her to her feet.

"The insolence," he spat, "to dare accuse my own son of murdering his mother."

As Freya struggled to prise his hand away from her neck, Raedwald drew a dagger in his other hand and Freya was sure he was about to take some dreadful revenge.

Elialdor dived at the Owl king with as much strength as he could muster, wrestling him to the ground. Freya stood, blurry-eyed and coughing, but stumbled over to them and pulled the prince away, seeing the knife that Raedwald still held in his hand.

Elialdor glanced towards her and his gaze softened. Raedwald stumbled to his feet and seemed unwilling to approach them further.

"I thank you, little prince," he laughed, "for

saving my life. In my anger, I forgot she was still human. If you really wanted to kill me, you should have let me destroy the worthless creature."

"You are not worth such a high cost," the prince snapped, standing between him and Freya.

"And I will not throw away any of my men's lives for such a girl, so she will at least stay alive at Listgard. You and your friends, on the other hand," he laughed slightly. "I can only imagine Eanfrith's face when I send news of your death."

Slowly and menacingly, Elialdor drew his sword. Elamra seemed to be lost in some kind of trance, staring blankly at Raedwald, and still holding Winnie in his arms.

"Oh, come now," the Owl laughed, "you surely can't think you can win against so many of us."

Freya could not deny the possibility of being successful was so slim as to be impossible. If Raedwald couldn't kill Freya straight away, she felt certain he would make another tribe member do the dirty work like he had tried with Elamra. The raven was still staring straight ahead, and Freya wondered why he was not speaking, or even looking at, the Owls in front of them. She even considered closing her eyes and allowing her shadow to take them out of the situation, but she would not allow herself to use such violence.

In the time it took for Freya to consider all their

options (which were very few), she failed to see several shapes in the sky ahead of them, coming closer and closer until they were almost upon them. Pulling herself out of her rapid thoughts, she looked up just in time to see a huge mass of brown feathers dive on Raedwald.

The Owl king let out a furious cry, trying to shake off the sharp yellow claws until he turned into a sleek barn owl, clawing at the giant bird and hissing menacingly. The other Owls could not come to his aid as more of these immense birds were dive-bombing them, distracting them from their king's attacker.

In the mass of feathers, it was difficult to see who was the stronger and Freya struggled even to make out what bird it was. It dwarfed the Owl with its finger-like wings and powerful hooked beak. Although the Owl king was much smaller, he was a formidable fighter, and Freya watched with fear and fascination as Raedwald's claws scratched at his opponent's fine feathers.

Eventually, with a thumping beating of wings that created a heavy breeze where Freya was standing dumbfounded, the bird knocked Raedwald away. The Owl was thrown into the battling crowd and did not appear again. As the giant bird turned to Freya and her companions, she realised it was an eagle. Its proud stare seemed more regal than the Owls or the Crows, and the rusty coloured feathers were no longer a tangled mess but a beautiful thick coat.

The eagle grew and became distorted, it's face growing and its legs becoming longer, while the claws grew shorter. In a matter of seconds, they were standing in front of Eli, Enna's father. Through all the days that Freya had spent at Enna's bedside with the old man, she had never seen him as a king, only as a father. Now she stood staring at the man before them, too awestruck to say a proper thank you.

"I don't want to ask what you are doing in a place like this," Eli said sharply. "You know this is a holy place for the Owl tribe? You could have been killed before I arrived."

"How did you know we were here?" Elialdor whispered, gazing beyond the eagle at the masses of feathers. The Owls really did not stand a chance against such numbers and skill.

"You have been followed throughout all your little adventures," Eli explained. "It just took a while for your follower to report back to me. When he said you had arrived here, I knew what would happen."

"It is very good of you to come to our aid," the prince bowed his head. "We have never been allies."

"It was not the Crows I came to help." Eli's harsh manner made Freya blink.

The prince did not speak but it was clear that his dislike of the eagle was not soothed by the king's comment.

"And this creature...?" Eli turned his gaze to Rald.

"Has saved my life twice now." Freya continued, placing a hand on Rald's shoulder which, she noticed, was shaking.

"Take care, Human," Eli whispered. "They do not do good unless they expect something in return."

Freya frowned and Eli bowed his head in what might have been an apology.

"Please." He smiled at all of them and looked over his shoulder to where the battle had almost finished. The Owls were few and far between, many of them lying unconscious on the grassy floor. "Please come back with me. You will be safe in our land and, tomorrow, you can leave for your home."

"That's very good of you," Freya replied when it became clear that Elialdor was not going to speak.

"But him," Eli pointed to Elamra, who was still in a daze. "One false move from him that will endanger my people and you will never return home."

After such a kind invitation, Freya was shocked at the change in tone. She looked back at Elamra who seemed not to have heard the threat, and wondered why Eli had felt the need to say it. Why, when the eagles had saved all their lives, would Elamra even think of attacking them?

They could not turn down the offer, however, and accepted it, but the eagles who had now finished fighting, eyed them suspiciously. It was clear that the dislike and distrust went both ways, and Freya realised why Eli had felt so uncomfortable staying at the castle.

One eagle took Winnie, and Freya almost threw herself between them, unwilling to let such creatures near her friend. Elamra was transformed without him even knowing and together they made their way from the abbey into the darkening sky.

The barn owl looked even more out of place and kept looking around himself as though he expected one of the eagles to break his wings. He made no sudden moves and, every time he tried to move to the edge of the crowd, more eagles kept blocking his way.

Freya wondered, as they were flying higher and higher, what people on the ground would think if they saw so many eagles flying above them. Perhaps the tribes weren't aware of how strange it would look to humans, but they did not seem too concerned.

CHAPTER NINETEEN
The Messenger and the Murderer

Freya could not really remember arriving at the eagle castle. She didn't know if she had fallen asleep mid-flight and one of the others had carried her, or if she was getting so used to flying, she didn't need to be conscious anymore. Both ideas frightened her.

When she woke up, she was alone in a stone room with tapestries and paintings on all walls except one, where there was a large fireplace. The fire was lit even though the sun was beaming in, warming anywhere the sunbeams landed. Freya wandered over to the large bay window to look at the view. The castle seemed to be built into a mountain side. There was nothing below them and the view looked out onto mountains which seemed too many to count. There was no chance of any humans stumbling across them here. Freya was not sure if anyone could get to such a mountainous region.

Determined to find out more about this strange place and, above all, find her friends, she left the room. The door led onto a gallery that overlooked something which resembled the Great Hall from the Crow's castle. Finding the large sweeping staircase easily, she crept down the stone steps into the vast room. Above her were galleries beyond galleries, and the roof seemed to be supported just by the will of the people living here.

It took her some time to take her eyes off the astounding sight, but her determination to find her friends managed to outweigh her awe at the surroundings. She wandered off through one of the side doors, peeking in first to see a library, with books surrounding all the walls. The only places not covered with books were the three small windows on one of the walls. It was clear her friends were not here, and Freya closed the door quietly, not wanting to pry.

She checked the next room and, this time, had more luck. This was a smaller room which had soft chairs around a roaring fire and, when Freya opened the door, the rich smell of peat smoke hit her and welcomed her into the room. In one of the chairs nearest the fire sat Eli, looking at the person opposite him. Freya could not see who it was as the chair was facing away from her but, also sitting on the soft chairs in the room, were Winnie and Rald. Freya felt her heart leap with relief and excitement as she realised Winnie was awake. She rushed straight over to her.

Winnie smiled but Freya's brow creased in concern as she started coughing.

"She's just a little weak," Elialdor said, and Freya turned to see that he was the one sitting opposite the eagle king.

"I'm fine," Winnie spluttered, glaring across at the prince. "I'll be fine."

"I was so worried." Freya hugged her, being careful not to squeeze her too tight.

"Sit here." Elialdor showed Freya into the chair by the fire and Winnie smiled across at her. Freya looked around the small room and back at the prince, who was now kneeling by Winnie, trying to make her more comfortable, rearranging the soft cushions so one rested behind her head.

"Where's Elamra?" Freya asked, recalling his blank look the night before and Eli's harsh words.

"He has gone to check the eagle defences," Winnie grinned. "He wanted to confirm they were enough."

"The sooner he leaves the better," Eli growled, shuffling in his chair.

"Thank you for your hospitality," Elialdor replied, "but the sooner we all leave, the better."

Eli bowed his head but scowled at the prince.

"I need some fresh air," Winnie whispered.

"Freya, will you come outside with me?"

Freya did not need a second invitation. The tension in the room was too much for her. As she and Winnie left, Rald gave them such an envious look, Freya almost asked him to come too, but she wanted to speak to Winnie alone.

Winnie seemed to know where she was going and led Freya to the door. She was almost scared that if they opened it, they would fall off the edge of the mountain, but there was a ledge in front of it. The ledge was large enough for two people to walk side by side, but Freya was terrified of heights, so she let Winnie lead the way and walked right behind her, trying desperately not to look down the sheer mountain side.

The ledge led to the side of the castle where there was a small garden, almost like a roof garden, but it was terraced down the mountain ledge. There were no trees, no grass and everything that was growing seemed to fit in with the harsh landscape.

"The eagles are not too fond of gardens," Winnie smiled. "It doesn't matter to them like it does to us."

"The gardens at your castle are the best bit," Freya laughed.

"Crows love to be outside." Winnie laughed too but quickly sat down on a bench that was made from a reddish rock.

"Elamra was concerned about you last night,"

Freya mumbled. "He carried you out of the abbey."

"So, I have him to thank then," Winnie smiled. "He would never have said."

"He likes you." Freya rested her hand on Winnie's cold fingers.

"I should hope so," her companion grinned. "We've been through a lot together."

"Well, I think he more than likes you," Freya edged towards the topic.

"What is it with humans and their dislike of the word 'love'?" Winnie laughed but stopped abruptly and her brow creased.

"Well, he loves you then."

"Yes," Winnie nodded, "I think he does, in his own way."

"And do you love him?" Freya spoke seriously.

"In my own way," Winnie could not help but smile.

"And you've known each other for decades." It was more of a statement, but Winnie shook her head.

"Centuries," she smiled.

"Then why are you not," Freya trailed off for a moment, "well, together?"

Winnie did not speak at first. She looked at her friend and shook her head.

"This strange world we brought you into," she whispered, "you should never be grateful for it, you know."

"I've met some wonderful people." Freya smiled, but she could not disagree with her friend.

"Some of us suffer just like humans do," Winnie said. "Only, we are more powerful so...it's a lot more dangerous."

"Suffer?" Freya asked, feeling like she was so close to getting the answers she needed. "How?"

"Oh, I don't mean physically suffer," Winnie sighed. "Although sometimes it shows itself in this way."

Freya did not say anything, but her blank look provoked more information.

"Elamra's family have always been affected," Winnie explained. "Well, his father's side anyway. They are so powerful - so useful to have on your side! But there is a darkness within them. Sometimes the darkness becomes too strong to ignore and they give into it. That is, I'm told, what happened last night but Elamra, determined not to harm anyone he cared about, shut off from it all and put himself into a trance. We were able to bring him out of it this morning."

"He chose to go into that state to protect us?" Freya repeated, as though it would help it sink in. "We could have done with his help!"

"If he had fought Raedwald, there would be no way of switching off that blood-lust. He could have harmed any one of us. He made that decision to protect us."

Freya said nothing. She sat staring at the small terraced garden in front of them. Elamra could have been killed when he was in that trance. He could have been killed and he could have done nothing to stop it, but she understood that. She knew that she could have fought the Owls successfully but had promised herself never to give in to the violence of her shadow.

"As I'm sure you can understand," Winnie said, "I would not mind this, but Elamra is determined he will not..."

Winnie stopped talking and turned around abruptly. Freya looked too and realised that Elamra was standing only three foot behind them. Elamra's face was not angry, just disappointed, as though Winnie had done something terrible in telling Freya the truth. When he opened his mouth, however, it wasn't to utter any harsh words, even though his face turned from disappointed to angry, making Freya take a step back from this dangerous being.

"How are you feeling now, Winnie?" He asked.

"Better, thank you, Elamra," she smiled. "Much better for getting some fresh air."

"Perhaps you should not get too much," he replied. "The air is quite thin up here."

Winnie nodded and ushered Freya back along the ledge without a second look at Elamra. As they walked past him, Elamra sharply grabbed Freya's arm and, although her heart started beating louder with anxiety, she smiled across at him. The smile seemed to soothe his angry face and the look was replaced with something like concern. He was on the verge of speaking but apparently thought better of it and let go, watching as Winnie led Freya away.

"What was all that about?" Freya asked shakily when they closed the door behind them.

"He wasn't angry with you," Winnie smiled, wandering towards the small room again.

Freya didn't feel much like conversation anymore but followed Winnie into the room, where Eli and the two princes were sitting in complete silence. She didn't want to know what curt words had passed between them to create such an uncomfortable atmosphere.

Freya ushered Winnie over to the fire and she sat opposite Eli, who bowed his head respectfully but did not meet either's gaze. Freya sat down on the floor next to Winnie but Rald stood from his chair.

"Please," he smiled, "sit here. I would be much more comfortable standing."

Freya would have refused but, after her confrontation with Elamra, she did feel like she needed to sit. She thanked him and Rald wandered over to the fireplace, staring into the flames as though he could read something in them.

"How can I thank you enough for saving us last

night?" Freya smiled at Eli. The eagle looked up and smiled back but was interrupted by Elialdor.

"Oh, he didn't do it for us," the prince laughed. Freya looked at the floor and wished she hadn't mentioned anything.

"Correct," Eli growled. "I did it for her." He nodded briskly over to Freya, who looked around to see if there was anyone behind her but saw no-one.

"Me?" she laughed. "Why?"

"Because of all those days you spent at my son's bedside," he said. The prince scowled.

"It was the Crows' generosity that helped your son wake up," he snapped. "You'd do well to remember it."

"And it is the eagles' generosity which means you are still alive." Eli stood up from his chair, his face grey and cold, and the Crow prince did the same. "You would do well to remember it."

Eli took a step towards the angry prince but was stopped by a loud knock on the door.

"Come in!" Eli shouted, letting out his anger on the poor newcomer. The door opened and Elamra walked in, causing Freya to shrink deeper into her seat. He was leading someone into the room and Freya didn't realise who it was until Rald took several steps back, so he was standing behind Eli's chair. The newcomer laughed.

"Yes, you might well run and hide." It was a woman who spoke, and Freya turned to see a tall thin lady with the same colour hair as Rald. Her features were twisted in criticism of the poor Owl prince.

"Did my father send you?" Rald asked, with the utmost contempt.

"Yes," the woman replied and smiled at Eli.

"I'm afraid I can't offer you a chair," the eagle said. Freya wondered if he was this abrupt to all the tribes, but the Owl hardly noticed.

"I came unarmed." The woman scowled at Rald for a moment before she turned to Eli. "I am just a messenger."

"And, as such, you have been welcomed into my castle graciously. I trust you were not mistreated?"

"No, thank you," she replied. "But imagine my shock that it was a Crow who intercepted me, not an eagle."

"Intercepted?" Elialdor stood up and walked towards the woman, who glared at him. "You make it sound like you were trying to steal your way into the castle."

"Were you?" Eli stood up and positioned himself between the Owl and the prince.

"I am disgusted by your accusation," the woman sneered.

"What is your name?" Elialdor's tone had changed since he realised he would get nowhere by showing his true feelings.

"Hild," Rald's sharp voice said from behind

them. "She is a favourite of my father."

"You sound somewhat jealous," she laughed. "He was always disappointed with you as a son. And I can see why."

"Enough," Eli snapped. "You are here as a messenger, but I will not have any snide comments from you. Your prince is my guest and you should remember that."

Freya was expecting a quick, nasty remark from Hild but was surprised. The Owl's eyes narrowed with anger, but she said nothing.

"Now," Eli smiled, "you have come with a message from Raedwald. What is it?"

"It is this." Hild raised her head. "The most noble Owl king knows that you are trying to find his queen's murderer. He appreciates this. He says that, if you succeed, the war between the tribes will stop. He will be open for negotiation."

There was silence for a time. All the Crows and Rald looked utterly shocked but this was nothing compared to the look on Eli's face. Surely, Freya thought, he must have known what they were doing at Edweth's tomb, but the look of confusion and shock told her that he hadn't had a clue. The colour had drained from his face and he swayed slightly. Hild did not seem to notice.

"Perhaps you should sit down," Freya said gently to Eli and he looked at her. His face was now deathly white, and he used Freya's support to make his way to the chair, his lips parted and slightly blue.

"This is good news," Elamra nodded and Freya turned to him, hardly daring to meet his face, "but we know who it is, and Raedwald does not believe us."

"King Raedwald," Hild snapped.

"He is not my king." However haughty Hild made herself, she could not look down her nose at Elamra as he was so much taller. He looked down at her, neither angry nor upset, but she scowled up at him.

"You only said it was Ranald to provoke him, and you know this," she said. "King Raedwald wants you to find the truly guilty one."

"It is a very noble offer," Elialdor nodded. "We will, of course, consider it."

"You wish to stay the night?" Eli asked, his throat tight and his voice hoarse.

"No," Hild replied, "thank you. I will return to Listgard with the positive news."

She did not wait for any reply but turned and walked out of the room, her head held high. For several moments, there was no sound in the room except the wind in the chimney. Everyone looked utterly stunned: all except Eli, who looked more like he was about to pass out. Freya knelt beside the eagle king and he smiled at her, but his eyes did not seem focussed on her.

"This is fabulous news," Rald said at last, when he had recovered feeling in his stomach.

"Yes," Winnie whispered. The possibility of the war between the Owls and Crows ending seemed unimaginable.

"Is it?" Eli whispered. "What will you do?"

"Find the murderer," Elialdor laughed, "and hand them over to Raedwald. Too many Crows have been killed in this feud. If there is a chance it can end, we will take it."

"I can't let you do that." Eli shook his head and rested it on the tips of his fingers, his brow creased.

"What?" Rald spoke softly. "Why?"

Freya looked from Rald to Eli, noticing the old man's white face and trembling hands and voice. She stood up and took a step back from him, bumping into Elialdor.

"You did it," she whispered. "No, you can't have done. Edweth said it was her son."

"She was not well-respected for her honesty, child," Eli smiled.

"What?" Rald snapped, rushing forwards so he was now standing in front of the king. Freya moved between them. "You killed my mother?"

"No, he didn't." Elialdor looked around the room. "Of course he didn't. What reason would he have?"

"I loved your mother," Eli said to Rald, but Freya continued to stand between them. Rald gasped and took a step towards him, shaking his head.

"No." Rald's whole body was shaking, although Freya was unsure if it was anger or fear that caused this.

"I loved her," Eli nodded, "but she loved your father. They were one, Raedwald and Edweth. I was jealous."

"You killed my mother out of jealousy?" Rald whispered. He was turning pale and the fingernails on his hand were growing longer and sharper until they resembled claws. In a flash of blue light, Rald was sent flying backwards and hit against the tapestry. Freya turned to Elialdor, who closed his fists together and the blue light vanished.

"I'm sorry, Eli," the prince said, "but if there is a chance of stopping the war against my people, I'll take it."

"No," Eli straightened his back and stared across at Elialdor. "No, I don't think you'll get that opportunity."

As he spoke, the door opened, and five other people crowded into the room. Freya glanced across at Eli in horror. Surely, after coming to save their lives, he would not kill his innocent guests?

"I'm sorry, child," Eli looked at her, "but I cannot have anyone knowing the truth."

"I don't believe you," Elamra growled, and Winnie instantly stood up and moved to his side.

"Don't worry. They will not harm you unless

you try to escape." Eli sat back down on the comfortable chair and the other eagles advanced on them. "I'm just sorry I could not offer you a more hospitable stay in my castle, but I have to ensure you cannot get out of here to tell Raedwald. Imagine what he would do if he knew the truth. I have to say - him thinking the Crows committed the crime has been a useful distraction."

"A useful distraction?" Elialdor snarled. "While my people were dying, you stood by and never once came to our aid!"

Eli did not reply and none of them could fight against the strong sea eagles. They went further and further into the castle and must have travelled a long way into the mountain. There were no windows, so the only light came from the torches that were dotted here and there on the walls, creating long shadows. Freya could hear sobbing from behind which must have been Rald. The poor boy, she thought, to live so long and never known who had killed his mother, only to be imprisoned when he finally learnt the truth.

CHAPTER TWENTY

The Devil and the Deep Blue Sea

The room they were placed in was dark, with no windows and no torch. At least, Freya thought as one of the eagles pushed her in, they were all together. How much worse it must be to spend any length of time in this room alone.

The eagles slammed the door closed, rattling the keys in the lock as though they were taunting the prisoners. Freya sat with her back resting against the wall and tried to make out the shapes of her friends.

"At least he didn't kill us," she said, hoping that a reply might help her locate them. "We're still better off than we would have been in Listgard."

"Yes," a sarcastic voice replied close to her, which could only have been Elialdor, "we just get to spend the rest of our days locked in a room with no light. Oh, by a murderer as well. How delightful!"

Then there was silence except for the sobbing in the far corner of the room. Freya was almost glad it was dark so she couldn't see the distraught Rald but, as Freya thought again about how much the young Owl had lost in the last few days, she felt she needed to comfort him. Following the sniffs and sobs, she edged over the rough ground. On reaching him, she said nothing, she sat beside Rald and put her arm around his shoulders as his breathing grew more ragged and he took in gulps of air before he started crying again. Freya just sat there, still with her arm around him, not knowing what to say that could make the Owl prince better.

"We need to get out of here," Winnie said at last from somewhere in the room. "We need to get back to the Crows."

The sobbing continued and Freya thought it even got a bit louder.

"Don't worry about that," Elialdor snapped. "You'll be safe with the Crows. We won't send you back to your father."

Elialdor clearly thought this would stop the sobbing and sniffing but it didn't work. The prince's tone of voice was probably to blame.

"We do need to get out of here," Elialdor groaned.

"We need more skill than I have. Or you,

Aldor. Or Rald," Winnie said softly.

"What's that supposed to mean?" Elamra's gruff voice made Freya jump, but she also wanted to hear the answer to that question.

"I mean," Winnie began, "that there are two people in this room who can get out of here single-handedly."

"No," Elamra snapped.

"We need to get back to the castle," Winnie persevered. "Imagine all the fighting between the Crows and the Owls stopping. We need to do this."

"You're not the one who will be putting everyone in danger by doing it, Winifred," Elamra argued.

"No," Winnie replied. "I will be the one who is put in danger. But I'm saying it will be worth the risk."

"I won't." Elamra remained quite firm and Winnie grunted in annoyance.

"Then we will spend the rest of our days in here," she snapped, "and our tribes will remain at war, perhaps even destroying themselves in the end."

"I understand what Elamra is saying." Freya was shocked to find herself agreeing with the man. "I can understand why he doesn't want to use the power he has."

"It can be used for good as well as bad, Freya." Winnie sounded hurt, which cut deep into

Freya's own feelings.

"Not when it's used for violence." She stood her ground and there was silence in reply. She knew she might have let her friends down, but she couldn't bring herself to use violence like before, having learned how dangerous it was.

"Can you open the door with the blue light?" Freya asked, hoping for an alternative.

"I'm sure the eagles would have thought of that." Elialdor sounded unimpressed but Winnie urged him to at least try.

Elialdor shuffled as best he could to the door, holding faint blue light balls so he could see where he was going. When he got to the door, he fumbled for the keyhole and placed the palm of his hand flat upon the hole. His hand started to glow brighter and brighter, but nothing happened. After several attempts, he grunted in frustration and sat down, clearly trying not to say 'I told you so'.

No-one said anything.

Elialdor started amusing himself by tossing blue light balls up to the ceiling. By the faint light, they could see that they were surrounded by hard rock and the only entrance and way out was through the impenetrable door.

Minutes passed and the prince continued messing around with the light in an attempt to stop himself listening to Rald's shaky breathing. He had stopped crying but was breathing raggedly. Freya looked at the boy next to her. By the strange light, she could just see him curled up against the rock. She felt a rush of pity for the poor boy: he only seemed her age, and yet he had been through so much tragedy.

Elialdor's lights were beginning to irritate the rest of them, and Winnie and Freya snapped together for him to stop his silliness. The prince said nothing, but the light balls vanished, apart from one.

"I said 'stop it', Aldor," Winnie groaned.

"I did," Elialdor said, puzzled.

Freya looked up. She could see that the faint light in the room was not blue, but reddish orange. *Torchlight!* Suddenly intrigued, it took her a few moments to realise where it came from before the prince announced it to the room of prisoners.

"It's just from under the door," he said wearily, making his companions sigh.

"Just a moment," Winnie began, and everyone looked up again, although they couldn't see where she was. "Aldor - what was it you said about a wren princess?"

"Karrie." Elialdor sat forward. "Winnie, that's a good plan, but I think even a wren wouldn't fit under that gap."

"But surely, if you can change someone to the size of a wren, you can change them to something smaller."

There was a pause while the prince thought about this and everyone else awaited his reply, holding their breath.

"It would be dangerous: I don't know if it would work. And I wouldn't be able to be the one if I'm to turn the person back to normal afterwards."

"I will," Freya volunteered, feeling guilty that they were in this position, although confident that she had made the right decision not to use her shadow.

"Freya," Elialdor warned, "there may be dangers we don't know. I might not be able to get you back."

Freya was silent for a moment and nobody spoke. She felt the force of the prince's words as though they had hit her in the chest, as she tried to imagine life if he could not restore her to full size. But what were the other options? One: they would all be trapped here forever, and she would never see her parents again. Two: she asked her shadow for help and risked everyone's lives. She realised she had already made up her mind when she thought about the alternatives.

"I'll do it," she said at last and was met with silence. "Really. There's no other option, is there?"

"Very well," Elialdor sighed and coughed, nervous. Not allowing for any time to change his mind, knowing he would talk himself out of it, the prince fumbled over to where Freya was sitting, darting blue light balls in her direction so that he could see.

He cupped his hands together in front of him, as though he was holding water in them, and closed his eyes. At first, the blue light was faint and dim, but it grew brighter and brighter until Freya had to close her eyes. Elialdor continued until the others shielded themselves. The light was growing hotter as it grew brighter. Although it did not seem to affect the prince, Rald and Freya, who were closest, could feel the intense heat cause drops of sweat to gather on their foreheads.

Elialdor, with his eyes closed, was oblivious to this discomfort until, finally, he thought that the spell light was strong enough to shrink someone down to the required size.

Freya felt the heat come closer and continued to close her eyes. With a gulp of fear, she realised that the shadow was forming before her. She tried to open her eyes but could not.

"You know how dangerous this could be," the shadow's voice called, but there was no mouth that moved, no eyes that looked at her.

"I know," Freya whispered, "but I have to do it."

"You are more powerful than you admit. Use that power. You want to - give into it."

Freya could not deny that the shadow's

suggestion was a good one. With the heat of Elialdor's light, she felt the fear of what it might do to her. Surely it would be safer for her if she fought her way out?

She paused and could feel the shadow watching her.

"But that's it," she whispered. "It would be safer for *me*, not safer for my friends."

If she allowed her power to be used, they would be out of here by now, but at what cost? She did not want to hurt anyone, even the people who had locked them up in here.

"I won't," she said at last. The shadow said nothing, but Freya had a strange feeling that it was smiling. It became smaller and smaller until it faded completely. As soon as it had gone, Freya felt a rush of warmth throughout her entire body and, although she was closing her eyes, her vision was filled with an intense blue light. This time, she couldn't escape it. As the light danced around her, Freya felt herself shrivelling. Her arms were becoming closer and closer together and her legs were too small to support herself, so she had to curl up on the ground.

The light grew blinding, and Freya felt like screaming that she couldn't get away from it but, just as she thought she might give in to unconsciousness, it vanished completely, leaving her in pitch darkness.

She opened her eyes.

Initially, she couldn't see anything because of the sudden change, but gradually, things started to come into focus.

In front of her, someone was collapsed on the ground, but it took her a while to understand that it must be Elialdor. Instead of the Elialdor that she was used to, he was gigantic. No, immense. She was astonished to find she was the same size as his fingernail. His hand was stretched out towards her but unmoving. She tried to reach him but had to run as her legs were so much smaller than usual.

It took what seemed like a century to run to his face, but she let out a sigh of relief as she saw his huge eyes blink open and close. Her relief was short-lived, however, as a sigh from the prince sent her flying backwards until she landed painfully on the flagstones. She stood with difficulty and didn't approach Elialdor again.

But the prince wearily knelt up, looked at her, and smiled.

"Freya?" Elialdor's voice wobbled. "How are you feeling? You're not hurt?"

"Are you?" Freya asked, seeing the prince's pale face. "Don't worry, I'll get you out of here."

"Here," Winnie whispered, her gigantic form crouching down in front of Freya. She held out her cupped hand and Freya crawled in.

"Don't drop me," Freya laughed. Elialdor gave a silent laugh, leaning his head against the floor of the dungeon and closing his eyes in exhaustion.

Carefully, Winnie carried the tiny Freya over to the door and put her down on the floor beside the tiny crack. The gap beneath the door had seemed impossible for a mouse to crawl under but Freya, now only a centimetre tall, could walk beneath the door while crouching.

"There is no bird that small," Winnie murmured, afraid the people outside might hear. "They must think this room is impenetrable."

"Now Freya," Elamra's clear voice contrasted to Winnie's careful tone. Winnie turned an annoyed face towards him and shushed him.

"Freya," Elamra whispered. The quietness seemed out of place for the giant man. "Outside this door, there are two guards. One of them has the key. You must take the key without him realising and bring it back underneath the door."

The plan sounded simple enough, but Freya felt sure it would not be so easy. But the choice was to try Elamra's plan or spend the rest of her life in the pokey room with no daylight.

"At least the Owls have the decency to keep their prisoners in light rooms," Freya muttered as she bent down and walked underneath the thick door. It didn't take her long to reach the other side so she could stand upright again.

"Although," she continued mumbling to herself, "I don't suppose anyone stays in their prison for long."

She shuddered as she remembered the end that *she* almost came to, at the hands of Raedwald and his smug son.

In front of her was a room with a doorway but no door. Through this gap, she could hear two men chatting, and the sound of knives and forks on plates.

Dinner time seems like a good distraction, she thought, and started making her way over to the doorway. Although she could have stepped into the room in one stride when she was her normal size, it took her several minutes to cross the desert of flagstones. This was made even harder by the draught that was sweeping along the floor, making it difficult for Freya to keep her balance.

After what must have been ten minutes, she reached the doorway and saw two huge men sitting at opposite sides of a small table, just finishing eating. Although their plates were empty, they made no effort to tidy them away, but pushed them to the side. One of them took a small cylindrical box from his pocket and put it on the table.

"Doubles score?" he said, and his friend nodded, taking what looked to Freya to be giant coins out of his pocket and laying them on the table for the other man to see.

What Freya was more interested in, however, was the sound the coins had made when they came out the pocket. There had been another sound too: still metallic but lower, deeper.

Hoping that her guess had been correct, Freya moved as fast as possible to the man. Fortunately, the man's large coat reached the floor when he was sitting down, so Freya grabbed hold of the material and hoisted herself off the floor.

The journey upwards, reaching for the fabric of the coat, pulling herself up, and reaching again, was shorter but far more difficult than traveling across the flagstones. Her arms felt like they were being pulled from her body, and she was grateful for all that seemingly wasted time playing on the monkey bars in the park.

On reaching the pocket, she carefully lowered herself in, and could not help an excited squeal of relief when she saw the large iron key resting against more coins. On hearing her, the dice game stopped while the two men listened. Freya kept silent and still. Contenting themselves that it was just a mouse, they eventually continued with their game.

For a moment, Freya sat on a large gold coin, getting her breath back.

Right, she said to herself, *time to go.*

She forced herself to stand up and walk over to the large key. Bending to pick it up, she tugged at it, but it wouldn't move. She tried again.

Nothing.

Of course, Freya thought as she collapsed on the

coins in a burst of failure and embarrassment. *How could I possibly have lifted the key? It's ten times my size and solid metal.*

Freya felt like crying but asked herself firmly what good it would do. Her friends were still locked away and, if she sat here in self-pity, they would stay that way. They were relying on her, she told herself.

But she had no idea what she could do. Sitting back on the coins, she closed her eyes to think.

Almost immediately, she could tell she wasn't alone. Faint, because it was so dark, she could see the outline of her shadow, but it didn't say anything as it had done before. Instead, it just seemed to wait until she spoke.

"Go away," Freya mumbled, knowing she didn't have the strength for this conversation.

"I'm not here to persuade you to fight," the shadow whispered. It sounded different - less confident than before.

"Then what are you here for?" she snapped.

"To help you," the shadow said, his voice just a breathy mutter.

Freya thought for moment. She was in this position because she didn't want to hurt people. If she had accepted the help her shadow had offered, they would likely have been out of the Eagles' castle by now, but she could not begin to wonder what the cost would have been. Still, she needed to help her friends, and there should be no harm in just listening to what the shadow had to say.

"How can you help me?"

"The blue light doesn't have to be used just in battle," the shadow replied. "Do you remember seeing the light in the infirmary at the castle?"

Freya shook her head.

"There, it was being used to heal people. It can be used for good. And bad."

"Okay." Freya dragged out her words. "Tell me how to use it for good."

"Just as I am, the blue light is *you*. It is your soul, concentrated into pure power. You can control that power, just as you can control yourself. Tell me what good things you've done before."

"If you are me, then you know," Freya snapped.

"I know, yes. I know every minute since you were born. I want to see if you can recall these events. You'll need to if you're ever going to be able to control the blue light."

"Okay," she mumbled, "I suppose…I got Mrs Taylor's prescription for her when she was ill."

"That's good, but not enough."

"I…I went to find Mrs Bellamy when Lucy broke her arm in the playground."

"Again, not enough."

"I…Ugh…I can't think of anything else, okay? I suppose I've not done enough good."

The shadow said nothing. Freya kept her eyes closed, feeling tears come behind her lids, and could feel the shadow's invisible eyes staring at her from within her mind.

She hadn't done enough good things in her life. She hadn't saved anyone's life; she had done nothing remarkable. She had gone to school, done her homework on time (usually) and got good marks, but she had never done anything out of the ordinary. Nothing until two weeks ago.

She sat up.

In her mind, she could feel the tension from the shadow, who was awaiting what she would say next.

"I refused to use my blue light for bad because I didn't want to hurt anyone. I could have chosen the easy way out, but it could have harmed my friends."

"That," the shadow nodded, "is enough."

Freya let out a sigh of relief.

"So, what do I do?"

"You concentrate on that thought. *That* will prove to you that there is the goodness in you to do this. If, at any point, you feel angry or threatening thoughts slip into your head, remind yourself *why* you are doing it."

"I'm doing it for my friends," Freya confirmed.

"Now, cup your hands together. Still with your eyes closed, locate it, in your mind, your heart. Focus on it. Keep focusing until it is all you can hear."

Freya tried doing what the shadow had said,
but every time she tried, she was distracted by
urgent thoughts and images of her friends sitting
alone in their dark cell. She could not move them
away.

"I need help," Freya gasped.

"No. You need hope," the shadow
commanded. "You need to see the hope in what
you are doing. Don't dwell on the bad things. Tell
yourself you are going to make them better."

As she tried to focus, she imagined her friends
escaping from their cell without harming anyone.
She could see Rald and Elialdor flying out of the
castle in their bird forms, with Elamra and
Winnie behind them, as a raven and a jackdaw.
She tried to feel the joy at seeing them all released
but, as she turned around in her mind, she saw
seven gigantic eagles pursuing them, their
wingspan dwarfing each of the other birds, even
the immense shadow of the raven.

Freya felt a rush of fear and power surge
through her.

"No!" her shadow snapped. "Don't give in.
Think only good!"

It was proving harder than it sounded, but
Freya gave it another attempt for her friends.
Again, she saw them leave their prison, again she
saw the eagles pursuing them but, this time, she
forced herself to see past it. Screwing her eyes

closed, she saw her friends arrive at the castle, she saw Rald being accepted by the Crows, she saw Raedwald and Eanfrith together, shaking hands. Concentrating further, she saw herself returning home and holding tightly onto her mum and dad.

A sudden thrust of warmth burst through her veins, and she felt heat appear in her cupped hands.

"Well done," she heard the shadow say, although her vision of her parents was still in her mind so she couldn't see him. "Now, go over to the key and, with the blue light, touch every part of it. Be careful not to miss anything."

Freya did this, unwilling to open her eyes in case she lost the blue light. She stumbled over coins and bumped her knee on the edge of what must have been the metal key. Quickly finding the bottom end of the object, she did as the shadow had said and touched every millimetre of the item. The key was cold, in contrast to the heat from her hands, but she put the shivers aside and continued in her dedicated task.

When, finally, she was convinced that the blue light had touched every part, she closed her hands into fists and could feel the heat disappear.

"Now open your eyes, and try to lift the key again," the shadow commanded.

Freya opened her eyes and tried to accustom them to the dark again. When she did, nothing seemed to have changed: the blue light was not there, the key looked the same, the coins had hardly moved. Cautiously, Freya moved over to the key and, with all her strength, tried to lift it up.

The key sprang up so easily that Freya was sent flying backwards through the force of her own strength, landing on the soft material of the pocket. In her head, she was sure she heard laughing and, while she rubbed her sore muscles, she couldn't help but joining in with the laughter. A second later, she cupped her hand over her mouth, and then let out a sigh of relief when she realised the two guards were too noisy to hear her that time.

Again, she made her way over to the key but was careful this time, knowing that it was much lighter than before. It took none of her strength to lift the now-weightless item.

Without wasting time to wonder how this could have happened, Freya grabbed hold of the key again and started climbing out of the pocket, holding the material in her hands and gripping the key between her feet.

It took more effort climbing like this than before, even though it was a much shorter distance. She hadn't realised how much she had moved her feet when she was climbing, but it took her a long stretch of time to reach the tip of the pocket.

As soon as she did, she sat over the fold,

gasping for breath, trying desperately not to look down. She didn't see the hand coming towards her until it was only an inch above her head.

Freya stopped herself screaming just in time and, seeing no alternative despite her fear of heights, jumped from the pocket towards the floor. The eagle did not seem to notice but delved into his pocket, taking out three more coins which he placed on the table.

"I'm out of luck tonight," he said, "so this will probably be my last game for now."

Freya hardly heard him. She was speeding towards the ground, still holding the key and watching the floor get closer and closer.

It was like a nightmare of jumping out of an aeroplane without a parachute, or leaping from the top of a flight of stairs, but she knew this was not a dream.

You never hit the floor in a dream.

CHAPTER TWENTY-ONE
Strength of Mind

Freya desperately grabbed at anything she was speeding past. She was rushing towards the floor but, because of her tiny size, she had not yet hit the ground.

Grasping at anything she could, she reached out to the material of the coat, feeling the fabric touch her fingers but unable to get hold of it. She tried again, lunging herself at the coat and, this time, held onto it for a moment. She had been falling so fast, though, that the weight of her fall pulled her downward again. But at last she had slowed down now, so she tried one more time to grab hold of the coat, as she was now only a few centimetres from the floor.

Lunging towards the coat once more, she reached out her tiny hand as far as she could and grasped the fabric tightly. Feeling it slip through her hand, she threw her other hand over and hugged the material, so she gradually came to a stop, only an inch above the ground.

Freya collapsed in a heap on the floor, looking up at the ceiling and breathing deeply, trying her best to calm her heartbeat. That had been the most dangerous thing she had ever done in her life. She thought back to all those times in the last two weeks when she hadn't felt as out of control as just now.

As she calmed down, she became aware that she was lying next to the eagle's feet. All it would take was for him to move slightly and all that effort would have been for nothing.

Dragging herself to her feet, Freya moved her shoulders backwards and forwards. They were sore with the effort of clinging on to the material, but the worst problem was that the fear had made her legs into jelly. Then she forced herself up and immediately dropped down to the floor. She stood up again.

Every time she moved, her feet felt like they could not support her, and she stumbled in the direction of the key, which had fallen only a little way away.

As she moved more, she felt strength returning to her legs, but her heart was still racing with each step. She reached the key without a problem and picked up the weightless object, dragging it behind her as she made her way across the flagstone floor back to the cell.

The purpose which urged her on this time meant that the journey back to the cell didn't take as long as it did before.

When she got to the door, she pushed the key under the gap before her and heard whispering on the other side. When she was convinced the key could be retrieved at the other side, she crouched down and walked into the cell herself.

"I really hope this is the right key," she laughed, and Winnie rushed over to see if she was alright.

"I'm fine," Freya said, "or, I will be, when we get out of here."

"Freya," Elialdor smiled at her, "I'll try and get you back to your normal size."

"Wait until we check the key," Elamra grunted. Rald, she noticed, was staying silent, but the sniffing had stopped so he must have been feeling hopeful about their escape mission too.

Winnie took the key from under the door and tried it in the rusty lock. After a bit of jiggling, the key went in and turned. She let out a quiet laugh and turned to the rest of them.

"It works," she smiled. "Now, let's get ourselves out of here."

Elialdor knelt before Freya.

"I'm going to try and turn you back now," his voice was shaking.

He's afraid, Freya thought to herself. Until now,

she had forced herself not to think hard about the consequences of remaining this size but, with the prince's hesitation and obvious fear, she began to consider it as a possibility.

Without saying another word, Elialdor closed his eyes. The same blue light appeared in his cupped hands that Freya had used with the key. Again, she could feel the heat from it, but it was stronger, more aggressive. The look of concentration and pain on Elialdor's face worried Freya, but she said nothing. The prince needed to do this, just as she had needed to overcome her shadow.

Without warning, the prince threw the blue light at Freya. The light itself was far bigger than she was, and she was knocked backwards by the force of it against her chest. She heard Winnie shout, but she needed to close her eyes, as the light was blinding.

It seemed to her as though she was covered in flames, the heat tearing at every part of her but not burning her. Closing her eyes against the light seemed futile now: it was so bright that, even with her eyes closed, the strength of the light reached them as a bright orange glow.

She was hardly aware of her limbs growing, or the light diminishing. She felt as though her head was going to explode but she opened her eyes as she felt a hand on her shoulder - a normal sized hand.

She looked into Winnie's face which was staring at her, concerned.

"I'm fine," Freya answered Winnie's expression. "How is Elialdor?"

They both looked over to see the prince taking deep breaths, trying to steady his head.

"Aldor," Winnie whispered as she and Freya crept over to him.

"I'm fine," he gasped, "now we can get out of here."

Freya was unsure. She did not think it was sensible to go while Elialdor was feeling so weak, but she knew that the eagles would soon realise the key was missing.

Winnie turned the key further in the lock and, gently and quietly, pulled the door open, looking out into the corridor.

The door made a squeak as it opened so they all froze, waiting for the inevitable noises from the guards. But they never came. Feeling as though luck was on their side, they crept into the hallway. Across from the cell, the two guards who had been playing with the dice were locked in a heated argument. Freya could not make out all the shouting, but it did mean they managed to slip down the hall, unnoticed. Winnie led the way with a very wobbly Freya. Rald and Elialdor were next, with Elamra at the end.

When they got to the end of the corridor, at the foot of a flight of stairs, Elialdor lifted his foot higher for the step and collapsed with the effort. He would have fallen to the floor but Rald, who was standing next to him, grabbed him around the waist to support him.

Elialdor could not speak, although Freya was unsure whether this was due to exhaustion or shock that it had been the Owl prince who helped him.

Rald didn't speak either but he looked up at the others with an unremarkable expression, showing that he had seen nothing noteworthy in this act of helping a fellow tribesman.

There was no time to explain to him the kindness he had shown, as the noises in the guardroom were growing softer – clearly, the argument was ending - and their disappearance would soon be noticed.

They continued up the stairs and Rald continued to support Elialdor, who remained silent. The corridor was all but deserted and Freya began to realise that they were the only prisoners this castle had seen for some time. The difficult part, she thought, would be when they tried to move through the upper castle and not just the dungeon.

After seemingly endless corridors which they stumbled down, they came across a heavy door. Swinging it open, they realised they were returning to the main part of the building. They were entering a high-ceilinged room that, while imposing, was only half as big as the Great Hall in the Crow's castle.

Four people stood at the other end of the hall. They had not seen the door opening but they would certainly see the five prisoners escaping.

"What do we do?" Winnie hissed. "We can't get out unnoticed."

"Th-think about when we arrived." Elialdor stammered. "The exit to the castle is…just through that door… If we can just make it through this room without being stopped…we're free."

"They will pursue us," Rald whispered and Elialdor reluctantly nodded in agreement.

"I'll distract them." They all turned to Elamra as he spoke.

"No," Winnie shook her head, putting Elamra's suggestion out of the question. "No, we need to get out of here unseen. We have to find another way out."

"Soon, the guards will raise the alarm, and we won't be able to get out," Elamra snapped.

"Look in these rooms," Rald suggested, and everyone turned to him as though he had gone mad. "I mean it. The kitchen will probably be along here somewhere. In all likelihood, there will be a chute or something that leads outside."

There was a pause.

"It's worth a try," Freya agreed. "It's better than being seen and chased."

"Take that side," Winnie suggested to Freya. "I'll take this side. You three - stay here and stop anyone from coming this way if you need to."

Winnie and Freya moved off down the corridor, opening each of the doors slightly to look inside. Most of the rooms Freya came across were storerooms, filled with wooden crates and brown sacks full of vegetables and fruit. One room was full of glass bottles containing what looked to be wine. The collection rivalled her granddad's wine rack!

The fifth room she came to was a small stone cubby-hole, about half the size of her bedroom at home. Three basins covered one wall and in the middle of the room was a barrel of water.

She crept into the room, seeing in the darkness that there was no one else there, and looked around. On one of the walls, there seemed to be a trapdoor, not much bigger than a cat flap. She walked over and pushed it open. At once, she felt a rush of cold air cross her hand, and she grinned triumphantly.

Looking closer through the trapdoor, she saw a small chute and, beyond, the edge of the cliff face.

This was where they could leave the castle.

She called Winnie softly and they went to fetch the others.

On seeing the size of the flap, Elamra's face fell.

"We will never fit through there, Freya." He sounded unimpressed.

"Not in our human forms, no," Freya agreed, trying hard to ignore the man's tone. "But as birds, we will."

"It's worth a try," Elialdor agreed and tried to stand on his own without Rald's help. Rald took a step back, hoping he succeeded. In a moment, both princes had disappeared, and Freya smiled at the barn owl and raven. The poor raven looked dishevelled, reflecting Elialdor's current strength.

"Will you be alright flying back to the castle?" Freya wondered aloud.

"I'll be fine," the Raven Elialdor spoke, "but we should go now."

The others transformed into their bird selves. Freya still needed a little help from Winnie but was becoming more confident with it.

"Ladies first," Elialdor croaked.

Winnie hopped over to the trapdoor. Her jackdaw figure pushed it open and was gone. Freya fitted easily too, and Rald came next. Elamra and Elialdor, being the largest birds in the group, had a little more difficulty but, before long, they were gliding away from the cliff-face castle.

When the castle had almost vanished into the distance, Freya was sure she could hear the tolling of bells.

"Warning bell," Winnie explained mid-flight. "They've noticed we've gone."

"Will they come after us?" Freya was unsure she could escape from the bigger, faster birds.

"If they do, they won't catch us," Freya was sure she saw the jackdaw smile. "We'll soon be at the castle."

CHAPTER TWENTY-TWO
The Uncomfortable Truth

When Freya opened her eyes, it was to find they were resting on the ceiling in her bedroom in the castle. When she tried to remember last night, all she could remember was flying from the castle as fast as possible. She could not recall anything else.

Sitting up, she realised that, although her shoulders and arms ached, she felt more rested than she had in days. She also realised that she was not the only one in the room.

Elialdor was laying at the foot of her bed, still asleep. Winnie was asleep in the armchair, her head to one side, while Rald and Elamra were talking quietly, sitting in the corner of the room by the door. When they saw that Freya was awake, they stopped talking. Rald smiled over at her and Elamra gave the briefest of nods in her direction.

"What happened?" Freya asked, feeling foolish. "I can't actually remember coming here."

"That will be because you fell out of the flight mid-way to the castle," Elamra muttered. "Don't worry, so did Elialdor. I think using the blue light exhausted both of you. It's perfectly normal."

"So how did I get here?" Freya asked.

"Winnie brought you," Elamra mumbled. "And Rald."

"Thank you." Freya started laughing and Rald looked confused before he began joining in. Elamra just watched both of them.

"That's the second time I've stopped you falling from the sky," Rald laughed.

"It ended better this time," Freya nodded.

The sound of the laughter woke up Elialdor, who jumped awake with a start. Winnie muttered something before sitting forward slowly, rubbing her wrist as though it was sore. She grinned when she saw Elialdor and Freya awake.

"Freya! Aldor!" she smiled. "We were so worried, weren't we, Elamra?"

Elamra said nothing but grunted. Winnie ignored him.

"Thank you," Freya replied, also ignoring the raven.

"We should see my father," Elialdor mumbled, sounding as though he wanted anything but to see the king. "We need to tell him about

Raedwald's deal. And Eli's confession."

Freya could understand the need to bring the truth to light but she found the idea of transferring Raedwald's anger onto someone to be unsettling.

"No," she said at last, "we need to do something first."

Elialdor looked at her, knowing that he too wanted to put off telling his father the news, but sure that he could not put it off for long.

"We need to tell Enna," Freya demanded.

"You're right," Elamra said, startling everyone else in the room. "The prince deserves to know."

"He'll try and stop us," Rald argued, a slight distaste slipping into his voice.

"Perhaps, but I don't think so," Elamra replied. "Besides, it is his right."

The five companions got to their feet, Rald somewhat reluctantly, and moved over to the door.

"We'd better hope we don't see anyone," Elialdor muttered. "I don't want my father knowing we have arrived and not gone to see him."

The sun was just rising, so there wouldn't be too many people around and Elialdor chose to go a way that led to the glass room where they were unlikely to see anyone, especially in the early morning. The castle was strangely quiet, but Freya was not sure whether she just noticed it more now because she felt a growing sense of unease as she considered telling Enna and the king the news.

They walked on in silence until they reached the glass room, the early morning sun creeping in through the roof and falling on the fountain. Freya hardly saw the beauty before her eyes but Rald, seeing it for the first time, stared open-mouthed at the rare gift from his tribe.

As though he was in a trance, Elialdor walked over to the hospital door and pulled it open. There were no sounds coming from the room and the prince crept in, knowing without looking that the other four were following.

Once inside the infirmary, however, he came to a stop, causing Freya to bump into him. Elialdor looked down at the floor and wouldn't meet anyone's gaze, but Freya could guess what was going through his mind.

"I'll speak to Enna," Freya sighed, unwilling to put the burden on anyone else.

None of them argued, not wanting the awful task themselves. Besides, Elialdor thought, Freya was in a much better position to speak to the eagle than he was, having spent so many hours at his bedside before he recovered.

Freya found Enna asleep on his bed at the other side of the hospital. She sat down on the chair beside him, remembering the times she had come here and talked to Eli. To think now that he was the one who had caused the rift between the Owls and Crows made her feel sick.

As though the young eagle could hear her thoughts, he mumbled slightly, and with a very quiet snore, woke up suddenly. It took him a while to focus on her and Freya wished it would have been longer, if only to put off the conversation she had to have.

"Freya," Enna smiled and sat up, "it's so good to see you again. I thought you had left us."

"No." She looked down at her fingers. "I returned."

"You don't look very happy about it," Enna grinned, but it slipped after a moment. "What's happened?"

"I have to talk to you, Enna," she replied, "about your father."

"What about him?" he asked.

"It's about something he did many years ago. I don't know if you were born."

Enna's eyes narrowed and Freya realised it was kinder now to tell him straight away.

"Your father confessed to killing Raedwald's wife," she said, watching Enna's face. It turned almost as pale as Eli's had done, and he began shaking slightly.

"There's more," he whispered as he stared hard at her.

"Yes," Freya nodded. "Raedwald has said he will stop his war with the Crows if we bring him the murderer."

"You're going to…" Enna trailed off.

"No," she said. "Even if we wanted to, we couldn't. He has his own tribe, his own castle and defences. We wouldn't be able to, but Raedwald might."

"You're going to serve him up on a plate for the Owls?" Enna's lips grew thin and Freya could not blame him for the angry flash in his eyes. She would certainly have been angry in his position.

"We're only doing what is right," Freya mumbled. "Your father killed Edweth because he was jealous."

"No," Enna snapped. "No, you are saying this because it's easy for you to believe it."

"Eli put on a pretty convincing show." Freya felt she had to defend her words. "He locked us in his little prison and would have left us there."

"Because you were going to bring a war on his people," he hissed. "I would do the same."

Freya sighed and rubbed her eyes.

"I agree," she whispered. "I would do the same if my friends were in danger."

Her words brought a change in Enna. The look of anger was replaced first by a look of astonishment and then something which might have been acceptance. He raised his hand and Freya thought he was going to lash out at her, but he laid it on her arm and smiled.

"I'm sorry," he said. "I forget you are just as

out-of-place here as I am."

"I will do everything I can to keep you out of this." Freya laid her hand on Enna's and squeezed it gently. His words could not stop her from telling Eanfrith, as her friends' welfare mattered more to her than Eli's, but she could understand Enna's anger and pain.

Walking away from Enna's bed before he could speak any further, she found her friends and leaned against Winnie, needing a friend's support. None of them asked how the conversation went.

"We should go," Elialdor said at last.

No one wanted to leave the room, but no one could deny that the prince was right.

"You best stay close," Freya said to Rald.

"Yes," Rald nodded, his eyes widening, wishing he could escape, "I've already been told that."

They wandered through the castle towards the Great Hall, seeing more people this time and, while many people paused to whisper to each other, nobody stopped them on their way.

They entered the Great Hall with a mixture of emotions: the prospect of the end of the war was refreshing but the thought of betraying another tribe and introducing the son of their enemy to the king, was cause for some concern.

Eanfrith was sitting as though waiting for them to enter. He sat up as they approached, and his eyes narrowed as he rested them on Rald. Rald looked like he wanted to fly away but knew it would be utterly fruitless. Freya stretched out her arm and tapped him gently on the shoulder, smiling in what she hoped would be an encouraging manner.

"So," Eanfrith sighed, "you've decided to come and see me."

Elialdor looked up at him with false puzzlement before they all bowed low.

"Come now, my son. Did you really think that we hadn't seen you arrive last night? I was expecting you to see me before this morning."

"I'm sorry, Father." Elialdor stood up. "We bring news: both good and bad."

"We should have been back sooner," Winnie explained, "but we needed to find a way out of the cliff-face fortress." Eanfrith looked at each of the companions, then focused his gaze on his son, his face lined in confusion and anger.

"The Eagles? What happened?" he snapped. "What did you do?"

Freya listened as Elialdor explained everything, from Edweth saying her son killed her, to the eagles rescuing them from the Owls. He did not mention that Eli had confessed.

"So, the eagles saved you?" The king leaned back on the throne. "Why, then, did you have to escape? What is this good news you promised?"

Elialdor spared a glance for his four

companions who were all looking directly at him.

"We received a message from Raedwald," Elialdor said finally, realising that the burden of telling the truth had fallen on his shoulders. "He states that, should we find Edweth's murderer, the war between our tribes will stop."

There was a strange change on the king's face. It seemed to take a few moments for the statement to sink in. He raised his eyebrows and then smiled, a broad smile, letting out a sigh of relief that centuries of bloodshed may come to an end. It took him a while to regain the ability to speak.

"This is great news, my son," he smiled. "To think that, when you reign, it might be a peaceful world you watch over."

"There is more, Father," Elialdor whispered, dreading the news he had to impart. The king's smile slipped, and his brow creased in concern at his son's tone.

"Yes? What is it?"

"My lord," Elamra spoke as Elialdor opened his mouth. The king turned to him. "It was then that Eli, the eagle chief, confessed to killing Edweth. This is why we needed to escape. He locked us away in case we told anyone, as he fears Raedwald's wrath."

"Eli?" Eanfrith's voice had become even more hoarse.

"He claims he loved her," Elamra explained.

"He killed her out of jealousy."

"Jealousy?" the king repeated. "A thousand years of war, all because of some man's jealousy? And he never paid the price. We paid it for him."

Freya was not sure whether the king had meant to say his thoughts out loud, but he said them so quietly all five of them had to strain to hear it.

"We have his son in our castle," the king said at last. Freya looked at him in alarm.

"We have offered him protection, Father." Elialdor sounded shocked.

"Enough, boy," Eanfrith croaked. "You don't understand these matters. How can you?"

"No, I don't understand," Elialdor spoke quietly, as though he knew what he was saying was dangerous and unwise. "I don't understand your coldness towards a guest of ours. He is a guest."

"Enough!" the king shouted, his voice echoing through the room so that everyone stopped to listen. "Is it not enough that you bring an enemy into my house? You would question my actions too. You are not king yet, Elialdor."

"This boy helped us," the prince pointed to Rald who had been steadily moving backwards from the king. "He saved our lives."

"Another one?" Eanfrith raised an eyebrow.

"Yes, Father," his son scowled, "another one. He is a servant in Listgard and would be killed if he returned. I offered him a safe place here."

"A servant?" the king repeated.

"Yes, a servant." Elialdor held firm and Freya was both impressed and concerned at how easily he lied. "He would be of little concern to Raedwald. I know you're thinking of using him as a hostage, but I can assure you there is no point. Raedwald would just want you to kill him and take the burden on yourself."

"Very well," Eanfrith nodded, "he can remain, if he is a good servant. But he will have to work for it."

Rald bowed for as long as he could manage, which seemed to impress Eanfrith a little. Freya could not help but wonder why the king had agreed so easily, but perhaps he was more reasonable than she had thought.

"But, my son," his voice was gentler now. "I understand your anxiety with using our guest as bait, but you must see that it is for a greater good. Peace is all I crave now."

"Father," Elialdor walked up to him and knelt down, taking his father's warm hand, "I understand. All I ask is that you do not break the boundaries of war. Turn Enna out on his own, never admit him again, but do not break your honour in harming him."

"Perhaps," Eanfrith whispered. "Perhaps you may not make a bad king after all. Very well. I…"

Whatever the king was about to say was cut short by the large double doors opening at the far end of the hall. Elialdor sighed with irritation as he realised that it was Enna who had admitted himself, and now strode up to where they were all standing. He had a look of grim realisation as he knelt before them, before standing up straight.

"Do you know what we have been discussing?" the king growled.

"I can guess." Enna bowed his head. "But I am here to tell you that you're mistaken."

The thunderous look on Eanfrith's face and Freya's look of fear did not seem to bother him.

"Please, continue," Eanfrith commanded.

"You believe my father is guilty of cold-blooded murder," Enna stated. "You do not know him. If you did, you would know that he is lying."

"As his son, you do him credit. As a guest," the king's voice was dangerously quiet, "you dishonour yourself. Leave this castle. You may never set foot here again."

"My lord," Enna persisted, "you misunderstand. I know that my father did not kill Edweth."

"Sentiment!" Eanfrith hissed, but Enna shook his head furiously and tutted in irritation.

"Will you listen?! I know it's not him because," he paused as he took a deep breath, "it was me."

The shock that the inhabitants of the room had felt when the young eagle prince had addressed their king in such a harsh manner was nothing compared to this blow. Freya stared at Enna, who seemed certain of his own guilt, while Elialdor, Rald and Winnie all looked horrified. Elamra and the king, however, were not convinced.

"Well, fourteen hundred years of war and now two people confess in as many days." Eanfrith looked critically at Enna. "Forgive me if I don't believe you."

"You must!" Enna snapped. "I am telling the truth. If you go to war with my father, you will be committing a terrible sin!"

"I feel somewhat touched by your dedication to your family," Eanfrith smiled. "But, make no mistake, if you insist on this path, you will wish that Edweth had killed you instead."

"You don't seriously mean to turn him over to Raedwald?" Elialdor took a step away from his father.

"I mean to do whatever is best for my people. If he," Eanfrith gestured to the eagle, "insists on lying to protect his tribe…"

"Then that is an incredibly noble thing to do!" Freya intervened. The king gave her a sharp look but said nothing.

"Why will none of you believe me?" Enna now sounded desperate.

"Why would you kill her?" Rald asked bitterly. "You must have only been a child."

"I was." Enna muttered, bowing his head. "I found out when I was very young that my father had been Edweth's lover. I am her son."

The five others exchanged glances, but the king was oblivious.

"I wanted to show that I loved her," Enna's voice became even quieter. "I went to talk to her, to let her know that I knew who I was. I thought she'd be pleased."

"She wasn't," Elialdor prompted, as the eagle trailed off.

"She was angry. She said that I would never be her son and she could never risk her husband finding out the truth. She'd managed to hide her pregnancy from Raedwald by visiting the Owls' allies." At this, Enna raised his head and looked directly at Rald. Elialdor shuffled slightly, fearing the eagle prince might betray them by revealing Rald's identity. "She tried to kill me."

"Edweth was a powerful woman." The king shook his head. "If she wanted to kill you, she would have succeeded."

"No," the eagle shook his head, "I have been cursed with that same condition Freya suffers with. I don't always know my actions, and I certainly never meant to kill her. I simply raised my hands to shield me from her power, and I..." Enna took a deep breath. "Her hunting knife. It turned against her."

"You killed her," Rald gasped, "and left her."

"I was frightened. If Raedwald had found out, I would have been killed. If I helped her survive, she would have killed me without hesitation. I ran away."

"And now you're telling the truth to stop us from harming your father." Freya rested a hand on his shoulder.

"He murdered..." Rald trailed off as he turned angrily towards Freya.

"Why do you believe him?" The king asked, eying them all with suspicion. "What are you not telling me?"

"When we saw Edweth, or her ghost, at least," Elialdor sighed, "she said that her son had killed her. We assumed she meant Ranald but..."

"Eli admitted that he loved Edweth," Elamra finished as the Crow prince trailed off. "With this confession, it all makes sense."

The king looked around each of them and they looked back to meet his gaze. Freya couldn't tell what he was thinking, but he paused for a moment to look at her. Willing him to forgive Enna and pardon him, she stared back.

"Then all that is left," the king commanded, "is for us to hand you over to Raedwald and stop needless bloodshed."

"You're joking, right?" Freya snapped, as Enna closed his eyes in acceptance.

"I do not joke when the safety of my tribe is at stake," the king hissed.

"He was a child," Freya laughed at the absurdity of the king's actions, "and it was self-defence. Do you know what it's like to have no control over your actions? I do."

"Freya," Elamra whispered, but she would not stop.

"I killed someone. In this very hall," she cried. "I had no idea what I was doing. What could Enna have done? Been killed himself?"

"He should have come forward sooner and saved countless lives," the king shouted. Enna nodded, which only infuriated Freya more. "You will take him to Raedwald, and he will make his confession before the Owl."

"Raedwald will kill him," Freya gasped, unwilling to believe the king's unconcern.

Eanfrith sat back on his throne and put his head in his hands.

"You think I'm not concerned by this, child," he muttered, "but, if you had seen the war destroy families like I've seen, you would be just as quick to find a solution."

"Father," the prince knelt before him. "Father, Freya is right. If you do this when you know that Enna was not responsible for her death, you will never forgive yourself. Please."

The begging in the prince's voice made his father look up. Freya was astonished to see that there were tears in the old man's eyes.

"I *need* to make peace," the king sighed. "For you, my son. I need *peace*!"

"I understand." Elialdor rested his forehead on

his father's gnarled hands. "But do not buy peace at this cost."

Freya, watching the father and son, had a sudden flash of inspiration.

"Let us talk to Raedwald," she requested. All eyes turned towards her.

"What will that achieve?" The king shook his head but waited for Freya to answer.

"I don't mean that we should tell him who killed his wife." She looked across at Enna who was listening intently. "I would never say that. But we could buy some time. Buy some peace."

"How?" Elialdor stood up. "You've met Raedwald. You know how he is. He'd never agree to it."

"I think he will," Freya smiled. It was clear to the others that she had an idea, and just as clear that she wasn't going to share it any time soon.

Enna looked around the gathered people in front of him, trying to ignore the crowd which had gathered. He had not been expecting this: he had been expecting to be killed, or taken to Raedwald, who would surely have killed him in the end.

"Very well," the king sighed. "Go to Raedwald and explain that you have been unable to find the murderer." The king sighed. "Try and negotiate a truce for as long as you can. Meet on neutral ground. He cannot harm you then. And," he turned to Elialdor.

"Father?" The prince asked as the king stopped talking.

"Take care, my son."

The prince stood up and bowed his head, before he turned on his heel and took Freya by the hand, leading her out of the hall. Elamra and Winnie followed without a word and Rald looked like he wanted to join them but realised it was perhaps not the best idea. He would just have to trust that the king kept his word and did not use him as a hostage: he was certain his father would only be pleased if the Crow threatened to harm him.

Enna stood with his head bowed and his shoulders crouched forwards. The king leant forward on the throne and rubbed his eyes with the back of his hand.

"The war will continue," was all he said.

CHAPTER TWENTY-THREE
An Unlikely Offer

The four individuals stood silently on the edge of the field. It was a cold spring morning and everything around them was alive. The birds were twittering and there was rustling in the hedge behind them that Elamra seemed unconcerned about so Freya was not too worried. However, she was very worried about seeing Raedwald again. Last time, and the time before, he had tried to kill them, so she was dubious whether he would keep to the laws of honour that the Crows seemed so sure about.

Freya was unsure why they had chosen this spot. They could not see very far as the field sloped up and down, so there was nothing to stop the Owls from ambushing them. Given their past actions, she thought her friends thought higher of the Owls' honour than they deserved. They had sent a messenger to Listgard and could only hope he had not come to any harm.

None of them felt like talking as they waited, and the silence gave Freya a chance to think. She thought of Rald: disowned by his father and placed at the mercy of his lifelong enemy. She thought of Enna and how everything made sense now she knew the truth. Eli had said he never really belonged to the eagle tribe, and Enna had confessed himself that he had done some terrible things. Perhaps he had remembered his actions in a dream, as he told Freya would happen. She could not imagine how Enna was feeling and hoped with all her being that she would never find out.

Finally, she thought of her plan and wondered if it would work. She hoped so fervently that it would. It seemed like a long shot, but she could think of nothing else she could do. Surely, buying the Crows some peace time was needed, even if it was temporary.

She wasn't sure how long they stood there but her legs had started to ache. Finally, she felt a rush of wind above her head and looked up to see three silent barn owls circling back to them. They landed on the floor and briskly - more quickly than Freya had ever seen - changed into their true forms. Raedwald stood in the middle, with Ranald and Hild at either side. Their gaze was fixed on Freya and her companions. Ranald scowled across at them, clearly wanting to attack them there and then, and Hild had the same haughty look she had done last time they met.

Raedwald, however, took a step forward and smiled as he bowed his head. Elialdor did the same.

"You have thought about my promise, I see," Raedwald addressed them all. "I'm pleased. Have you found the villain?"

"Sir," Elialdor bowed, and Freya grimaced at the hypocrisy, "I regret to inform you that we have been unable to find him."

"But you know who it is?" Raedwald eyed them all and Freya found she could not hold his gaze.

"Edweth said it was her son." Elialdor told the truth, meeting the Owl's eye.

"And you believe it was Ranald," the Owl king laughed, but his son looked angrier. "Or perhaps you have changed your mind and believe it was the other one?"

"Rald was with us when we saw Edweth," Elialdor explained. "She would have known, and she met him like he was her pride and joy."

Freya was expecting a quick remark from Raedwald, but none came. His lips parted slightly as though he was about to say something, but no sound came out. It took her a few moments to realise that this was him showing his grief, or rather trying not to show it. His sharp eyes became clouded over for a matter of moments, but they cleared quickly.

"I wish to speak to the human girl," he declared, and Freya took a step back, frightened but pleased to have the opportunity to try her plan.

"Freya is here merely for support," the prince shook his head, "she will not speak to you."

"I am *merely* wanting a word." Raedwald looked directly at her now. "You may stay here if you wish, princeling. I do not care."

Elialdor was about to protest, but Freya walked forward before he could get into an argument, intrigue driving her to know what Raedwald was going to say, and determination for the truce. The Owl king gave the prince a look of something that might have been gloating triumph as Freya walked up to him.

"Touch her and you die," snarled Elialdor but Raedwald just held up his hands.

"After what I hear she is capable of, I wouldn't dream of it," he laughed, but Freya scowled at him as her thoughts were brought back to her shadow.

"What do you want?" she snapped. Raedwald smiled plausibly and pulled her to the side so they were further out of earshot.

"I admit I'm intrigued." He stared at her but this time she met his gaze confidently.

"Oh, yes," she scowled, "how am I still alive

when I've spent so long with the tribes?"

"No." Raedwald took hold of her hands. Freya could see Elialdor give a jolt towards his sword, but she shook her head quickly. She needed to know what the Owl was going to say.

"Then what?" She tried to sound unconcerned but realised she had started shaking as Raedwald looked deeper into her eyes.

"You are being torn apart inside, aren't you?" he whispered. "You think you are going mad and cannot talk to anyone about it. I have never known a human with this same condition as many of us have."

"I know about Elamra if you are trying to turn me against him." Freya's voice shook.

"Stupid girl. No," the Owl dismissed the comment as a mere irritation, "I am merely offering my help."

"Help?" Freya spluttered on the word. "Your help? You tried to kill me."

"Yes," he conceded. "I find you repulsive, impetuous and entirely out-of-place in our world, but I still admit that I am most intrigued. I want to help."

"You're making no sense." Freya turned away, but Raedwald held onto her hands so she had to look back at him, trying not to show any fear.

"This condition," he persisted, "it will tear you apart inside. You need shelter. All I am saying is that, if the Crows abandon you, you may come and rely on the Owls."

Freya gave him a disbelieving look. She believed that Raedwald thought she was utterly repulsive so she could not understand why he had given her such a strange invitation, especially after being so keen to kill her only yesterday.

"Remember it," Raedwald whispered and let go of her hands. It took Freya a few moments to gather the courage to talk.

"Seeing as you're so keen to *help*," she sneered, "I have a suggestion that may help you."

"I'm listening." Raedwald's eyes narrowed.

"You want Edweth's killer," Freya began. "I want peace for the Crows."

"Go on."

"Give the Crows a truce. Agree to, say, six months?"

Raedwald laughed at the suggestion.

"That sounds fantastic," he laughed, "for the Crows. What would I get out of it?"

"Apart from peace?" Freya suggested. "Think about it. The Crows crave peace. It's all they think about now. If you were to give them six months of peace, they would be overjoyed. They would be so happy that they wouldn't want it to end."

Raedwald didn't speak, but he had stopped laughing and was now staring in concentration at Freya.

"At the end of the six months, they will be so

desperate to keep the peace that they will hand over Edweth's killer. You've waited for centuries. Will another six months be too long?"

"Intrigued," Raedwald muttered. "Yes, you intrigue me, girl."

"Do we have a deal?" Freya persisted, ignoring the shiver that crept up her back towards her neck. There was a pause - a long pause that Freya's nerves couldn't handle.

"Yes," Raedwald declared. "Yes. I believe we have a deal."

After that conversation, Freya could not make her way towards her friends fast enough. She held on tightly to Elialdor and Winnie, who embraced her warmly, but she was brought back by Raedwald's laughter.

"I don't know what words you shared," Elialdor said with distaste, "but know this: if you ever come near her again, your sons and all your tribe will pay the price."

"Your friend," Raedwald laughed. "Your friend has negotiated a truce for six months. I've agreed to this. There will be peace for this time and, if you hand over my wife's murderer in that time, the peace will be everlasting."

With a flourish, Raedwald waved his hand in a strange pattern in front of him and blue sparks began flying everywhere. When the Owl had finished, Freya realised he was now holding a rolled-up piece of paper and a feather, which must have been a pen.

"Here," Raedwald held it out to Elialdor, who took it suspiciously, "I have signed it. Now you must sign it."

Elialdor looked through the paper, reading it as fast as he could. His brow furrowed as he read on and on.

"Six months?" He asked and Raedwald nodded.

"Not a minute less," he paused, "and not a minute *more*."

Elialdor read the truce once more before he took the pen and signed his name below Raedwald's.

The Owl king made more signs in the air, and further blue sparks flew around the air before another roll, with the exact same words and the exact same signatures, fell from the paper.

"One for your tribe," Raedwald grinned, "and one for mine. Now, go back to your castle and rest easy. We have peace." With his last words, Raedwald held his arms out as though the peace was something they could all see.

"Remember my offer, girl," Raedwald smiled coldly at Freya. "And, princeling, after the truce is ended, if you are refusing to honour the bargain we struck and do not bring me the villain who killed my wife, the war will continue long into your reign."

"You would not know what to do with peace,"

the prince replied. "I expect the war will continue whether we give you what you want or not."

"You question my honour?" Raedwald seemed amused.

"Yes," Elialdor replied. "Yes, I question everything about you."

The smile slid from the Owl's face and was replaced by a scowl. With one final look at each of the three of them, he transformed into a barn owl and glided away silently over the field, higher and higher into the sky, followed by Ranald and Hild in their Owl forms. The Crow party watched them until they drifted out of sight. Freya felt sure that she would see him again and would never forget his words.

"Peace," Elialdor breathed, and collapsed on the grass, staring up at the sky.

"I have never known peace either." Winnie knelt beside him.

Freya looked at both of them in their elated state. She thought about what she had said to Raedwald and wondered if she had been mistakenly right. Would they love peace so much that they would betray Enna?

But, she thought, that was six months away. Six months to find a solution and six months to enjoy peace before the war started again.

By then, she was sure, they would have a successful plan.

"We should return," Elamra announced,

watching as the sun disappeared behind some clouds and it instantly became colder. Elialdor agreed and they glided away in silence. Freya could not help but wonder what everyone at home would think if they saw her transform into a bird. She had certainly got better at it throughout the two weeks.

She had thought more about home today than she had in some time and wasn't sure whether she missed it. No one had ever tried to harm her at home. Since she had stumbled into this strange place, her life had been put in danger six times. Now there was peace, she would feel safer returning home. However, the thought of leaving her friends unsettled her. How could she leave when they had been her whole life for weeks?

The castle came into sight within minutes and they landed softly in the garden, transforming into their human selves again as soon as their feet touched the grass. Without a word to each other, but each grinning, they walked to the Great Hall and were surprised to find that Enna was still there, standing at the side of the room with a look of sincere shame. He walked up to them as soon as they entered.

"You know I never wanted this," he whispered to Freya. "I wanted to take the blame. It is only right."

"Right that you should take the blame for something which was hardly your fault?" Freya laughed. "I would never have allowed it if it was up to me."

"But still," Enna's voice became even quieter, "I deserve it."

"No," Freya said. "I know what it's like to be completely out of control. It wasn't your fault."

"I did it," Enna persisted, but Freya just shook her head. She could not accept that anything he had done in that state was his fault.

She would not hear any more of Enna's guilt but walked away from him purposefully, following Winnie, Elialdor and Elamra to the throne where they knelt in front of the king.

"So, you made it safely back," the king smiled. "Good. Seeing as you have made this castle a sanctuary to disgraced tribesmen, you should at least have returned to help."

"I appreciate your actions today, Father," Elialdor returned the smile. "I'm sorry we have not found a solution to this war."

"The only solution, my son, is to win."

"We have been trying for hundreds of years," the prince reminded him. "But we do have some good news. Freya should tell you, as it is all down to her."

"Freya? Tell me."

"We have secured a truce for six months," Freya declared, feeling both happy that they had peace and worried it would not last forever.

"Six months?" The king breathed slowly.

"Child, this is the best news I could have hoped for. In that six months, we can regroup and decide how best to move forward. Centuries on, and it has taken a human child to bring us our first slice of hope."

Freya didn't know what to say, so she looked across to her friends. All their eyes were on her. Rald, who was standing at the side of the room, was watching her with intrigue. The gaze, although not in any way malicious, reminded Freya of his father, and she looked back to the floor.

"Six months," the king muttered again, and then stood up from his throne with a spring in his step. "We shall have a feast! The biggest feast this hall has had in centuries! And you, Freya, shall be our guest of honour."

Elialdor grinned across at Freya, who felt everyone's joy and hope as a burden she could not handle. Only she and Raedwald knew the reason for the truce, and she felt sick at the thought of sharing a secret with him. She was not aware of anyone until she felt a hand on her arm. She spun around and looked into Elialdor's smiling eyes.

"Whatever bargain you made with Raedwald," he whispered, so quietly that only the two of them could hear, "we have six months to sort it out. Don't worry. Now is a time for celebration!"

Freya grinned: the prince was right.

"I'd be overjoyed to stay," Freya said, "but, now there is peace, I'd like to go home for a bit."

The king paused but kept smiling.

"Of course, child," he said, "you're not our prisoner, you are our guest. As you say, it is now safe for you to return home. But," he added, "I believe it is only fair to say we will need your help in the future."

"And I'd be so happy to help," Freya agreed. She looked across at Winnie, who smiled, and to Elialdor. The prince had a sad smile, but it broadened into a grin instantly.

"But first, we will celebrate," he said.

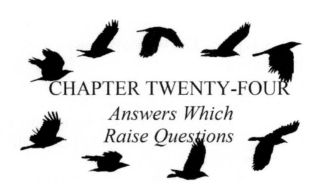

CHAPTER TWENTY-FOUR
Answers Which Raise Questions

Remembering the tragedy after the Crows' last banquet, Freya approached the night's festivities with concern. It had been two days since she had agreed on the truce with Raedwald. The truce paper had been shown to all in the castle, and word had been sent to all the other tribes in Britain. They had been invited to the feast but the doves, after the last one, had declined, although the chaffinches and jays had agreed to come. They were the closest in distance to the Crows, so it was easiest. Other tribes, such as the woodland tribes, had agreed to send a representative of one or two people.

She sat, as guest of honour, at the high table next to Elialdor. At her request, Winnie and Rald sat there too. The king had initially been very discouraging of the Owl 'servant' having a place at the table, but Freya was obstinate. This was the last evening she would be spending with her friends for a while and she wanted it to be a fantastic one.

Enna was sitting on one of the other tables, his face grim and set. He had not spoken much since the truce. It was his last evening there too, as he was returning to his own tribe in the morning.

Elamra stood at the side of the hall, not partaking in any eating or drinking, but watching everyone with a mixture of interest and suspicion. The others paid him no notice, although Winnie spared him a smile every now and then. He would smile back and bow his head, and then look away.

Halfway into the evening, Freya allowed herself to admit she was enjoying herself. It seemed that Raedwald, determined to be handed Edweth's murderer, would honour the truce. They really did have six months of peace ahead of them, and Freya could be proud of her part in it.

There was dancing and so much laughter, and Freya held mixed emotions as she stood in front of the castle the following morning, watching the sun coming over the high walls.

In front of her stood Winnie, Elialdor, Rald, Elamra and the king. All five of them smiled at her as she stepped up to them to say goodbye, knowing that she would have to work very hard to keep her eyes dry. Winnie was having the same problem and Elialdor was holding his chin up as high as he could. His mouth was firmly shut, and his nose kept flaring as he tried to keep control of his emotions. Rald just looked at her with his wide eyes, and Elamra was actually smiling at her.

Freya smiled back and bowed in front of the king.

"Thank you," she smiled. "I've learned a lot in the last few weeks. I hope I can help you if you need it."

"Your help will always be needed and appreciated." The king took her hand. "If you ever need *our* help, you just have to shout for us. We'll hear, and we'll come."

With this promise, Freya felt a little more comfortable to ask for something which had been on her mind.

"Rald," she whispered to the king. "Rald is frightened in your company. Look after him."

The king looked at her for a moment as though she had gone insane, but then smiled.

"Perhaps it is your kindness that has helped us so far. Very well, Freya. Do not worry. He will be well cared for. Besides," his eyes began to twinkle, "it will give me much pleasure to know I have an Owl in the castle who prefers the company of Crows. Raedwald will be delighted."

Freya smiled, confident that, if only because of

this, Rald would be safe with the Crows. She turned to him next.

"I don't think you have to worry." She hugged the Owl, who returned the gesture.

"Thank you, Freya," Rald whispered, "for everything."

Freya shook her head. She didn't feel like anyone should be thanking her. All she had done was buy them a bit of time.

"You've bought us all peace, if only for a time," Rald said, as though he could read her thoughts. Freya moved to her other friends. Of all of them, she would miss Elialdor and Winnie the most.

"We're going to see you home," Winnie declared, leaving no room for discussion. Freya was glad as she couldn't face saying all the goodbyes at once.

Waving a goodbye to the king and Rald, the others changed into their bird forms and set off into the sky. Elialdor stayed close to Freya as they flew higher and lower, whirling through the clouds as though they were trying to make the journey last as long as possible.

Freya wondered if she would still be able to fly without her friends' help. She loved flying and, while she was looking forward to seeing her mum and dad, a part of her hoped the flight home would never end. All too soon, however, the tops of the roofs and the shopping centres came into view. Although it was only a few weeks that

Freya had been away, it seemed strange to be heading towards such a modern town.

They touched ground just around the corner from her flat and went into an alleyway to transform. Freya had not thought of how out-of-place her and her friends would look in the town, but her three companions did not seem to mind the strange looks they received from the people. As Freya looked at the clothes they wore, she wondered why the tribes did not move with the times and wear normal clothes, until she remembered that they were a threat to normal people simply by being around them. This turned her to thinking why she, of all people, was unaffected.

They had now reached the door to the flat, and Freya hesitated before ringing the bell.

"Are you joining me inside?" she asked.

Elialdor shook his head, unable to speak in case his emotions over spilled. Elamra simply smiled and Winnie embraced Freya.

"I know we shall see each other again," she smiled, "but this is still hard."

"I know," Freya agreed, but could not say anymore as she felt herself choking on emotion. She turned to Elialdor as the prince took her hands gently.

"I see now why they say a human can make all the difference to a tribe." He hugged her while Freya tried to work out what he meant. "You have helped us in so many ways. You have given us some of your humanity."

"Goodbye, Elialdor," Freya whispered, unable to say anything else.

"As my father said, we will always be here for you," he whispered. "Call my name, or call Winnie, or any of us and we will come immediately. And remember...this can be used for good too."

Freya shivered slightly as Elialdor concealed a blue flame in his hand. She looked around to see if anyone had seen the strange sight, but no-one was now sparing them a second glance.

"I should go," she whispered. Knowing that if she stayed much longer, the goodbyes would only get harder, she gave Elialdor and Winnie another embrace and nodded to Elamra, before ringing the doorbell.

There were footsteps from inside and her mother opened the door. Freya turned around to introduce her friends, but they were not there. Quickly scanning the street, all she could see were two ravens and a jackdaw flying away from her. As she watched them go, she felt a sudden assurance she would see them again soon.

"Ah, you're home," her mother said, looking out at the street to see what had caught Freya's attention. "How was the party?"

"Party?" Freya asked, somewhat bemused.

"Yes," her mother smiled as she stood back to

let her in, "I thought you were going out with your friends."

"Yes." Freya grinned, feeling instantly better in her mum's company. "Yes, I was."

She did not feel like talking and sat in the kitchen silently as she watched her mum make a cup of tea. Merely to be in her company again calmed her. By the time the evening came, she had started to feel like the last few weeks had been a very lifelike dream.

She never needed to speak when she was around her parents and was content watching her Mum and Dad that evening talk about what they had done that day. Dad was back at work and, although it was Mum's day off, she had used the time that Freya wasn't there to visit her grandma in the old people's home. This always made Mum chatty and Freya was happy to sit and listen.

Their trip together seemed to have worked. Either they were keeping up appearances for Freya's sake, or they were enjoying each other's company more.

The happy chattering, and the simple conversation made Freya's mind drift further and further away from the tribes. Her parents had not noticed her absence for more than half a day and, although her Mum spared her a few concerned looks, she was not worried as she always did this when Freya had been out with friends.

Feeling her mind overcrowded with tiredness,

Freya wondered which of her friends she was supposed to have been out with.

Walking upstairs to her room, everything in the house seemed ten times more beautiful. She had no idea of how much she had missed her home but, now she was back, she never wanted to leave. Looking at every picture and relishing every ornament, she sauntered up the stairs.

Her sleepy eyes came into focus suddenly as she saw a picture that she had been so used to, she now never saw it. It was a photo of her mum, taken several years ago before Freya was born, during her college years. Her mum frequently talked about those years, and Freya loved to hear about it, but something caught her eye as she ascended the stairs. It wasn't her mum - it was the man standing next to her. The photo was grainy, but the man's thin, pointed face, and sleek hair which came to a distinct widow's peak was unmistakable. She had seen this ageless man only yesterday.

She stood staring at the picture for minutes until she managed to drag herself away to her room, shutting the door as though she was afraid that the picture might come to life. Thinking back over the last few weeks, she tried to find a rational explanation as to why there was a picture of her mum with Ranald hanging up on the stairs. The only thing that came to mind was her confusion at being the one human they chose. As certain things began to make sense, other things became more confused and distorted from her earlier memories.

She wrapped herself up in the covers, curling up into a tight ball as she heard the nearby sound of a hooting owl.

I hope you have enjoyed taking part in the first part of Freya's journey.

Reviews are worth more to an author than **gold**, so please do leave an honest review on your chosen book website.

Read the first chapter of Book 2 for **FREE** by subscribing to the email list

www.clemencycrow.co.uk

As a subscriber, you can take part in numerous giveaways, get up-to-date news of books and events, and even have the chance to read the whole 2nd book before its release date!

Also published by

Rosie Jane and the Swodgerump by *Susan Crow*

Rosie Jane and the Swodgerump tells the story of naughty Rosie Jane and her best friend, Jessica.

At the seaside the girls discover more than shells and sand. But why is the Swodgerump there? And will Rosie Jane remember why Swodgerumps are so important...?

The Backwater by *Judith Crow*

When Rebecca Williams' mother dies, she is sent from the city to rural Lincolnshire to live with her father. What she finds is a quiet, unassuming man who lives alone on a large country estate.

Lonely and nervous, Rebecca makes friends with a boy she meets at the lake. However, as their friendship develops, she discovers that her new friend is haunted by a secret which Rebecca must first unearth before it can be laid to rest.

A ghost story inspired by the guidelines used by the great M. R. James, but with the freshness in tone of the twenty-first century, The Backwater weaves together the guilt of the living and the anger of the dead to produce a chilling but tender story of one girl's struggle to find her place in the world.

Lightning Source UK Ltd.
Milton Keynes UK
UKHW010729050619
343910UK00001B/69/P

9 781913 182038